Happy Moth
Grace.

Enjoy.

Arrows, Indians and Love

Barbara Raué

Barbara J Raué

PublishAmerica
Baltimore

First printing

Hardcover 978-1-4560-7313-8
Softcover 978-1-4560-7312-1
PUBLISHED BY PUBLISHAMERICA, LLLP
www.publishamerica.com
Baltimore

Printed in the United States of America

Also by Barbara Raué

Coins of Gold

Contents

Prologue – Building the Road to Boonesborough

Most early settlers in America lived along the east coast with their settlements less than one hundred miles from the Atlantic Ocean. By the late 1700s, many people wanted to move west to find new places to live and work as the coastal areas were becoming crowded.

The Appalachian Mountains form a natural barrier to east-west travel, from Pennsylvania to Georgia. Settlers from Pennsylvania tended to migrate south along the Great Wagon Road through the Great Appalachian and Shenandoah Valleys. Daniel Boone, the great adventurer and pioneer, was from Pennsylvania and migrated south with his family along this road. From an early age, Boone was one of the long hunters who hunted and trapped among the Native American nations along the western frontiers of Virginia. They were called "long hunters" because of the long time they spent away from home on hunts in the wilderness. Boone would sometimes be gone for months and even years before returning home from his hunting expeditions.

In 1775, Daniel Boone is hired by the Transylvania Company to blaze a trail from Virginia through the Cumberland Gap into central Kentucky. In 1750, Dr. Thomas Walker was one of the first explorers to reach the Cumberland Gap; he mapped the area and gave the Gap its name. The route of the Wilderness Road makes a long loop from Virginia southward to Tennessee and then northward to Kentucky, a distance of over two hundred miles. The Cumberland Gap, at an elevation of 1600 feet, is a pass through the Appalachian Mountains, the pass covering a distance of twelve miles. It is a key passageway through the mountains, an important part of the Wilderness Road.

Daniel, dressed in a fringed hunting shirt, leggings, and moccasins is a muscular man five feet ten inches tall. His brother, Squire Boone, has done a lot of exploring and is eager for this adventure of exploring new frontiers and building a road. Richard Calloway, Daniel's neighbour in the Yadkin Valley in North Carolina, is several years older than Daniel. Richard served as a captain in the French and Indian War and was a colonel in the local militia in North Carolina. He is almost six feet tall, proud of his sixteen hands tall horse, and makes quite an impression in his army uniform as he leads a troop of men on a mission. He is very opinionated and Daniel has to deal cautiously with him at times.

Benjamin Anderson, Samuel Barker, the four Bryan brothers, David, Henry, Jonathan and William, John and Leonard Bullock, Edward Bradley, James Bridges and Samuel Coburn are some of the other members of the group. Daniel chose his team of men very carefully. When Michael O'Neill is recruited, he recommends his blacksmith assistant, Timothy Eadon. Timothy has been working with Michael for the past six months and is learning the trade quickly. Timothy is a tall man, with well-muscled arms and chest, having dark blonde hair and blue eyes. Daniel welcomes Timothy as part of the group. Michael Stoner is a surveyor and hunter and will be helpful in determining some of the specific routes of the trail for sections that don't currently exist; his services will be valuable when they arrive at the town site.

The men are to spend several weeks together and they all have to cooperate and get along together in order to successfully accomplish their job of completing the road to the settlement site on the Kentucky River. As they are chosen, they gather together at Long Island in the Holston River in eastern Tennessee. The men are camping together, preparing their food over campfires with each group being given a specific chore to do. Richard Calloway is in charge of one group; the other three groups are led by three captains, William Twetty, William

Bush and John Holder. One group is sent out to hunt for meat to eat; another group collects firewood; the third group carries enough water to the campsite to meet all the needs of the whole group; the fourth group cooks all the meals. The next day, roles are switched so that the men will have a better understanding of the chores that will be required on a daily basis, chores which will be in addition to the actual building of the road using axes and saws.

As the group grows, those who were there from the beginning show the new men what needs to be done. For some of the men, it is a real challenge to produce a meal over the campfire to feed a large group of hungry men. Robert Boggs, John Boyle and Jacob Baughman have never cooked over a campfire before; each is matched with a partner who is skillful in this so that they can learn from watching and assisting. Jacob Crabtree, and Benjamin Culbirth have to learn the new skill of stalking animals and killing them for food and preparing the meat to be cooked. Two days before they are to start building the new road, Daniel calls them together to explain in greater detail what they will be doing.

On March 10, 1775 the thirty men mount their horses, armed mainly for hunting as they are not expecting any problems with the Indians, and followed by black servants, loaded pack-horses and hunting dogs, start out to connect buffalo trails, Indian paths, trails of hunters and Indian traders and the great Warrior Path. The trail is blazed every mile by using a hatchet to mark the direction of the trail. They are building the first continuous road through the wilderness to the Kentucky River. They are a cheerful group as they set out, full of excitement of their part in preparing for settlement of new country. The road that Daniel and the axmen cut is a crude road. It is steep and rough and can only be traversed on foot or horseback.

Timothy Eadon does not feel nearly as confident as his leader, though sharing the eagerness for adventure and desire to see new places. He is still feeling the pain of rejection in his past, and often shows a deep sadness during time around the campfire at night. Mike O'Neill has a harmonica and when the conversation dies down he plays some lively tunes; he has quite a repertoire and helps provide a wind-down time for the men. At other times, Daniel reads passages from one of the books he is currently reading. One of the first evenings around the campfire after working hard all day on the road, the men begin sharing about their plans and their families. Several have very young children at home, others have teenagers, others have brothers and sisters and parents they are eager to bring west. Some appear to be all alone in the world, but none seems more burdened than Timothy. He clams right up whenever the conversation gets personal, making it very plain that his past is not to be discussed.

The men work hard during the day blazing the road, which sometimes requires them to build a whole section, completely clearing it of trees and brush. All the men have great physical strength on their side, evidenced by how quickly the miles of road are completed. It takes about one month to complete the road to Kentucky. They swing their axes from morning to night day after day. Some are chosen to hunt for meat to feed the group, while others are content to chop the trees and make progress on the road. They toil onward, chopping down saplings, cutting away vines and overhanging branches, removing logs and fallen trees, connecting paths, filling sink-holes, burning ways through dead brush, logging streams for future people to walk across, cutting paths through what seems like almost endless canebrakes of tall grasses with woody stalks.

On the 25th of March, after an undisturbed journey of two weeks and only fifteen miles from their destination of the Kentucky River, Boone's party is fired on by Indians and Captain Twetty and Felix Walker are killed. Thomas McDowell, Joshua Barton and Joseph McPheeters are killed on a second attack two nights later, with Samuel Tate escaping through the stream where the small group had camped a short distance from the main company. At this time the group thinks that the natives are already breaking the treaties that have just been signed.

This reminds Daniel of his earlier attempt to settle in Kentucky with Rebecca when their son James was killed. David and Sarah Gass and their five children, James, Jennie, John, Mary and Sarah had been part of that group in 1773 when they travelled from North Carolina. After a surprise attack by the Indians, the party turned back to the home of the Gass family at the western-most point of civilization. The Boone family lived in the cabin with the Gass family for two years and then Daniel took David with him to build the Wilderness Road.

After these attacks, guards are placed on duty to warn of Indians and to protect the belongings of the community. A messenger is sent back along the trail to tell Richard Henderson of the attacks, as he is travelling with the much slower wagons and pack horses that are carrying the supplies for the settlement. Daniel presses on to the site chosen for what becomes Boonesborough. Tim works right alongside Daniel on the road detail, admiring him as an extraordinary leader, one with determination and drive. Daniel has an "I'll never quit" attitude, and is always looking for adventure. Tim keeps his ears and eyes open, wanting to learn from this man, a man who has explored many areas, a man who has hunted extensively, a man with a dream, a man eager to inspire others to join him in the settling of Kentucky. Tim also likes to seek out adventure, is an excellent marksman, and has muscles of steel from his work as a blacksmith. Tim is sometimes fearful, especially after the first Indian attack, wondering if they should turn back. The second attack almost has him hightailing it for the east, but Daniel's optimism wins Tim over. Gradually Tim's courage grows as his survival skills increase.

The night after the second attack, the men start talking about the recent wars. A few of the men are older and served under the British in the Seven Years' War between the British and French as they fought for control of America; they had the Indians fighting with them. Richard Calloway has risen to the rank of Colonel, having fought at Fort Frontenac in the battle on August 27, 1758. He, as well as Captain Twetty, was part of the delegation of British officers who made peace with some Indian tribes, namely the Shawnee, Iroquois and Delaware. Captain David Gass was in active service in the militia of Virginia. Timothy Eadon can carry on a conversation on many topics including the political situation. Many had heard about the Boston Tea Party and the men in the group cheer as they talk about the brave young men.

As they approach the plains of Kentucky, the men are very pleased with the country they see. The grasses blowing in the breeze have a bluish tinge to them and are luscious looking and covered with patches of white clover. The sky seems bigger with all the stars shining brightly. The appearance of the country exceeds their expectations. Finally, the work on the road is finished. At last the men stand by the Kentucky River, like a dream they held onto as they laboured onward.

The trails of four tribes, of the Creek, Wyandot, Cherokee and Shawnee, meet in Kentucky around Boonesborough. The Cherokee are most interested in peace with the white settlers. Kentucké, the Promised Land, is the hunting ground for meat for the tribes.

Richard Henderson is a big, strong man with a barrel chest, and a loud voice; he was a lawyer and judge in North Carolina, a cultured man, self-reliant and a hard worker; he is a man of ambition looking for new ways to earn a living. Following behind the road-making crew a few weeks later, Richard is making the trip with supply wagons to the Gap and then using pack mules for the one hundred and thirty miles further to the settlement site. Henderson has forty mounted riflemen with him, including William Cooke, who is 27 years old with black eyes and hair. Richard has a large group of black slaves, a drove of cows, and forty pack-horses, and a train of wagons loaded with provisions, ammunition, material for making gunpowder, seed corn, garden seed, and a varied store of articles of prime necessity at an isolated settlement. His brother Samuel Henderson is travelling with him, along with Nathaniel and Thomas Hart, Robert and Samuel McAfee, John Williams, William Johnson and John Luttrell. William Bailey Smith is a tall, rollicking, energetic, brave but unstable bachelor who likes to tell stories by embellishing the details to make them sound better or scarier than the actual facts; he is a surveyor whose services will be useful in designing the layout for the settlement. They are joined at the Cumberland Gap by Captain Joseph Martin, William

Calk and four others.

Some of the supplies have to be stashed at the Gap for a second trip as there is too much to take the first time. At Martin's Station about forty additional pioneers join Henderson. As they travel on their way, they meet about a hundred refugees fleeing Indian attacks with a few of Richard's party deciding to turn back, while the rest, despite the danger, keep going toward Kentucky. Some of the rivers are flooded and the pioneers have to swim across with their horses.

After a month of travel, covering three hundred miles, they arrive on April 20, 1775. Henderson sets about to erect a fort that is large enough and strong enough to accommodate the present settlers and protect their supplies, desiring cabins to be completed before the arrival of more families who are expected in September. Daniel and Richard with the help of his slaves prepare the soil and plant corn soon after their arrival, along with some vegetables like potatoes, carrots, onions, beets, turnips, beans and cabbage requiring little daily attention. These vegetables grow well in the rich virgin soil. The fruit trees growing in the woods provide apples, peaches, plums and pears. There are blackberries, gooseberries, blueberries and others berries growing in the open areas. In the combined groups, there are eighty men; some claimed land outside the fort and begin clearing land for homes and planting crops.

The plan for the whole fort is drawn up first with the help of Michael Stoner and Oswald Townsend, surveyors with some experience who are a good help in determining the dimensions that will work well. The size of the blockhouses is decided with the plan for the ten foot high stockade walls on either side of each of the blockhouses in the four corners. The stockade wall pickets are the least needed features of the fort in time of peace and are neglected at this time. On the two ends, there are five cabins each. On the long side walls, the front and rear gates are in the middle and are wide enough to take a loaded wagon through. The back gate heading towards the Kentucky River is generally closed. The front gate is to be open during the day with sentries on duty on the walls for viewing the area for the greatest distance and one or two sentries by the gate. There are four cabins between each blockhouse and the gates. Both cabins and stockades are provided with little portholes for muskets to be fired through in times of attack.

After staking out the location for the fort, it takes a week to clear the area of trees, shape and notch logs, and split logs for shakes for the roofs before the building begins. Richard and Daniel divide the eighty men into four groups. The first group hunts for meat for everyone. The second group cuts trees and prepares logs for building, while the third group works on the foundations for the fort. Chestnut is the most popular wood to make into logs to build the cabins. It is also easy to split into shingles for the roofs; the roofs are built to slant inwards. Once enough logs have been cut for all the cabins, stones are gathered for the fireplaces as one is needed in each cabin for cooking and warmth. The blockhouses require a two-storey fireplace. The fourth group is given six days to go out and explore, trap and hunt for furs. Each week the groups rotate to keep variety and interest for the men. Henderson's cook Dan recruits helpers as needed to prepare the meals.

Daniel and Richard work with a small group to dig a deep hole about six feet in the ground, and ten feet square. They frame it with logs to a height two feet above the ground, and then put a roof on it. The roof is covered with clay to protect it from sparks as the building will be used to store gunpowder and ammunition.

Holes for the foundation logs are dug and then the foundation logs are hammered in deeply and the holes filled in. The first row of logs for all the cabins around the perimeter is attached to the foundation. The back wall of each of the cabins forms the outside wall of the fort. The rapport between Timothy Eadon and Flanders Calloway grows as they work together cutting trees, trimming the branches off, tying a group together and having the mules pull them to the settlement location. After the first week they have enough logs ready to build a cabin and they eagerly set about the building. The inner foundation holes are dug where the markers had been placed and the outline of the cabin is now completed, with an opening at the inside for the door. Logs are notched to fit into each other.

By the end of the second week, much progress has been made and many of the cabin walls are at least half their height and the fireplaces are beginning to take shape. What a thrill it is for Daniel, Richard, Timothy and the others to look over the area and see the town shaping up.

Henderson has one blockhouse on the back of the fort which runs roughly parallel to the Kentucky River. Richard has the General Store on the lower level with the family living quarters on the second floor. His kitchen is next door with eating and cooking all done there, and his black cook, Dan, takes care of what is officially known as Richard's Café, but popularly called Dan's Café. There is an extra storage room in the back of the kitchen and a bunkhouse for a dozen bachelors to sleep.

Richard Henderson brought Ching Lu and his wife Su with him to do the laundry for his family and any of the bachelors who want to use their services. Ching and Su are short in height, have long pigtails in their black hair, and their round faces are always cheerful as they smile a friendly greeting to everyone passing by. The laundry building is located next to the café with an outdoor fire and kettle for use in the mild and clear weather. Clothes are hung inside to dry and then pressed by Su.

As some of the young bachelors are more interested in furs than in building and looking after a cabin, and as others are used to having their mothers feed and clothe them, Flanders Calloway, Joseph Combs, Joseph Hughes, David McPhee, Timothy Eadon and John Martin are content to bunk in the back of the café and have Dan prepare their meals and Ching and Su look after their laundry. They are a very eclectic group of men from varying backgrounds, all eager for adventure, all care-free, all strong muscular men. Both Josephs are shorter than average, while Flanders is a tall handsome man. Some have left parents and siblings in the east to venture out into the western frontier, but David and John are without family connections. Timothy and Flanders have similar principles and find it easy to converse together on various topics. Jesse Benton and Pemberton Rollins use the bunkhouse until they have their land cleared and a cabin built. William Miller and David and William Robinson help in the building of the tavern and bunk in the back section for awhile.

By the beginning of June all the cabins and the blockhouses are complete, although gaps between the logs will be filled in later by the people living in each cabin.

Daniel Boone, Mike O'Neill, Richard Calloway, David Gass and other men are eager to return to their homes back east to bring their families and belongings. Captain William Hayes heads back to North Carolina to marry Daniel's daughter, Susannah Boone with the plan to settle in Kentucky. The men have opened up the land of Kentucky but now it is time to bring their families. The men talk eagerly of overcoming challenges and settling on the abundant rich farmland. The women are all too aware of the dangers and hardships that lay ahead. The wagon ride is uncomfortable and jolting and often the women and children walk alongside the wagons. When the wagons are left behind at the Cumberland Gap, hardships increase on the more difficult, narrow trail.

Daniel comes with a group of thirty people on his return on September 8 but the Boone's are the only family in the group. Rebecca and their family of six children, Jemima, Levina, Israel, Becky, Danny and Jesse are glad to have finally arrived and soon settle into their cabin in the fort. An ash-hopper, soap kettle and clothesline are set up for use. The rest of the men arriving with them are neighbours from North Carolina.

Richard and Rachel Calloway and four older sons and daughters, Zechariah, Isham, Elizabeth and Caleb, and six younger children Frances, Lydia, Theodosia, Kezia, Richard and newborn John arrive three weeks later on September 26, with a party that includes Barney and Helen Stagner and their four children ranging in age from ten to one, John and Jane Pogue and two twin daughters just beginning to walk, and William and Laura Pogue with their two young ones. John and David Gass arrive with their families. They all stay in the fort over the winter and plan to build cabins and clear land for their farms in the spring.

Soon afterward Mike and Mary O'Neill arrive with their three children; Colonel John Floyd, Jesse and Nancy Benton, Bland and Patricia Ballard, Pemberton Rollins, Benjamin and Naomi Anderson and others are not far behind.

William Pogue sets up shop making wooden drinking cups, washtubs and butter churns, all necessary items for the people. The Pogues build two cabins in the spring for the two brothers and are the closest neighbours to the Stagners. William moves his shop beside his new cabin. Once a month, he brings churns, washtubs, pails, washboards and other wooden items into Boonesborough to sell. At first he sets up a stand for his wares but it isn't long before he starts to sell everything to Richard and Pleasant Henderson at the General Store. Each time he comes in, he checks what items are needed. He loves to spend an hour in the early morning in his workshop and at least an hour in the evenings. Laura enjoys her trips with him into town, a chance to visit with other women, and for the children to play with other children.

The four Bryan brothers are off to get their parents and two sisters, returning in the spring of 1776 to set up a mill on their farm about five miles outside Boonesborough. In the spring, the Bentons and Ballards build cabins and clear land of trees to grow food. They raise sheep which are sheared for their wool. Nancy and Patricia card the wool, spin the yarn and then use it on their looms to make blankets. Jesse and Bland are shoe and boot makers and raise a small herd of cattle for the meat and the leather. Nancy always likes to have one cow for milk for the family. Chickens provide a supply of eggs but have to be kept in a closed pen with a roof or the foxes will be sure to have a tasty meal.

Pleasant Henderson is the opposite of her husband, being a quiet, somewhat shy woman especially in a group, with mousy gray hair and pale blue eyes. One-on-one Pleasant is cheerful and outgoing and a real asset in the store after her arrival in October. She organizes the stock, knows where everything is located and can help a person find even the unusual, seldom-asked-for items that every general store seems to have.

The two Hart families share the blockhouse at the opposite end of the fort on the Kentucky River side. Nathaniel and Sarah Hart and their four children, seven year old Kezia, five year old Nate, three year old John and Mary Ann a baby of eight months take the upper floor, while his brother, David and Donna, with their children, John, Mary, Chenoa, China, Kizia and Cumberland make their home on the ground floor. Thomas Hart married Susanna Gray in North Carolina. When they arrive in Boonesborough, they have two children, Eliza is seven and Tommy is three. Thomas starts a business making rope and burlap sacks from hemp. Their cabin is located next to the blockhouse on the end of the fort.

On the same end of the fort, at the opposite corner, Thomas and Colonel John Luttrell with their families have the blockhouse. John served first in the Virginia militia, helped out with the siege of Boston, and in the militia service he met Judge Henderson and got to know him. Richard contacted him when the trip was planned to go to Kentucky. John decided to join with Henderson to check out the country. He left his wife and two brothers, Hugh and William, to look after his farm while he made the trip. When they arrive at the settlement site, John works alongside Richard and Daniel to build the settlement. Being a Colonel in the militia, he is offered one of the two storey blockhouses for his assistance in sentry duty at the new fort. He decides to accept the offer and heads back to Virginia to get his family and to talk his brother into joining them. John's wife, Susanna, is a lovely woman with long, soft brown hair that John loves to run his fingers through. Their three sons, James, Simon and Peter, ages 18 to 14, are eager for the adventure of pioneering, while his daughter, Susanna, the apple of his eye, is rather sad to be going and leaving all her friends behind. She is glad to hear that her cousins, Becky, Maryanne, and Polly will be coming with them on the move, along with her Uncle Thomas and Aunt Jane.

When the four Williams brothers are offered the fourth blockhouse for acting as sentries, William, Edward, Jarrett and John are all bachelors. John is an agent of the Transylvania Company which purchased the land from the Cherokee Indians. They all have sweethearts back home in Tennessee and decide to take the plunge and ask them to marry them the following year. It gives them time to get the blockhouse built and make some furniture. They often frequent Richard's Café having their meals prepared for them. When the women arrive the following year, they make the block house a home, adding feminine touches and bringing cheer and laughter to fill in the lonely times.

There are more bachelors than young girls, giving the young women many choices, providing competition for the men. The women, both young and older, enjoy wearing a new bonnet, providing splashes of colour around the fort. A festive occasion, such as a wedding, provides opportunity for more brightly coloured dresses to be worn, emphasizing their beauty, causing male eyes to turn their heads and follow them with their eyes. Before long some young fellow will be knocking on a new door, hoping to begin courting.

In the spring of 1776, Richard Calloway joins with his brother William and nephew John to start a station across the Kentucky River. A large group of men gather together to build six cabins grouped close together. The layout for all of the cabins is determined first and the foundations for all of them dug. This is an ambitious undertaking and cannot be accomplished in a day. One group of men is cutting trees and trimming the branches, another group is notching the logs. Once there are enough for the first cabin, some of the men switch to building the cabin. Within hours, the house is taking shape. Once the logs are prepared, a cabin can be raised in a day, but the fireplace still has to be built. Since all the helpers cannot afford to be away from their own homes for a long period of time, two days a week are dedicated to the construction of the homes. The remaining days are dedicated to getting the ground ready for crops and beginning the planting. They clear the land to plant corn, wheat, oats, barley, rye and a large vegetable garden. Until the homes are ready, the families continue to live in Boonesborough. Furniture is made during any spare time.

Richard and Rachel with their six youngest children have their large two storey cabin built first. The next week, a second large two storey cabin is built for William and Elizabeth and their nine children. The cabins for Richard's son Zechariah and his wife Amelia and the one for Isham, Elizabeth and Caleb are smaller and are both completed the next weekend. These smaller cabins are designed to be able to easily have an addition added when the family grows larger. William's son John has six children with the youngest born the previous October and another spacious cabin is built for them. After all the crops are planted, men gather to build a small cabin for Elizabeth to use after her marriage in August.

During the cabin raisings, it is a time for the women to gather together and visit as they prepare the food. The men stop for a quick meal at lunch and then head back to work. The women call the men for a meal at the end of the work day.

Not all of the cabins in the fort are continuously occupied because some of the settlers live on lands nearby, and some have farms across the river. The fort is very crowded when an Indian alarm is given and the settlers pour into the fort.

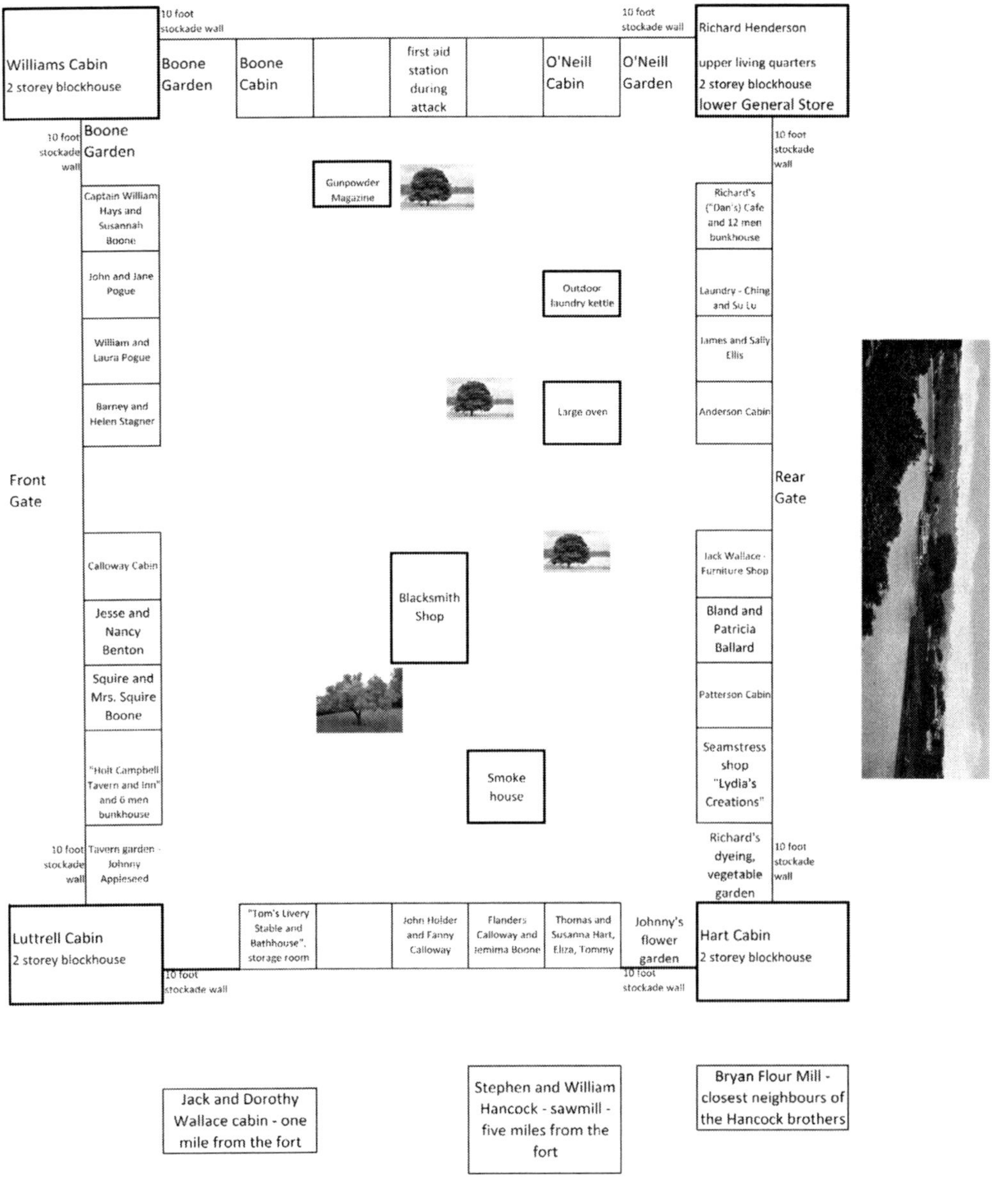

Layout of Boonesborough

Chapter 1 – The Letter

A letter dated February 15, 1776 from my sister, Mary! I can hardly wait to read it. It has been so long since the family heard from her now she has moved farther west. Elizabeth Worthington carefully opens the envelope, shaking in her excitement to read the news. As she reads her joy swings to consternation as she realizes the reason for the letter is to request something of her she is not sure she wants to give.

Elizabeth is five feet four inches in height, with hazel eyes and a beautiful complexion. She has shoulder length, dark, wavy hair. She has lived all of her life in Boston, Massachusetts enjoying a life of leisure due to the family wealth. She can sleep in as long as she wants to each day, party until the small hours of the morning and buy as many dresses as she has events to attend. She can eat whatever she pleases, visit the shops, go calling on her friends or have them visit her. She has turned twenty and has no big plans for her future other than helping her mother with her charity functions. She has been well-educated and has a keen mind, sometimes feeling frustrated with her empty life, such feelings being infrequent and short-lived. She enjoys playing the piano and harpsichord, singing, and doing needlework.

Now Mary asks her to leave her parents and Boston and go into the wilderness. Does Elizabeth really want to do this? She has always admired Mary, who is ten years older than her. Mary married Mike O'Neill and moved first to North Carolina and then to Boonesborough, Kentucky.

Mary didn't go into too much detail about the hardships she has been facing. Elizabeth knew some items were scarce and Elizabeth and her parents put packages together on a regular basis to send to them. There wasn't regular mail delivery but there were ways to have packages delivered. Elizabeth wrote to Mary and Mike every week but sometimes had several letters ready before there was a way to send them.

After reading and rereading the letter, Elizabeth went to find her mother to see what she would have to say. Elizabeth's mother Sally is a short, petite woman who is overshadowed by her tall, commanding husband, Jacob. Sally's hair hangs below her shoulders and has many strands of gray amongst the brown. Sally usually wears it rolled into a chignon at the back of her head. When company is coming over, Elizabeth helps to put her mother's hair up in a becoming arrangement to offset her heart-shaped face.

"Mother, I got a letter from Mary this morning."

Her mother had been resting with her feet on the chaise longue in the conservatory where she had been working with the plants and flowers. She perks up, "Will you read it to me?"

"Mom, Mary and Mike have asked me to go to Kentucky to help her for the next few months until after their baby is born."

With Elizabeth's pronouncement her mother's face drops and pales. Sally remembers how difficult it was to have her firstborn daughter Mary move so far away from home, and wonders if she can stand to have a second daughter leave her, even if only for a few months.

"I don't know what to do. I'm not sure I could live the way Mary does Mother, living so far from a city, living in the wilderness. On the other hand, Mary really needs me. She wouldn't have written otherwise. Mike even wrote in the letter asking me to come. They are really in rough shape."

"I don't know if I can stand to have you leave, Beth."

"Let's talk to Father tonight and see what his thoughts are on the situation."

To help alleviate the turmoil in her heart and clear her head, Elizabeth decides to stroll to town. She changes into a floor-length pink gown worn over a petticoat that peers through the front opening of the skirt showing the fancy embroidery work; the sleeves are tight to the elbow and have lace trim. Even though she hoped to clear her head, thoughts continue tumbling round and round. *Should I go? Could I stand to go? How much help would I be? I can't cook, have never washed clothes or ironed. I have spent some time with younger children of the neighbours. Do I want to go? Would I be happy with myself if I said no and didn't help my sister out in her time of need?*

Boston is an intellectual and educational centre with theologians and statesmen settling here and founding the Boston Latin School and Harvard University in the mid 1600s. Boston is a leader in shipbuilding, has an excellent harbor and is the leading commercial centre in the colonies with the largest seaport. It trades with the rest of the world in goods of all kinds with many of the goods made in Boston. Overseas trade has increased, and mills have been built along the rivers for logging, forging iron and processing wool.

The French and Indian War between Great Britain and France in North America began in 1754 and erupted into the worldwide conflict known as the Seven Years' War (1756-1763). The French and their Indian allies fought along the frontiers between the British colonies from Virginia to Nova Scotia. In 1755 the capture of Fort Beauséjour on the border separating Nova Scotia from Acadia was followed by the British deporting the French inhabitants. Many Acadians were transported thousands of miles away from their homes never to see their families again. After all the bloodshed, Britain became the dominant colonial power in the eastern half of North America.

In the early years of her life, all Elizabeth knew was living under British rule. Most colonists considered themselves loyal British citizens. Relations between the Thirteen Colonies and Great Britain steadily worsened after the Seven Years' War which plunged the

British government deep into debt. To avoid having to lay off many soldiers, and not being able to have a standing army in England, they sent the soldiers to the colonies. The British parliament passed laws to increase tax revenue from the colonies to help pay for the soldiers stationed there. Jacob Worthington could see that times were changing. He sees the need for colonists to be less dependent on British goods.

The Stamp Act of 1765 required that printed materials in the colonies be produced on stamped paper produced in London. These printed materials were legal documents, magazines, newspapers and other papers used in America. The British government felt that the colonies were the main beneficiaries of the soldiers and should pay a portion of the expense. A tax had to be paid for the purchase of these papers. Many colonists considered it a violation of their rights as Englishmen to be taxed without being able to send representatives to Parliament. The British Constitution guaranteed that British subjects could not be taxed without their consent, which came in the form of representation in Parliament. When Jacob and Sally Worthington's oldest daughter, Mary, was married in 1765 to Michael O'Neill, they had to pay a tax to obtain the marriage license. British merchants who sent exports to America were also against the Stamp Act tax and Britain repealed it the following year.

Jacob has a very prosperous importing and exporting business. In the past few years, he has been building up the manufacturing part of his business, concentrating on items that are needed by fellow colonists such as traps, guns and ammunition, cooking pots, farm and garden implements, wagons and wagon wheels. He also increased production of paper at his pulp and paper mills to supply some of the local needs.

In 1767 an import tax was imposed on tea, glass, paper, paint and lead; the taxes were called the Townshend Acts. The colonists, spurred on by the writings of John Dickinson, Samuel Adams and others, protested against the tax. The Boston merchants boycotted English goods. Women started the Homespun Movement in 1769. Instead of purchasing clothing made from imported British materials, women turned to spinning their own yarn and weaving cloth to make into clothing for their families. The Pattersons, friends of the Worthingtons, owned a dry goods store in Philadelphia. With the boycott on British imports, Lydia and Richard chose to close their store. They both took up spinning and weaving as a means of some income, and taught their daughters these skills.

After colonists began to boycott British goods, Parliament altered the revenue measure on March 5, 1770. Duties on all items except tea were repealed. The tea tax was retained because it was the most lucrative and was kept to show the colonists that Parliament still had the right to tax them. When Bostonians were informed of the British parliament's decision, there were three ships laden with tea in the Boston harbour. The merchants of Boston were not willing to purchase the tea with its attached tax and wanted the three shiploads returned to Britain. British officials in Boston refused to return the ships to England and this led to the Boston Tea Party. On December 16, 1773, a group of colonists, some of them disguised as Mohawk Indians, boarded the three vessels and dumped all the chests of tea into the Boston harbour. Jacob Worthington's son Robert, a young hot-head, was one of these men, along with his best friend Samuel Brownley.

The Worthingtons and Brownleys are two of the many families who switched to drinking coffee which was easier to import from the south. The Worthingtons have been good friends with the Brownleys for many years and their children have grown up together.

Britain closed the Boston Port until the destroyed tea had been paid for, and put in place four other laws known as the Coercive Acts which the British Parliament hoped would, by making an example of Massachusetts, reverse the trend of colonial resistance to parliamentary authority. One of the acts was The Massachusetts Government Act which took away the rights of citizens of Massachusetts to elect men to the executive council and gave the king the right to appoint men to govern; it also forbade town meetings without the consent of the royal governor. The fifth act enlarged the boundaries of Upper and Lower

Canada to the Ohio River, shutting out the claims of the thirteen colonies, removed references to the Protestant faith in the oath of allegiance, and guaranteed free practice of the Roman Catholic faith.

Many colonists viewed the acts as a violation of their rights, leading them to organize the First Continental Congress to coordinate a protest. All those involved agreed to boycott British goods and, if that did not get the Coercive Acts reversed after a year, to stop exporting goods to Great Britain. The Congress pledged to support Massachusetts in case of attack, which meant that all of the colonies would become involved if war broke out.

Jacob Worthington had already switched some of his importing and exporting to the leading port in the south at Charleston, South Carolina and had switched much of his exporting to France and Spain. In order to continue to prosper, he always had to be aware of current events but also to think ahead to what would likely result from his decisions.

On the night of April 18, 1775, British General Gage sent 700 men to seize munitions stored by the colonial militia at Concord, Massachusetts. Paul Revere, a prosperous and prominent Boston silversmith, helped organize an alarm system to keep watch on British troop movements and is well known as one of the midnight riders who alerted those in the countryside that the British were coming. The militia fought the British troops at Lexington and Concord and as the British retreated back to Boston, thousands of militiamen attacked them along the roads, inflicting great damage before British reinforcements arrived to prevent a worse disaster. With these two battles, the American Revolutionary War began. Robert Worthington and Samuel Brownley eagerly joined the militia. The Homespun Movement served the Continental Army by producing needed clothing and blankets. Spinning, weaving and sewing were skills used by the women to assist the revolutionary cause.

The militia converged on Boston and the eleven month siege began with the New England militiamen surrounding the town of Boston to prevent movement of the British army garrisoned there. Many cannons from the colonist captured Fort Ticonderoga were brought to Boston and used to fortify Dorchester Heights overlooking Boston and its harbour. The cannon threatened the British naval supply lifeline. The British realized they could no longer hold the town and chose to evacuate it, withdrawing their forces on March 17, 1776. The British headed for their naval base in Halifax, Nova Scotia.

Even with all of the strife, Mr. Worthington loves life in Boston, the largest city in the colonies. The homes are made of brick and stone instead of wood since many of the colonists had not forgotten the lessons learned from the great fire in London, England. Boston is situated on a peninsula four miles across, almost square, and surrounded by Massachusetts Bay which is large enough for 500 sailing vessels to anchor. Tradesmen, blacksmiths, schoolmasters, weavers, shoemakers, cabinetmakers, millers, preachers, lawyers and physicians are welcome in Boston. Even though farmers are welcomed and needed in America, they are encouraged to come to America through Boston, but are encouraged to move on to the interior where they can find the land they need for their farms.

Sally Worthington efficiently runs her household. She knows how to cook but has no need to do so since her marriage to Jacob as he has hired a cook for this job. Because of the servants that the Worthington's have, their daughter Elizabeth has never learned how to cook, preserve food, do the laundry, or clean the house. Sally enjoys working in the garden with the vegetables and flowers and Elizabeth has been helping her for years. The Worthingtons have a fine library which includes books for the young people and Mary, Elizabeth and Robert were encouraged from a young age to borrow the books to read. The books have been available to their friends as well. Elizabeth always has a book beside her bed and reads from it as often as she can, loving to learn about history and what is happening in the world. Jacob encourages his wife and daughter to read the daily newspapers and they have many lively discussions on various topics. Jacob taught Elizabeth how to keep the business ledgers, beginning to work with her from the age of twelve; her columns of figures are very neat, and she is good at adding and subtracting figures.

At supper Elizabeth and her mother are both picking at their food, remaining mostly silent with sad faces. It takes a bit but Jacob finally notices and asks what is wrong.

Elizabeth says, "Father, we wanted you to enjoy your supper before we burdened you."

"Out with it, Elizabeth. What's the problem?"

"I got a letter from Mary this morning and the contents of the letter have been weighing heavily on me all day."

"Is Mary alright?" Father looks up as he pauses during his eating.

"Yes and no."

"What do you mean?" he asks with a perplexed look on his face.

"Mary has written, and Mike too, asking if I will come to help them out until after their baby is born. Mary has not been feeling well and the three small children are more than she is able to manage. Mike is helping all he can but he has to work each day to support the family."

"Do you want to go?" Father asks, getting right to the heart of the situation.

"I don't know, Father. I don't know if I could live in the wilderness. It seems too much to ask of me. What about you and mother? You would be all on your own. "

"Sounds like Mary reached down deep to ask you, realizing I'm sure that she is asking you to make a sacrifice. Don't worry about your Mother and me. We'll manage. Your brother Robert is talking about moving back to Boston to help me with my work. I'm not sure how soon that will be though. He has had many adventures and is now ready to return home to learn the family businesses."

"You will be able to take some supplies with you for Mary," Mother pipes up. "That is if you decide to go. I must admit it was quite a shock when you first told me. I'm strong enough to manage without you for a few months."

"I'll think about it some more," Elizabeth adds quietly.

"How soon would you be ready to go? I mean, how long would it take you to get ready? I suppose you would need different clothing than you wear in town," Father comments. The gowns she wears in Boston are quite elegant, many still with hoops to hold the full skirts wide. Many have frills and ruffles and lace. Panniers are side hoops to extend the width of the skirts at the side while leaving the front and back flat, providing a flat panel where woven patterns or rich embroidery can be displayed. This ensures that the woman takes up three times as much space as a man and always presents an imposing spectacle. A pioneer woman has to do all the chores of daily life and cannot have hoops interfering. Their work clothes don't require anything fancy as they have to stand up to many, many washings.

"It sounds like you and Mother think I should go. I'm still not sure."

"Give yourself time. You have to make up your own mind." Both parents nod in agreement.

"Thanks Father and Mother. I'll go to my room now."

Jacob and Sally talk for a while longer, agreeing that they will encourage Elizabeth in whatever she decides to do. They are thinking of items they can send to Mary and Mike, either with Elizabeth, or as a package to send with a group going to Kentucky.

Elizabeth stands at her bedroom window leaning on the windowsill gazing out at a beautiful green lawn interspersed with flower beds with a riot of colours. The crocuses had popped their heads through the light dusting of snow two weeks ago and are shining in deep purple, bright sunlight yellow and solid white. The yellow daffodils are just opening and nod in the breeze providing a pleasing border along the pathways. The tulips in their bright red and pale yellow are a welcome sight after the long winter months. Elizabeth knows spring is nearly here when she sees the first robin and hears its musical notes. The cardinal will not be outdone, welcoming one and all with its sweet whistling notes. The branches on the maple trees are still bare but soon tiny leaves will begin to form. The lilacs will be perfuming the air in another month or so, and the blossoms on the apple, cherry, peach and plum trees will appear to stretch as far as the eye can see. Tonight as she stands at her window, even though it is still light out, Elizabeth doesn't see the beauty as her thoughts are troubling her.

She thinks and thinks long into the night, deciding at last that she will go to Mary. With her decision finally made she feels as if a huge burden has been lifted from her shoulders allowing her to fall into a restful sleep.

Mary included with her letter a list of items to bring. In the morning over breakfast Elizabeth and Sally discuss the items that Elizabeth will need to bring for herself and also a few things for Mary, Mike and the children. When she puts her mind to it, Sally adds many items to the list, knowing that her daughter is always careful not to ask for much, never wanting to ask for handouts, feeling how important it is for them to manage on their own.

Elizabeth can feel her excitement over her new adventure begin to mount! After telling her parents of her decision to go to Mary's, she heads over to see her best friend Katie Brownley. Katie is excited for her and is eager to pitch in and help her in whatever way she can. The two girls realize that they are going to need more help and so they call upon three other friends, Brenda Smiley, Barbara Townsend, and Patricia Fulton. They stroll to the local café to enjoy a cup of coffee and a fresh pastry. When their treat is set before them, Elizabeth shares about her upcoming trip.

"My sister, Mary, sent a letter which I received yesterday," Elizabeth tells her friends. "Mary needs me to help her look after the family until after she has her next baby."

"How long will you be away Elizabeth?" Brenda asks.

"I'm not sure but likely until next spring. Mary expects the baby to arrive in October and by the time she is ready to resume all her family duties it will likely be too late in the year to travel east," Elizabeth explains.

"We will really miss you!" Barbara says, and the rest of the girls nod their heads in agreement.

"When do you leave?" Patricia questions her. "What do you have to pack to take along with you?"

"Father is trying to make arrangements for travel companions through his business connections. He is hoping to have something concrete by the end of the week," Elizabeth explains.

"What can we do to help you?" Brenda asks, and the other girls look at Elizabeth eagerly, all ready to assist.

The five girls took music lessons together learning to play the piano and harpsichord. Patricia was the most musically inclined, excelling at playing. She had the ability to make the music come alive. She even composed a few pieces of her own music. Katie and Brenda took advanced dance lessons while Elizabeth and Barbara took only the basic instructions and spent more time with singing lessons. They all learned to draw and paint in water colours, all showing a little skill at it, but none of them brilliant. In their needlework classes, they learned embroidery, starting with simple samplers and progressing to detailed work on pillowcases, dresser scarves and table runners. They started with basic sewing and progressed to being able to use a pattern to make some of their own clothes although not the elaborately embroidered gowns that came by ship from overseas. They learned how to knit and made scarves, mitts, gloves and socks. Crocheting was finer work which Barbara and Patricia were most patient with, while Elizabeth often got frustrated with the thin cotton yarn and how slow the progress on a project seemed to be. Sally Worthington worked with all the girls on their handwriting and they are all proud to be able to write letters to relatives in England and friends who had moved away from Boston.

As they drink their coffee, the girls discuss some of the things they can help with. The refreshments have been enjoyed and they all stand up to head to Elizabeth's to get started on preparations for her journey. Sally has made a list of treats Elizabeth can take along for the family.

Elizabeth had already started a list and her friends help her add items to the lists, both necessities, and things that will be nice to have if there is room. She will take three chests with her, one for her own needs, one to share with her sister and family, and the third will be for supplies for the trip. Elizabeth will take two barrels of flour, two sacks of sugar, cornmeal, oatmeal, some homemade jam from their strawberries and raspberries made by their cook, a crock of pickles, crackers, bacon, dried meat, potatoes, rice, and beans. As a treat, she will take some chocolate.

Brenda and Barbara take on the job of looking over her current clothing to see which outfits can be adjusted to be suitable for her use during her time away. Lace trim is removed on some of the cotton dresses and will then be serviceable for Elizabeth. Hoops and fancy petticoats will be left behind; plain petticoats made out of sturdy homespun material will need to be made. The dresses made out of satins and silks will not be suitable because they do not wash well. Some of the dresses need to be shortened as the extra material is not needed to go over the hoops. Brenda and Barbara set to work on this assignment. Elizabeth has to take time out of her hectic pace to try on the outfits once they have been altered to make sure they are suitable. Elizabeth is an attractive girl and many of the outfits give her an extra glow and look just as nice on her without the hoops.

The local women are using dyes to add subdued colour to the material and it is now available in many soft shades of green, blue, purple, yellow and brown. Elizabeth met with Alice Chalmers, a leader in the Homespun Movement, and Alice is able to get her a supply of material. Elizabeth has time to do some sewing before leaving but plans to bring extra cloth along, as well as needles, thread, pins, and scissors.

Patricia and Katie check out Elizabeth's shoes and dancing slippers and realize they are not sturdy enough. They take Elizabeth to town to get two pairs of sturdy brogues. Each day they encourage Elizabeth to walk for awhile in the new shoes as it has been explained to them that Elizabeth will be doing a lot of walking on this trip.

By the second week of March, Elizabeth's father has been able to make travel arrangements. There are two covered wagons making the journey that will begin on April 4. Elizabeth will be leaving on April 1 to make the three day journey to meet up with the wagons. Now the girls have a specific date they are working towards.

In the middle of their preparations the girls pause for a few hours of celebration on March 17 when the British withdraw their troops from Boston, effectively ending the shipping blockades and allowing free movement of all the citizens throughout Boston once again. Patricia Fulton's parents invite everyone to their home. The children of the five families have grown up together and many days and evenings throughout each year have been spent together.

As the items are collected, they are put in the front parlour. The piles grow larger each day. Elizabeth's friends help her sort the items. Elizabeth's personal items are placed together, with the necessities in one pile and the extras in a smaller space not far away. The food items for Boonesborough are placed in another pile, along with items specifically for Mary, Mike and the children. The four girls work together packing the trunks, finding small items to stuff into all the small spaces. Unbeknown to Elizabeth, the girls tuck in some special items from each of them that Elizabeth will find when she unpacks her trunks. The piles of remaining items diminish as another item is packed. There is much laughter and giggling going on as the hours speed by each day. Often Sally Worthington smiles as she walks by the parlour door, glad that the girls are having a fun time. It is great for Elizabeth to have friends to be able to share this busy time with and to have help getting everything packed. Sally puts together items that she wants to send to Mary and she has a few items for the children, if there is room. Elizabeth always moves all the items her mother adds to the non-necessity pile to the trunk she is taking along.

It will take a month of travelling to reach her destination. The food items to be used on the month long trip are placed separately beside the third trunk. Some items will be packed on the day before as they are perishable and will be used up within the first week of travel, such as bread, fruit and meat. For the first three days, there will be inns available for sleeping and eating, but after that they will be in wide open country, sleeping under the stars and cooking over a fire. She has quite an adventure ahead of her.

Katie, Brenda, Barbara and Patricia put together a going away party for Elizabeth on the evening before her departure. Jacob and Sally Worthington join the group at John and Catherine Brownley's home. James and Joan Fulton, Abraham and Sarah Smiley, John and Dorothy Townsend and their sons and other daughters are all part of the merry group. Earlier in the day as a gift for all their help, Elizabeth had each of her friends choose one of her dresses to wear for the evening. The girls are all about the same size and only vary in height by an inch or so. Katie chose a soft pink gown with the deeper pink petticoat showing at the front with elaborate embroidery adorning it; it looks lovely on her with her long brown hair which she chose to pile on top of her head. Brenda has a reddish tinge to her hair and looks lovely in the pale green dress she chose; she put her hair up in a ponytail. Barbara has the darkest hair which is full of curls and waves; all she has to do is brush it and it attractively frames her face; she chose a deep purple gown with a pale mauve petticoat; she chose side panniers that stretched the gown out a foot to each side; it is a good thing the doorways are extra wide as it is difficult to get through them with some of the wide outfits. Patricia has beautiful blonde hair that is styled in ringlets; she chose a deep rust coloured gown that deepens the green of her eyes; the sleeves are tight to the elbow with a wide lace ruffle.

The mothers are all elegantly attired in various colours; they all enjoy dressing up in their fanciest clothes. John and Catherine Brownley decide to wear complimentary outfits in shades of deep maroon. John's shirt front and cuffs are elaborately frilled with the coat-cuffs embroidered with silk flowers in silver thread. The neck cloth is knotted at the back and kept in place in front with a diamond pin. Catherine's stomacher is adorned with diamonds.

Abraham Smiley chose a deep forest green jacket and breeches.

His silk stockings are worn outside the breeches and gartered just below the knee. He has a hunting scene on his snuff box. Sarah chose an emerald green dress with a pale green petticoat richly embroidered with flowers.

James and Joan Fulton chose shades of brown for their outfits with yellow accents. Dorothy Townsend chose a deep yellow gown to complement her husband's tan coat and breeches.

Elizabeth is the belle of the ball in a deep royal blue which accentuates the beauty of her complexion; the light blue petticoat is intricately embroidered. All the girls are wearing jewelry brought out of the family safes for the special occasion. Each of the girls takes turns playing the piano so the group can dance. The fathers all want the chance to dance with their daughters and their friends. The brothers enjoy dancing with the girls, and each has their eyes on one of them. Food is enjoyed around ten o'clock, earlier than usual for a social evening but Elizabeth has an early morning start the next day. The Worthingtons bid their goodbyes at eleven o'clock and Elizabeth is soon in bed, trying to settle down for a good sleep, but finds it hard to do after the excitement of the day and the busy month that has preceded it. In the morning she will have a few final things to pack and then be on her way.

Chapter 2 – The Journey

Departure day, April 1, 1776, arrives with the sun rising on a clear day with a few fluffy clouds in the sky. Elizabeth gives her Mother an extended hug, each knowing it will likely be spring before Elizabeth will be returning to Boston. Sad though she is to be leaving home and the life she has always known, Elizabeth is excited about the prospect of seeing her sister. She is looking eagerly forward to the trip although she realizes some of the challenges she will be facing; she has read enough stories to know about some of the hardships she will encounter.

Jacob is travelling with Elizabeth for the first day and they talk as they travel along. "I wish I was joining you for the whole trip to Kentucky, but I know it isn't possible." He is thrilled with the adventure ahead for Elizabeth, shares in her excitement, encourages her, cautions her, and challenges her. Elizabeth shares with her father her fear that she won't be able to help her sister very much. Her father assures her that because she has the desire to help everything will work out well; she will quickly learn how to do what needs to be done.

"I will really miss you, Elizabeth. You have been a really big help in the last few years doing the ledgers for my business." The next morning, not ready to see her go off on her own, he says, "I'm going to travel on with you for two more days so that I can get you settled in the wagon that will take you on to Boonesborough."

Reluctantly on the third morning, having packed her belongings in the wagon the previous evening, they hold each other tight for a long moment. Jacob helps Elizabeth onto the wagon and stands to the side as the group prepares to head out. Father and daughter wave until they turn the corner and can no longer see each other, she fighting the tears, he crying silently after she is out of sight.

Elizabeth is travelling with a husband and wife, Jack and Dorothy Wallace, with two sons, Johnny and George, ages seven and nine. Three single men eager for adventure are the remaining members of the group. Paul Holt is the leader who has taken this route before and is guiding the group, with the assistance of Samuel Campbell and Thomas Allan.

Jack is of average height, brown hair and eyes, a quiet spoken, pleasant man with a good deal of enthusiasm for the adventure ahead. Jack is a carpenter and hopes to open a shop to make furniture for the settlers. Their boys are excited about the adventure, but apprehensive too, not knowing what to expect but sensing the tension between their parents. Dorothy is a short woman, just barely making five feet, a little heavy, with plain brown hair straight to the shoulders, with all of her curls being created with the use of rags rolled in the hair each night. Initially she is rather surly and doesn't share much while Jack is much friendlier. It seems like it is only Jack's idea to settle in Kentucky and that Dorothy resents him forcing her to come. This is definitely a poor way to begin a new life since working together will be essential to their success.

Paul is a tall man with a physique that demands the respect of those in his keeping; he is a good leader, firm with commands in circumstances which are life threatening, gentle when there are injuries that need tending; he is patient to explain the reasons for orders he gives. Samuel is of medium height with thick dark hair and dark eyes that sparkle; he loves to tell stories and cheer anyone up who is feeling down. Thomas is a short, stocky man only coming up to Paul's shoulders. What he lacks in height is more than made up for in his attitude. He is a team player who gives one hundred per cent effort. Whenever something needs to be done he is right there to do his part. When a wagon gets stuck in a rut in the trail, he puts his shoulder to it to help move it along.

As they travel, everything is new for Elizabeth, and the beauty of the land is wonderful to behold. In the mornings they are up before daylight to cook breakfast, often preparing lunch at this time as well, something they can eat without having to light a fire. After breakfast, they hitch up four oxen to each wagon and continue on the trail. A cow is tied behind the Wallace's wagon, and when the men aren't riding the horses, they are tied behind the wagons as well. A string of eight pack mules will be used later on the trip. Chickens are in a cage tied to the wagon. The road is bumpy and often Dorothy and Elizabeth walk behind or beside the wagon, with the children running ahead and back, burning off steam. Late afternoon they stop to make camp for the night. After supper if they are not too tired, they gather around the campfire and sing songs, tell stories and visit. The boys sleep inside the wagon with Dorothy and Elizabeth, while Jack and the other men sleep under the wagons or out in the open under the stars. The first leg of the journey takes them to the last town with an inn for accommodations for the night. From now on they will be in wide open country, the beginning of the frontier.

Before long everyone is calling Elizabeth Beth, and Sam and Tom have their names shortened as well. The next day begins early, starting with a good breakfast, the last someone else will cook for them, the next at noon to be cooked over a fire. Everyone has to work together on the trip, each doing their necessary chores. Bread brought with them from the inn supplements their meals that day.

Dorothy gripes, whines and complains about everything – the weather is too hot, the road is too bumpy, there is too much dust, it is cold at night. The first day out, she gets badly sunburned on her face and is miserable. She complains about the smell of the bear fat that Paul applies to her face, but doesn't complain long as the concoction is soothing to her skin. After the first week she is complaining less and what a beaming smile she has when she chooses to use it.

Sam is patient with George and teaches him how to milk the cow. Each night they try to camp beside a stream for water for themselves and the livestock. In any case, the water barrel hanging on the side of each wagon is filled whenever there is water available. George, Dorothy and Beth carry water for their daily use. They collect buffalo chips and wood for the fire to cook the food. They gather strawberries, and raspberries they find along the way.

Dorothy, Beth and Jack have never cooked over an open fire; Paul has done it a little, while Sam and Tom are quite efficient at it. The first night the ladies do the washing up. This is a novel experience in itself as they have no pump to draw water. They use a pail to gather water from the river and use sand to scrub the metal plates, succeeding in the cleaning up process. Johnny and George search for firewood at each stop; they are cautioned not to wander too far from camp. As the days progress, everyone knows what they have to do, cooperating and working together, with Dorothy warming up and beginning to enjoy the trip.

Beth is often impatient with herself as they travel along for she wants to be able to do everything correctly right away. Sometimes she is even impatient with others who are slow in doing things. Not being used to so much walking, after the first day Beth and Dorothy have blisters on their feet and bear fat helps to bring comfort as their feet heal. Each day Sam or Tom shows the women how to do some simple cooking over the fire but it isn't long before they both have blisters on their hands from burns.

They are thankful for the clouds in the sky as April is warm and sunny, but even so sunburn on the women's fair skin is inevitable. The boys tan quickly. The toughest thing for the women is the lack of privacy for taking care of their daily needs and for bathing. Beth is used to having hot water to bathe in, while on the trail the water in the streams and rivers is quite cold. There is no opportunity to heat water for washing. Washing clothes on the trail is a challenge and is done quickly in the stream but then they have to find a place to hang the items to dry, and there certainly is no opportunity to iron the wrinkles out. Although initially there is a lot of grumbling and complaining, both inwardly and outwardly, by Beth and Dorothy, they soon begin to take things in stride and make the best of what they have. They grow a lot in the month of travel.

After two weeks on the trail, they have a broken axle on one wagon. Tom knows what has to be done and sets about doing it. They have a spare along but it takes a few hours to accomplish the repair, since the process requires them to empty the wagon to make it lighter. Then the wagon has to be reloaded, ensuring that the load is evenly balanced for the best performance of the oxen pulling it. There are bumpy, rutted roads in places, streams to wade through and rivers to swim, hills to climb, slopes to descend, all placing strain on the wagon and the oxen. The animals definitely earn the oats provided for them at the end of each day.

Sam decides he will try to hunt some game, already thinking ahead to the thick juicy steaks they will have roasted over the fire.

By tomorrow late afternoon they expect they will be at the Cumberland Gap, a natural opening between the Appalachian Mountains. The road has been widened from narrow trails but only roughly smoothed from this point onward.

Flapjacks are a favourite for breakfast, with the aroma of a pot of coffee bringing everyone to wakefulness.

"Come and get it," Sam calls. "Help yourselves."

"We pull out in half an hour. We want to make the Cumberland Gap while the sun is still providing lots of light to make camp," Paul, the leader, directs; everyone appreciates him keeping them on track. The sun is shining as they begin their day's journey. Paul hasn't decided whether he is staying this time or returning east to lead other groups out to settle the beautiful country of Kentucky. As they travel together, Paul, Sam and Tom develop a great rapport, working well together, becoming a cohesive unit. They talk about doing something together when they reach Boonesborough. They don't want to farm but they aren't sure what else they might find to do together.

They are more than half way and have been on the road for just over two weeks. There is to be a two day camp here beside a stream; however, it is not just time to laze about and relax. The oxen and pack mules have to be loaded for the remainder of the trip as the wagons can go no further. Since Jack is a carpenter and cabinet maker, and knowing ahead of time the terrain they would be passing through to get to Boonesborough, Jack sold all of their furniture before the trip and Dorothy shed her tears and stamped her feet in anger that some treasured items had to be left behind. There really had not been a "we'll try it out" option for moving west. It was completely a one-way trip. They had to make a go of it.

"The next stage of the journey is a tough one," Paul tells everyone the next morning, "but we are nearing our destination. We will continue to work together to get the job done. The rest of the way we will not have the wagons. Whenever the women and children need a rest from walking, we will try to have an animal available for you. You are all doing a great job."

Everything in the wagons has to be sorted and packed so that the weight is evenly distributed and tied securely. By the end of the second day, all the packs have been assembled; the next morning, the animals will be loaded and the last leg of the journey will commence.

It is mid-morning before everything is loaded and the trip through the Gap begins. Everyone follows the animals in single file. The sections that were old Indian trails are the smoothest. By the end of the first day of travel, the group is all pretty happy that they have managed well. Everyone has kept up and no one is totally exhausted; it was a little easier than their worst nightmares. Beth and Dorothy send the boys out to collect firewood, the men shoot some rabbits, skin them and the women soon have a savoury stew cooking. Everyone will be camped out under the stars tonight as the wagons have been left behind. This is exciting for the boys, although a little unnerving for Beth and Dorothy. But just as they have been adjusting to all the demands upon them in the past three weeks, they accept this as another challenge to be faced and accomplished. After the first night, there are no hesitations.

On the second night, Beth looks up at the stars for a few minutes, noticing how many twinkling lights there are but not knowing anything about them. One day she would like to learn more about the stars.

The next morning as they are eating breakfast, Tom says, "Where we are planning to stop to camp tonight, there is a good fishing stream. Maybe we will have fresh fish for supper." He is a real outdoorsman who loves to fish and hunt, seeking adventure continually. This is his reason for travelling to Kentucky.

Beth gets the boys singing silly songs to pass the time, everyone joining in from time to time. Even Dorothy laughs at their antics as the oxen and mules move along the wilderness roads. They haven't met anyone else today, it being just the eight of them in this wide open country, the clean air invigorating them, the adventure drawing their eyes onward.

At supper time almost two weeks later Paul tells them, "One more sleep on the trail and nearly a full day of travel tomorrow and we'll be in Boonesborough for supper. I wonder what the cook will have on the menu at the Tavern?"

"We'll find out tomorrow," Sam replies.

"Jack, where will we be sleeping when we get to Boonesborough?" Dorothy asks her husband.

"If there is an empty cabin inside the fort we may be able to use it until we get a cabin built on our land. I will try to get a group of men to help me put up a cabin. The land will have to be cleared of trees where we want the house located. After the house is built, we will have to clear the land for crops. I may build a workshop beside the cabin, or I may be able to open a shop inside the fort. I'm excited, ready to begin the next stage of our adventure." Dorothy is quiet, waiting to see how things will actually turn out, not being nearly as optimistic as Jack.

The next morning Paul sings out, "Everyone up! Let's pack up and move out! We will be in Boonesborough before sundown. Gather some extra water because we won't be near water again until we reach our destination."

Beth is so excited, today is the day, Boonesborough here we come. Excitement is running high for everyone in the party, their journey drawing to a close, their new life about to begin, looking forward to it with eagerness. It will take some time to get used to everything, a thought which causes her some trepidation, but Beth is anxious to see her sister.

It is another beautiful sunny day, a day made for travelling, a day made for living.

"Westward ho!" Paul calls as they pull out from camp.

"We're on our way," sings out Beth and everyone echoes the phrase.

"One more day," rings out the echo.

"The sun is shining," Beth sings.

"Done is the dining," is the next line of the song.

Johnny and George are excitedly running along beside the animals with Beth, singing at the top of their lungs, "We're on our way, it's a beautiful day!"

When they arrive in Boonesborough, the three men and the Wallaces head to the tavern for a meal and for a room for the night.

Paul gets to talking with the tavern and innkeeper who is planning to move back to Philadelphia. Paul sees it as an opportunity for him to put down some roots. He talks it over with Sam and Tom and they agree to work together on it, with Paul as the innkeeper and Sam assisting him. Tom will run the Livery Stable. The livery stable is on the other side of the blockhouse on the end of the fort. There are often horses boarded there and when there is an army unit present, the livery stable is full requiring feeding and grooming.

The men are always ready for a drink at the end of a work day.

Visitors to town can rent a room and have a meal cooked for them, a real treat after weeks of travelling on roads beyond civilization. The rooms are often used temporarily by new settlers until a cabin is ready inside the fort, or until a cabin can be built on land outside the fort. Everyone available in the area gets together for a cabin raising to get the new family off to a good start. Those who arrive in the spring get a crop into the ground to harvest in the summer or fall. Those who come in the late summer and fall have to rely on what they bring with them, on what others grow that year and on whatever is available at the General Store or the Tavern. Johnny Appleseed joins them to grow a garden beside the inn for vegetables to serve with the meals. There is a door in the stockade wall of the livery stable to allow the horses to graze outside the fort. At the first sign of Indian trouble, the horses are brought inside and the door barred with iron closures made by the blacksmith.

"You know what will be a good use for this corner of the stable, next to the storeroom?" Tom says to Paul and Sam when they look around. "A bath house for the men would bring in a little extra cash."

"We could call it *Tom's Livery Stable and Bathhouse*."

"*The Holt Campbell Tavern and Inn* sounds like a good name for our lodging house."

Chapter 3 – Arrival

When the Wallace group approaches Boonesborough on May 1, 1776, many people rush out to greet them. Mike is there to meet Beth and lead the mules carrying her belongings to their cabin where Mary is waiting for her. Mike is so grateful that she has arrived safely to help out his wife who is still doing poorly. Mary is resting when Beth comes in, but she gets up to hug her sister tightly, so happy to see her. Mary is a petite woman with a pleasant, easy-going nature, always eager to help a neighbour out. She has had a rough time with morning sickness during her pregnancies, but this fourth child is giving her an extra dose of illness which lasts most of each day. Beth can see that Mary is putting up a brave front and soon suggests that she tuck her into bed, gently steering her toward the other room.

Mike introduces Aunt Beth to the three children, eight year old James, three year old Isaac, and one year old Sarah. Mike shows Beth around the cabin, including where the cold cellar is for storage of their food. It is a whole new way of life for Beth, having never had to cook before, let alone over a fire, although she did get a little practice on the trip to Kentucky. Cooking over the fire requires some knack to get the food cooked and to keep it from burning. Mike agrees to cook the evening meal while the children are playing quietly. This gives Beth a chance to unpack and find the gifts she has for the children. She has a wooden horse and wagon painted a deep shade of blue for James, a wooden buggy painted brown and cream with a horse to pull it for

Isaac, and a doll with a knitted outfit in apple green for Sarah. The children squeal with delight at these new playthings, James and Isaac thank Beth with big hugs, Sarah thanks her by hugging the doll and smiling adoringly at her aunt.

After supper, Beth handles the dishes and general cleanup while Mike checks on Mary asking if she wants a little to eat. Mary attempts to eat, but only gets down a few spoonfuls. Mike and Beth get the children ready for bed, tuck them in, Beth sings them a lullaby and they are soon sleeping peacefully. Mike and Beth visit for a short time before turning in for the night, it having been a long day of travel for Beth.

The next morning Mike gently wakens Beth with a shake to her shoulders, showing her the morning chores, this time letting Beth do some of the cooking. Before long the children come out, hungry, eager to start the new day.

"Everything is so strange to me; all of the chores will have to be learned. Let's see how Mary makes out after a few days of staying in bed. I'll start by looking after the children, keeping the cabin neat, preparing the meals with some assistance from you, Mike. Then we'll add to those duties as the day's progress. How does that sound?"

"It's just wonderful to have you here, knowing that anything you do will lighten my burden and enable me to get some work done at the blacksmith shop."

"I have everything I need for the morning. You go ahead and work. I'll manage with the children until lunch time."

Mike heads out shortly afterwards, with a lighter step than he has exhibited in the past few weeks, knowing Beth will be a big help, since the short time she has been in his home she has already helped immensely. He remembers her from the wedding ten years ago as a bubbly person when caught off guard, but shy around him. In those intervening years Beth has blossomed into a beautiful young woman, caring, eager to please, although still lacking confidence in herself.

Beth manages to put lunch together for the children and Mike, after which she puts the two younger children down for a nap. James is off to see his friends. Mary is awake so Beth gives her a little food to eat and has a visit with her. As long as Mary is lying down she feels better. It is wonderful to be able to rest knowing that Beth is taking care of the children and managing the meals. Mary is able to give her some additional food suggestions – how to make cornbread for supper, and pancakes for breakfast. Beth feels very happy to be able to help her older sister. She is eager to learn whatever Mary can teach her.

"Time for you to have a nap, Mary, and I'll start thinking about supper. A pot roast would taste good. Do you have any potatoes, onions and carrots? Is there a store in Boonesborough where you can buy supplies?"

"The Hendersons have the General Store and it is kept well-stocked with non-perishable items. Fruits and vegetables are available some of the time. We have some vegetables growing beside the cabin but there are some things still to be planted."

"Rest now. I'll see you after supper."

Beth hums to herself as she mixes the cornbread. She decides that tomorrow she will ask Mary how to make biscuits. *I wonder if Mary has tried making cookies. Oh, bread! I probably need to learn how to make that tomorrow as well. I wonder if Mary makes several loaves at a time to last a week. I'll try to plant the rest of the vegetables in the garden. There are lots of things to keep me busy*, muses Beth. *I wonder if I will be able to do everything.*

Mike arrives and plays with the children for a half hour while Beth finishes the supper preparations, then calls everyone to the table. After eating, Mike watches the children while Beth clears up, then it is time to get the children ready for bed.

"Aunt Beth will you sing for us again tonight? I really liked that last night," James smiles up at her.

"Sure I will. You lie down and close your eyes." Beth sings two songs and by then the children are sound asleep. In the meantime, Mike visits with Mary. While they are talking she actually eats her entire supper. Beth visits with Mary for an hour while she knits, working on an outfit for the new baby. Beth receives instructions on how to make bread and biscuits and is willing to give both a try. No one has ever needed her this much before.

The next day before breakfast, Beth has the bread prepared and set to rise. Then she makes pancakes and cooks bacon. Mike milks the cow and collects the eggs. When she is ready, Mike will show Beth how to do both.

"What a wonderful aroma to wake up to!" Mike exclaims as he comes into the kitchen followed by James, Isaac and Sarah. Everyone enjoys the meal, then Mike leaves for work and the busy day continues. The children spend a few minutes with their Mom and then there is time to play with their toys. Beth spends time playing with the children in between her other chores.

The next morning Mike asks, "Beth, if I heat the water and get you set up, do you think you can manage to wash the clothes? It's beautiful and sunny and looks like a good day for it." Beth is up to the challenge of another new experience.

She is doing well with all of the strange chores of the frontier, chores she has never even thought about before, chores that are a way of life, a necessity, chores that all pioneers have to learn, and learn quickly and well, chores of survival. Mike builds up the fire and puts the tub of water on to heat. Once the water is hot enough the clothes are added and given a good stir to get them clean. Soon the clothes are ready to be hung on the line Mike has strung up outside the cabin. It is an excellent day to do laundry, as it is warm with just a bit of a breeze, ensuring quick drying of the clothes and sheets. The clothes will be ready for ironing the next day. By late morning the clothes are blowing in the gentle breeze.

Mike is shoeing a dozen horses for the army today. The soldiers are leaving tomorrow after their horses are shod, planning to check on other settlements in the area. Some pioneers live outside the forts, coming in for protection only when the Indians are on the warpath.

Beth prepares a pot of vegetable soup and sets it to simmer by the fire for them to enjoy for lunch. Later Beth will make an apple cobbler for dessert to be enjoyed after the supper meal of beef steaks, potatoes and vegetables.

"James, Isaac and Sarah, let's go for a walk around town before lunch. James, you can show me around," Beth suggests after hanging the laundry out.

"Aunt Beth, I know some of the families. I'll introduce you," James agrees. "Israel is my friend. I think you will like him. First I will show you around the fort. The General store is close to our cabin. Mr. Henderson has a jar of candy sticks."

"I'll take you inside another day, but today I just want to walk around. Who lives next to the store? It looks like a café."

"That's right. Some men sleep in the back and have the cook make their meals. Flanders and Timothy always smile and wave when I see them. I don't know all the men. Next is the laundry man and his wife; they are friendly when I go by." They continue past the next few cabins. "I don't know the ones who live in these cabins very well. They don't have any children my age. Sometimes I watch Mr. Ellis drawing. There are several young children in the next cabin."

They pass the closed back gate and as they walk on James exclaims, "It looks like there is someone new in the next cabin." He looks eagerly towards the doorway as two boys about his age come outside.

"That's George and Johnny Wallace. I travelled to Boonesborough with their family. I'll introduce you. Hi, George and Johnny. These are my nephews and niece. James is about your age George. Isaac is three and Sarah is one."

"In the afternoon I'll call on you and show you around," James offers.

"We'll wait for you. We have been busy helping Dad and Mom get settled but we are eager to do some exploring," Johnny pipes up.

"See you after lunch," James calls as he waves goodbye.

"We have time to meet your friend and then it's time to head home for lunch."

"Okay, Aunt Beth. We can cut across the square and be at Israel's place in a few minutes." They arrive at the Boone cabin and James knocks on the door. Rebecca answers and James introduces her to his aunt.

"Welcome to our town, Beth. I apologize for not having come over to meet you sooner," Rebecca says in greeting.

"It's been extremely busy for me learning all the pioneering chores. I just finished the washing and decided to take the children for a walk around town. This is the first time I have been out since I arrived," Beth explains. They chat for a few minutes while James makes plans with Israel for the afternoon.

"We'll get together for coffee one morning later in the week when your chores are lighter," Rebecca smiles warmly.

"I will look forward to it. It's time now for us to head back. Mike will soon be in for lunch. Mary is getting some much needed rest and feeling better each day."

"See you in a couple of days." Rebecca waves, as the group heads towards home.

The bread Beth made yesterday goes well with the vegetable soup she prepared in the morning. Mary is awake and the children chatter away to her while Beth sets the table and dishes up the lunch. She takes a bowl of soup and a thick slice of bread to Mary, shoos the children out to wash up. Mike arrives as they are all sitting down at the table.

After bringing the sheets in and remaking the children's beds, Isaac and Sarah are ready for their afternoon naps. James heads out to find Israel Boone. The afternoon is Beth's down time. Mary and Beth enjoy a visit together.

"I think I will get up for a little while tomorrow. I'm feeling so much better."

"That's good news to hear," Beth smiles at Mary.

Chapter 4 – The Attack

At the end of the first week Beth writes a letter to her parents telling of all of her experiences on her trip to Boonesborough. She writes about Mary feeling somewhat better now and the fact that she is happy to have her sister with her. She writes about the beautiful scenery both on the trip and around the fort. She mentions some of the people she has met and describes her interaction with them.

The sisters find time to talk about their life in the East. Mary has no desire to go back, as she is very happy with her husband Mike who fits right into the life in Boonesborough as the blacksmith. He has plenty of work to keep him busy shoeing horses and making wagon wheels. He always tries to have several wheels ready for anyone who comes in needing one. As the settlement grows with farms outside the fort, roads are made for travel and the need is greater for wheels for wagons and carts. Mike goes on some short excursions into the wilderness with Daniel Boone and a small group of men to hunt for meat to feed their families. Those are special times for all the men who are chosen to go as it is a time for the men to spend time together out in the wilderness and stalk game. On the farms grain and corn are grown and the surplus is brought into the fort to trade for other items.

"Why is that noisy bell ringing?" Beth asks on May 23, 1776.

Mary, whose face pales noticeably at the sound says, "Indian attack! Everyone is being called to help defend Boonesborough."

"Well, I cannot shoot a gun. How can I help?"

"There will probably be people injured who will need nursing. Head over to the cabin two doors away and the others there will put you to work." Wow! What an introduction to the west. Beth just arrived here three weeks ago and now they are in danger.

Beth is in the midst of her first battle for survival against the Indians. She is not yet used to the frontier, but she is willing to do what she can. She hurries along to the cabin and meets other women who have just arrived; among them is Rebecca Boone, a leader among the women. Beth is assigned her first job of carrying pails of water in from the barrels outside in preparation for any injuries. When that is completed, bandages are prepared by tearing larger pieces of cloth into strips. Others are preparing tables in case the doctor has more serious injuries to deal with. There is a commotion at the door and the first injury is brought in, a man named Timothy Eadon who has an arrow in his right shoulder. It is a tricky operation for the doctor to remove the arrow. Beth is given the job of watching him after he is bandaged up. He has fallen into a deep sleep and doesn't need too much attention at the moment so Beth helps out nearby. In the meantime, the battle continues with the constant crack of muskets. So far they have been able to hold off the Indians. Timothy is beginning to moan and mumbles these words in anguish, "I didn't mean it!" Beth gets a cool cloth for his forehead noticing that he has developed a raging fever. She tries to keep him comfortable and as calm as she can. Every few minutes he cries out in anguish the same words as before. Beth decides to try singing to see if that will help to calm him. Her voice has a rich, sweet sound and everyone is calmed as the words pour forth.

There is cheering coming from outside. Beth wonders what that means but everyone soon knows that an army detachment has arrived to chase the Indians off and assist the settlers.

Luckily only five people were injured, with Timothy having the most serious injury. His fever is raging so Beth is kept busy trying to cool him off. When he relaxes into a more restful sleep, Beth sings another soothing song.

All the injured folk are taken to their homes by this time, except Timothy who is too ill to move. Daniel Boone came in to see Tim. Everyone is praying for his recovery. He is a well-liked young man who loves to play with the children. He is friendly with everyone and is a part-time blacksmith. Perhaps best of all, he is an excellent shot with a rifle, often joining Daniel, and a few others on hunting expeditions.

Beth nurses him throughout the night and in the early hours of the morning Janet Williams is willing to give Beth a break and she heads to Mary's for a few hours of sleep. After awakening and having some food, Beth returns to Timothy's side. The pattern continues for two more days, with Rebecca Boone coming for a few hours on the second day, and Janet returning on the third day. His fever breaks late the third night and he rests peacefully for the first time since the arrow was removed. Beth nods off in the chair beside him. Several hours later the doctor comes in, checks the patient and is happy to see that his fever has broken. He sends Beth back to Mary's to get some rest.

Shortly afterwards, Timothy opens his eyes and says to the doctor, "How am I doing? I feel pretty sore. Where am I hurt?"

"You had an arrow in your shoulder that I removed for you and you have been fighting a fever for three days."

"Was someone singing? I remember hearing a beautiful voice singing. Maybe that wasn't real."

"Mary's sister was here and she nursed you all night long. She sang from time to time and it seemed to help calm you as well as everyone else," Doc replies.

"I can't wait to meet her." Timothy asks, "When can I get up?"

Dr. Watson replied, "One of the men will be along soon and we'll get you more comfortable in the bed. I didn't want to move you when you were unconscious and feverish."

Johnny Appleseed arrives a few minutes later and Tim is transferred to the bed. This exhausts him and he falls asleep quickly, the best thing for him to help with the healing. While he is sleeping, Beth pops in to see how he is doing; she is greatly refreshed after a few hours of sleep.

It is a beautiful day for a walk, but with the recent Indian trouble, Beth has to content herself with walking around the town inside the stockade walls. She has an hour to herself before she is needed to help with the children. Mary is in good spirits today and feeling more energetic than she has for some time.

The men and some of the women are busy moulding more bullets because their supply is dangerously low. The muskets take one bullet at a time and then have to be reloaded, but in the three hour skirmish, a lot of shots were fired. Thankfully no one lost their life.

As she walks, Beth thinks about her parents back east and of their expectations for her. She is no longer sure that their plans for her are the right ones. She shakes off those thoughts as there is nothing she can do about things in the east while she is in Kentucky in the middle of a frontier town. She walks into the General Store and wanders up and down the aisles, surprised at the great variety of goods that are available. She chats with Pleasant Henderson for a few minutes.

Jack and Dorothy Wallace are heading towards the store. Dorothy is talking about the Indian attack a few days before. She finds it very disturbing that the attack occurred so soon after their arrival in Boonesborough. "That's why I was so against coming west with you, Jack. It's still so dangerous."

"It does make every day quite an adventure," Jack replies. "We learned what to do yesterday and everyone survived."

"I was plenty scared though."

"We all were, but we did what we had to do."

"I'm trying, Jack."

"You are doing well, Dorothy. I'm proud of you. There's Beth now. How is Tim doing Beth?" Jack calls to her.

"The fever broke and he is sleeping peacefully now."

"That's good to hear."

"How are you settling in Dorothy and Jack? Is your cabin ready yet to move into?"

"We were going to move tomorrow, but I think it is wise to wait a few days now to make sure that the Indians are not on the warpath. We are waiting for Daniel Boone's return to see what the situation is really like out there. He has a great rapport with many of the peaceful Indian tribes who are friendly with the white settlers," Jack adds to Beth's knowledge.

"I worked with Rebecca Boone during the Indian attack; she is a real leader among the women, not pushy, but she has a strong will. The rest of us are like putty in her hands, willing to do whatever she asks," Beth continues.

"I am still pretty timid," Dorothy comments. "I was so scared, but I was able to help Jack load his musket and work side-by-side with him."

"You were a big help honey and I was so happy to have you by my side. You knew what I needed without me having to ask."

"I guess that comes with being married for ten years," Dorothy smiles.

"I must get back to Mary now. Have a good day," Beth waves as she heads back to the cabin.

Sally smiles at her as she walks in the door and holds up her arms to be picked up, which is a joy to Beth. The next hour flies by playing with and entertaining Sally, Isaac and James before it is time to prepare the evening meal.

For the next couple of days there is extra baking to do and a dress for Beth to make for the square dance social planned for Saturday evening. If all remains quiet with the Indians, they will have a bonfire and dance in the town square. Charlie will get his fiddle humming and everyone from young to old will kick up their heels. Beth can hardly wait. Her powder blue dress is almost finished and the colour suits her dark shoulder-length curly hair and her complexion.

Extra food is prepared on Saturday morning to be enjoyed in the evening. Apple and pumpkin pies are made in quantities as these fruits were preserved from the plentiful fall harvest the year before. Cornbread and stew with carrots and potatoes are the aromas greeting everyone as they gather together. The women have changed into dresses with more colour than their everyday work clothes. The pinks, blues, greens and yellows with matching bonnets are a pleasing sight to the eyes. The men are all cleaned up and many have freshly shaved faces. Everyone is looking forward to the evening.

As people begin to gather for the fun evening, Timothy comes up to Beth to thank her for looking after him so well. She blushes to hear his praise. "Your voice sure was beautiful and soothing. I hope I'll be able to hear it again soon."

"If you are sitting near me during the sing-along that is planned after supper, you might get that chance," she says with a twinkle in her eyes.

"I'm not up to dancing tonight but I look forward to our next gathering and I hope you will partner me for a dance." Beth agrees and is then interrupted by William Bailey Smith to join in the first dance, a Virginia reel, which gets everyone involved with the clapping even if they are just watching the dancers. Tim stands on the sidelines and gazes his fill as Beth does the dosado, allemande left and allemande right, swing and promenade with different partners for the next several dances. What a thrill it is for him to watch her.

The next dance is a waltz and Joseph Kennedy comes to take Beth onto the floor. He is a brash young man having just recently arrived at the fort. He still thinks he knows it all and doesn't need anyone to tell him what to do, least of all a woman, as Beth finds out when she tries to tell him that a waltz is a slow, elegant dance rather than a fast, stomping one. His stomps many times land none to gently on her small feet. Unsuccessful in her attempts to get Joseph to slow down, she uses her energies to jump out of the way as his feet are about to land once again on her toes. Beth is glad when this dance ends and everyone is called to the buffet table to get some food.

Tim comes up to her and chuckles, "You made quite a sight with your little jumps out of the way of Joe's big feet!"

"He sure didn't like me to try to tell him how the dance was supposed to be done. Everyone else tried to give us a wide berth," Beth agreed with a smile on her face.

"You sure covered a lot of ground quickly. It wasn't easy for the others to always get out of his way. He bumped into a few people," Timothy chuckles.

"Every time he bumped into someone, he glared at them as though it was their fault."

"That was quite a whirlwind dance as you tried to protect your feet."

"If he asks me to dance again this evening, I will have to be very forceful in saying no. He will be hard to convince."

"He still has a few things to learn. It probably won't take too long out here in the wide open country," Timothy says. He joins her in the lineup for food and they sit down together to eat, enjoying their time together.

After everyone's hunger is satisfied, Mabel sits behind the harpsichord and strikes up a tune, leading the group in a lively sing-a-long. She starts with "Jesus Loves Me", then proceeds to a lively round, "Row, Row, Row Your Boat". Everyone knows the words and sings along. Songs like "Magic Penny", "Morning Has Broken" follow next. "Old MacDonald Had a Farm" is a hit with the children and they have fun adding in the names of animals they know from their environment, the buffalo, the deer, as well as cows, chickens, and sheep. "I Love to Go a Wandering," and "You Are My Sunshine" are also sung. Beth knows all the words and eagerly joins in, the notes ringing harmoniously from her throat. Many people around her quiet their own singing to hear the melodious notes. The last song is "Auld Lang Syne" and Beth sings it loud and clear.

"Your voice is even lovelier than I remember it from my dreams. Thanks for letting me listen. I have to slip away now as I'm on sentry duty with Flanders Calloway. I will be an extra pair of eyes to ensure we are not taken unawares. I will see you soon." Beth turns to follow him with her eyes until he is out of sight. Then she is drawn into the next dance.

The empty cabin makes a good nursery as it isn't needed tonight as a hospital. When the children become exhausted, they are bedded down in a space on the floor and the mothers take turns watching them.

Tim finds that everything is quiet outside the fort, no sign of any trouble and with the full moon there is enough light to see at least a little. The time close to dawn is always an anxious time because that is when the Indians often make a surprise attack. The sentries must be especially alert at that time so that as much warning as possible can be given to the men in the fort.

It was great foresight to start digging that well inside the stockade; they really need to complete it. Another piece of great planning is the area set aside for growing some vegetables. Outside the fort you never know if farming efforts will yield anything due to the unstableness of the situation with the natives. These thoughts flit through Timothy's mind as he keeps an alert eye out for any movement beyond the walls. The stars are out in full array. *I'll have to take Beth for a walk to point out the constellations and the different shapes I see in the stars. Maybe tomorrow night will be a good time.*

The next morning Tim swings by Mary's house to invite Beth for a walk around Boonesborough after supper. Then he heads off for the blacksmith's shop. His arm hasn't healed enough for him to do much, but he can work the bellows with his feet for awhile to keep the fire glowing hot.

Beth is humming to herself, smiling as she goes about the day's chores, anticipating this evening's walk. The day seems to be extra long, and yet on the other hand it seems to fly by, one of those unusual types of days. Supper is cleared away and there is Tim at the door. It is a beautiful, clear evening, a peaceful time with a gentle breeze blowing, the stars sparkling like brilliant diamonds in the sky.

"Look Beth, do you see the water scoop there? It's called the Big Dipper. That star always points north."

"That arrangement looks like the outline of a man and makes me think of Hercules," Beth comments.

"It's actually called Orion. There's a 'W', that's Cassiopeia." Timothy reaches for her hand to point out another one that seems to snake along. There are millions of stars.

"Timothy, how do you know so much about the stars?"

"My father was interested and read about them and taught me from the time I was young." Beth's hand is warm in his and he doesn't let go as they continue their walk.

In the following days, other bachelors ask Beth out for a walk down to the river, a walk around Boonesborough, or coffee and cake from Richard's Café. On moonlit walks, Beth converses with them, tries to get them to talk, but keeps her distance from them. At the weekly church services, different men ask her to sit with them. Some comment on her beautiful voice, others seem to be more interested in holding her hand and sitting very close. Before long Beth starts saying no to requests by certain individuals. She wants to share time with others who have some depth of character. She is more interested in friendship, someone she can relax and be herself around, rather than someone she has to be on guard with.

"One day we'll go for a longer walk outside the fort, but I'd like to be sure everything is quiet with the Indians," Tim says on another of their walks. "The attack two weeks ago was a surprise to us all as we weren't aware that there were any Indians on the warpath. It only takes one renegade to lead a group of hot heads to start a fight. We respect the Indians out here and show ourselves friendly, but some feel we are spoiling their hunting grounds here in Kentucky."

Soon Timothy and Elizabeth are seen each evening strolling around town, greeting whoever they meet.

Chapter 5 – Kidnapped

In spite of all the talk about Indian wars, Boonesborough is feeling fairly secure again in the early summer of 1776. Farther to the north a few settlers have been killed, but Daniel and Squire Boone come home from a surveying trip at the Falls of the Ohio without hint of danger.

The customary Bible reading is over when Jemima Boone, Fanny and Betsey Calloway invite Beth to go with them for a walk. The wildflowers in the meadow are a sight to behold that summer morning of Sunday, July 14. Jemima has a sore foot from a cane stab, a common injury as young girls and many women do not wear shoes during the summer and broken cane is very sharp. Jemima and Fanny are 14, Betsey 16 and Beth 20.

It is a beautiful sunny day. Jemima soothes her foot in a bucket of the cold spring water, as the girls laugh and talk about the boys in Boonesborough. Jemima has her eyes on Flanders Calloway, cousin of her friends. Betsey is engaged to be married to Samuel Henderson and Fanny likes Captain John Holder. Beth likes Tim and they are becoming good friends.

"Sam just gives me a really good feeling all over when I am with him," Betsey smiles dreamily as the young girls giggle.

"Flanders has beautiful, big, brown eyes that I love to gaze into," is Jemima's comment.

"Tim and I love to talk about so many things. He taught me about the stars. We just enjoy spending time together," Beth adds.

Jemima's foot feels much better after soaking it in the water so they wander into the meadow to pick some wildflowers. The meadow is a mass of brightly coloured blooms. The golden yellow buttercups are a contrast to the pale yellow lady's slippers, while the pale purple coneflowers and the black-eyed susans nod their heads over the colourful array. The deep red cardinal flowers are bright splotches of colour among the purple prairie clover and wild petunias. The bright pink bergamot blooms are beacons of colour next to the daisies and butterfly milkweed; so many lovely shades and so much variety.

"They are so beautiful!" exclaims Fanny.

"It's almost a shame to pick them. They look so beautiful where they are growing," comments Jemima.

"They will likely wilt before we get them back home," agrees Beth.

"We have about another half hour to admire them before we head back," Betsey observes.

As they wander among the flowers, they come close to the woods, laughing and having a good time, when suddenly they are surrounded by a small band of Indians, two Cherokee and three Shawnee Indians led by the Cherokee Hanging Maw. The girls hands are tied together and they are marched away towards the Shawnee towns in the Ohio country.

Wow! What a sudden end to the enjoyment of the afternoon. The young girls do all they can to leave a trail for a rescue party. Each of the girls tries to break branches as they are hurried along by the Indians. Betsey makes an extra effort to dig in the heels of her shoes whenever she can. This whole way of pioneer life is so new to Beth that she doesn't know how to leave a trail but she does help to keep the girls encouraged. They are all scared but Beth knows she has to keep up their spirits. She decides to start a song with the first line being repeated by the girls, then Beth sings the second line, and the girls repeat it. Beth has such a lovely voice that the natives enjoy it and don't hush them up. After the first song is finished, Beth starts another lively tune which the girls quickly catch on to. Beth makes up a song about their walk to see the flowers, keeping it light-hearted, now they are seeing the mountains with a ring of cloud around the top, a beautiful vista looking down into the valley with the lake below. Kentucky sure is a beautiful place.

After walking for awhile, Jemima refuses to walk any further with her sore foot bothering her so much. The Indians provide Jemima and Fanny with moccasins to cover their bare feet. At this time, the captors cut the girls' long skirts off at the knees to make travelling through brush easier. The material cut off is used to make leggings to wrap around their legs to protect their skin from brambles and underbrush.

The girls are tired by the end of the day and glad to finally be able to rest. They are given some dried meat to eat, have their hands untied while they eat, but the Indians are extra watchful of them at this time. As soon as they are finished eating, their hands are tied again and the rope tied around a tree. The four of them huddle together and Beth tells them a story until they finally fall asleep in exhaustion. It takes Beth a little longer to get to sleep as she thinks about being captured and wonders where they are being taken.

It seems like she has just closed her eyes when she is roughly nudged awake and told to get up. She wakes the other girls and they are soon on their way again. The girls are feeling a little more down today, so Beth encourages them with her music. The Indians don't like them talking together too much, but they don't stop them from singing. Beth makes up words of encouragement and as the girls follow along, they are soon giggling.

There is a quick stop late morning for some dried meat to eat and then the journey continues. There are many tears by the younger girls so Betsey and Beth have their work cut out to keep them encouraged. The girls are noticeably slower today but their captors can only hurry them along a little. They stumble and require short breaks often. Beth keeps them busy trying to identify the different birds they see and hear. Once they see a little fawn in a meadow. The summer flowers are abundant in the sheltered valleys, reminding them of their initial pleasure of the morning before when they started their walk from Boonesborough.

I wonder if anyone will try to rescue us, Beth thinks. The best she can do at the moment is to keep the girls' spirits up. It helps her to keep her mind off what is planned for them at the end of their journey.

As the Indians travel, they set many false trails to mislead anyone who is trying to track them in order to rescue the girls. This makes it very difficult for the rescue party to follow their trail, but Daniel Boone exercising his expert woodsman skills deciphers where they are heading. Half the group is led by Colonel Richard Calloway and are travelling by horseback. They are sent farther ahead to ambush the Indians. William Bailey Smith, Samuel Henderson, Nathaniel and David Hart and John Martin are part of the group. Daniel leads the others in a northerly direction that crisscrosses the trail from time to time that indicates, from the signs the girls manage to leave behind, that they are heading in the right direction.

On the third morning, having seen no sign of pursuit after travelling many miles, the captors are less cautious. They kill a buffalo, cut out a rump and make camp shortly afterwards to roast some fresh meat. Water from the stream is a welcome treat on this hot summer day. Thankfully most of their trip has been along a trail among the trees which provide shelter from the hot sun. Their break is a little longer, providing a time of recuperation to continue on, with Beth encouraging them to keep a smile on their faces, knowing that a positive attitude will be their best defense.

When Daniel and his men see the fresh carcass of the buffalo on July 16, Daniel figures that the Indians will be less cautious as they have covered thirty-five miles without any sign of white pursuers. The Indians believe that by this time they have outdistanced any pursuit. The pursuit has been much swifter than the Indians dream, due to the skills of Daniel, Timothy and others in the rescue party.

They know they are close now, and also know that when they go into the camp they will have to be swift in their actions in order to save the girls. John Floyd makes the first shot and one of the Indians falls into the fire, but is not seriously hurt and is able to get up and run off into the woods. Two other musket shots kill two Indians and the others flee. Daniel Boone, Timothy Eadon, Flanders Calloway, John Floyd, John and David Gass, John McMillan, William Bush and John Holder move into the camp and rescue the girls. There are lots of tears and hugging. Timothy holds Beth tight and says he is so glad to see that she is all right.

The kidnappers had told the girls there was an Indian band at Blue Licks and another on the Kentucky River. Daniel Boone wants to get the group back to Boonesborough as soon as possible; however, everyone is exhausted. The girls are worn out by the discomfort of two nights tied up to trees and the speed with which the Indians have forced them along. The rescuers are tired by the even greater speed with which they have followed. They travel only a short distance that day before making camp. The next two days they continue the journey for home. Along the way they find a stray pony, catch it and the girls take turns riding it.

The people of Boonesborough are happy to have the girls back safe and sound. Everyone is sobered by the capture. It was the Cherokees who had negotiated the sale of Transylvania to the white men, but there are many other tribes, the Shawnees being the major ones who are not going to peacefully let the white people settle in Kentucky. There is a constant battle to send them back to the east, but more and more settlers keep coming. The white man is here to stay.

Betsey Calloway's fiancé is certainly glad of her safe return and plans to do his part to keep her safe. Their wedding is planned for next month. Betsey's cousin, Flanders, realizes how much he likes Jemima Boone and starts courting her in earnest as does Fanny Calloway's beau, John Holder. Flanders and John have to wait a year until both girls are fifteen before they can marry.

Mary is happy to have Beth back home. "It was terribly frightening when you didn't come home the other day and it was discovered hours after it happened that you had been captured by a small band of Indians," Mary says as she hugs Beth to her.

"It was scary for us too, but I knew I had to try to keep the younger girls as calm as possible. I was able to sing to keep their spirits up, and got them singing as well. The braves must have liked the singing because they didn't stop us. As the second day began, the girls were noticeably more tired and so I started to make up silly songs and had them sing after me. I even had them laughing a few times. Then we were on day three with only a little jerky for food and some water from the streams we camped near."

"Who would have thought you would have had the stamina to do what you did and the courage to help the girls stay encouraged."

"It needed to be done and so I did it."

"You have really changed and grown since you have been here Beth. Four months ago back in Boston you couldn't have begun to imagine what life would be like out here. You have faced several challenges already," Mary continues.

The next day, July 20, Beth is called upon by Sarah Hart to assist her after the birth of her son Cumberland.

Chapter 6 – Wedding Celebration

In August the first wedding in the new state of Kentucky is to take place. All the women plan what they will make for the celebration meal, each contributing a special dish. Betsey Calloway and her mother work for several days on a lovely wedding dress in forest green homespun material.

Finally the day arrives, a warm summer day with the sun shining brightly for the outdoor celebration, with people coming from all over the territory to witness the ceremony. The bride and groom are standing in the shade of the tree in the centre of the town. Betsey is the daughter of Colonel Richard Calloway and Samuel is a brother of Judge Henderson. The bride carries a bouquet of wildflowers. Her sister Fanny is her bridesmaid dressed in pale apple green, and Judge Henderson is the best man. Samuel has purchased a plain gold band for the ring to give to his bride. Mabel plays the harpsichord from the doorway of the nearby cabin as Betsey walks down the aisle formed by the people. Squire Boone, a Baptist Elder, officiates to join Betsey and Samuel as husband and wife. Squire takes the time to explain the importance of the union and the need to be faithful to each other. When he announces it is time to kiss the bride, cheers go up from all the people gathered around. After the ceremony James Ellis uses his sketching skills to capture the bride and groom in picture.

Tables are set up under the shade of the trees and soon filled with lots of good things to eat for the wedding feast. The gardens of the settlers produced some lovely vegetables including corn on the cob with the big treat for the guests being home-grown watermelons of which the settlers are very proud. The lines begin to form and the plates are filled with the delicious food. After everyone has eaten their fill, the leftovers are taken inside the cabin for use again a few hours later for a late evening snack. The wedding gifts include practical items for the couple to set up their home. Jack Wallace made them a kitchen table, and several of the bachelors pitched in to have Jack make matching chairs. Rebecca Boone provided a copy of her favourite stove top apple cake and the pan to cook it in.

A bonfire is started and Charlie gets his fiddle tuned up and Ben has his accordion. Betsey and Sam have the first dance and then everyone else joins in.

Beth has lots of partners and has no chance to sit out a dance. Everyone is in a gay mood, excited for the newly married couple, happy with the harvest, enjoying the social time together.

Tim claims Beth for the next dance.

"Where did you learn to dance, Tim? It's a joy to be your partner."

"In the church in my hometown all the young people were taught the basic dance steps and encouraged to dance at all the social events. I had a natural feel for the music and really enjoyed swinging my partner."

The first stars begin to appear after the sun sets in the west in a beautiful display of colours, a lovely end to this memorable day. After late evening refreshments are served, the dancing continues long into the night. *I wonder who will be getting married next*, Beth thinks to herself.

A few days later a returning settler brings a copy of the Virginia Gazette with the Declaration of Independence which was signed on July 4, 1776. The document is read to the assembled people who cheer after hearing it. They formally declared their independence as one new nation, the United States of America, claimed their own sovereignty and rejected any allegiance to the British monarchy. Now they will be governed by a group that allows them to have some say in the way they are governed. No more taxes will be added without them being able to represent themselves. They celebrate with another bonfire that night and soon there is a new flag fluttering in the forest, a flag with thirteen alternate red and white stripes with thirteen white stars in a blue field.

"We are a new country now, the United States of America. It's a good feeling," Beth states.

"The British have not accepted us as a new nation. As more and more settlers move west, there will be less and less game for the Indians which we have already seen around Boonesborough," Tim responds with a realistic viewpoint. "The Indians are being recruited by the British to fight against us, even as they fought with the British and the French in the Seven Years War which gave Britain control of this country.

"After the outbreak of the war in 1775, violence has increased between American Indians and settlers in Kentucky. Indians, particularly Shawnees north of the Ohio River, raid the Kentucky settlements hoping to drive away the settlers whom they regard as trespassers. Isolated settlers and hunters become the frequent target of attacks and many are convinced to abandon Kentucky and return to the east," Tim adds to Beth's knowledge.

Chapter 7 – Anguish

Fewer and fewer of the bachelors are asking Beth out. Soon it is only Tim, and Beth eagerly waits for his knock on the door. Often when it is a clear evening, they will gaze at the sparkling beauty of the constellations, millions of stars twinkling like diamonds in the pitch black sky.

There are walks down to the Kentucky River on a sunny day, watching the sun sparkling on the flowing river. It is great to be alive. After Timothy teaches her how to ride, horseback riding is another outing for them. It gives them the opportunity to travel outside the walls of the fort. The first trip they go as far as Dorothy and Jack Wallace's cabin about a mile from the fort. As more and more people are starting farms, the roads are improving to get around.

On their next horseback ride they decide to make a day of it and pack some food to take along. Beth has been practicing riding around the fort whenever she has a little spare time. She is now ready to see a little more of the countryside. They head in a south westerly direction towards the settlement where the Gass family live. David and Sarah are raising their family, and five of his siblings also have cabins there. With the six cabins built close to each other, they stand a better chance of withstanding an Indian attack, but also the Indians are more apt to attack a lone settler than a whole group.

As Tim and Beth arrive, it is quite a sight that meets their eyes. The fields of grain are ripening; there are horses in the field and a few cows, pigs, sheep, goats and chickens to be seen. They are greeted warmly and welcomed by Sarah as they settle down for refreshments and a visit. Soon other members of the family begin arriving and there is an impromptu festive atmosphere with each family bringing over some food. Not many visitors come out this far, and everyone is excited to hear the latest news, to catch up on friends in Boonesborough, and enjoy a break from routine.

Beth offers her assistance to organize the food and put it on the table. The conversation starts to flow. "I knew your sister Mary back in North Carolina. How is she doing? It has been many months since I have been in Boonesborough."

"Mary had a daughter in October. Ellie is a sweet girl and is a joy to have in the family," Beth informs her.

"James must be growing up. He is about the same age as our James," Sarah continues.

"James is very talkative. He loves the adventures he has with Israel Boone," Beth adds.

"How is Rebecca? She was like a sister to me," Sarah reminisces. "She and her family lived with us for a couple of years before we moved to Boonesborough."

"I spend quite a bit of time with Rebecca. We enjoy each other's company and she often has my nephew at their cabin. Rebecca has assisted me many times in learning about pioneering ways," Beth says. "It has been quite a change for me living out here. My life in Boston was very different."

"After lunch you can tell me about Boston. Right now lunch is ready and we will call everyone to the table."

During lunch Beth is seated between 12 year old Sarah and 13 year old Mary. She enjoys a good visit with them in between mouthfuls. Both girls have friendly, happy dispositions and are following in their mother's footsteps. It won't be long before the boys are chasing them.

After lunch is cleared away, the men head out for a tour of the barn and the station. Tim is eager to see what the group has been able to accomplish. They are in the process of building a stockade wall around the cabins. Tim brought some of his tools along and was able to do some blacksmithing to repair a few broken pieces of equipment.

James and Sally Black have a cabin in the settlement. They have two sons, William and John. Sally is quiet but Beth draws her into the conversation after lunch. Much of the conversation is centred on the topic of Boston. Beth shares some of the experiences she had while growing up in the coastal town and more recently the occupation of the British in the town after the Boston Tea Party.

As the afternoon is far advanced, David urges Tim to stay the night rather than risk the possibility of running into trouble on the way back as the day draws to a close. Sarah had the same conversation with Beth earlier. When the men come back in, Tim and Beth agree to stay the night. Before leaving from Boonesborough in the morning, Tim had mentioned to Mike O'Neill where they were heading and that it was possible they would be staying overnight with the Gass family. No one will be worrying about them not returning that day.

After a hearty early morning breakfast, Tim and Beth bid their hosts goodbye and after an uneventful trip arrive back in Boonesborough in time for lunch with Mike and Mary and the children.

As they are walking along a few days later, Beth turns to Tim. "When you were injured and I was looking after you, Tim, you said something several times in anguish and I wondered what you meant when you said, "I didn't mean to do it.""

Tim stiffened, let go of her hand, and turned slightly away from her. That was something he wasn't ready to talk to her about, but it was something he knew he had to deal with.

"Time to take you back," he said tersely. Beth was sorry she had mentioned it because it spoiled their lovely evening together. She shared it with her sister the next day. Mary said that Tim had been a troubled man when he first came to Boonesborough but he had really changed over the past year. Hopefully this would not drag him down again, but obviously it was something he still had to deal with before he was ready to move forward with his life.

"You like him a lot, don't you Beth?"

"Yes I do. He is becoming a great friend," Beth clarifies.

Several days pass, days of soul searching for Tim, hours of thinking about the past, thinking about what he had done, but even more important, what he hadn't done. It is now time to talk to Daniel about what had happened.

He raps on the door and Rebecca invites him in but he declines, just asks if he can speak with Daniel. Daniel puts his jacket on and comes out to Tim.

"Let's walk aways. I have something I feel I must say." It isn't easy to begin, but once he finds the first words, the words tumble out like a waterfall cascading down the mountainside.

"We knew when you first came here that you were a troubled man," Daniel responds. "What you have shared with me tonight took a lot of guts. I suspect in the telling, and in the thinking you did leading up to it, that you have come to the conclusion that you didn't do anything wrong; it was the result of circumstances beyond your control. How do you feel now that you have told me?"

"I feel much better and relieved that you have responded so positively to me."

"You are a fine man with a strong character. Now you can finally put this behind you and move on with your life."

"Will others feel the same way you do?"

"Well, I won't be telling anyone," Daniel assures him.

"I mean if I told someone else would she see it the same way you do?" Tim persists.

"So that's what this is all about? You like Mary's sister," Daniel said with a knowing smile.

"Just as a friend, but I don't feel I can continue to be a friend to Beth until I talk to her about my past," Tim replies.

"I can't guarantee her reaction, but I'm sure when you are ready, you will find the right words to say. Now how about some coffee and a piece of Rebecca's apple pie?"

"I won't say no to that," Tim beams.

Rebecca has the coffee hot and serves the men after they settle down by the fire. Rebecca joins them for some light conversation, relaxing at the end of a busy day.

A short time later Tim stands up to take his leave. "Thanks Rebecca for your hospitality, and thanks Daniel for your friendship." Daniel gives him a light slap on the back and closes the door on his departing figure.

It is about one o'clock the next afternoon and Tim decides to call on Beth to see if she has an hour of free time. Mary tells her to go ahead.

"Let's find a quiet place to talk. There's a bench tucked away between the blacksmith's shop and the shed next door; if it's empty we should have some privacy there." It only takes a few minutes to settle.

"It's a beautiful sunny day." A pause. Beth waits, not hurrying him as she senses he wants to say something that will be difficult for him to talk about.

"I need to tell you about my past. I want to tell you. I lived back east and had a lovely red-haired sister named Kathryn." Tim pauses for a moment while Beth nods, waiting for him to continue. "When I was 15 I took off to explore and hunt. I was always intrigued by what was around the corner or over the next hill. I was gone for six months, returned with a light heart, having been thrilled time and time again with the beauty and wonder of the places I had been." He pauses, taking a shuddering breath before continuing. "When I opened the door these were the words I heard from my mother.

"If you had been here you could have protected your sister and she wouldn't have died. I hope you're happy now that your sister is dead."

Beth's face pales, hearing for the first time these harsh words of Tim's mother, instinctively knowing that the words are unfair, stemming from a mother's grief, a mother wanting to lash out at the first person who came through the door. Beth reaches for his hands, squeezing them in sympathy, beginning to understand some of his pain, wanting to ease his anguish if only she can.

Tim continues, "I went to Kathryn's grave and wept in anguish, 'I never meant you to die Kathy. I'm sorry.'" Even now Tim is choked up as he speaks to Beth, as though he is living through it again.

"How did Kathy die?" Beth enquires. "Surely you had nothing to do with it and couldn't have saved her."

"Kathy was hit by a runaway team of horses when she was walking home from town." Tim goes on to explain how bad he has felt over the past year that he was away from home when his sister was killed. He has been blaming himself for not being there, but now he has finally come to grips with it and realizes he was not to blame and could not have prevented it even if he had been home.

Beth listens attentively as the story progresses. It is sobering what Tim is sharing. She realizes the importance of her response to it. When he finishes the story, she takes her time responding, choosing her words carefully. "I am sorry to hear about your sister; I would have liked to meet her. Sometimes we say some awful things when we are hurting, as your mother must have been with her daughter gone from her. She took her hurt out on you, blaming you for something that was not your fault."

"It has taken me a year to tell anyone what happened. I shared it with Daniel last night and knew I was ready to talk to you about it. You are so easy to talk to and I enjoy spending time with you. Let's plan to spend a little time together each day." They hold hands as they walk back to Mary's.

"Thank you. See you tomorrow Beth." She smiles as she closes the door. That was quite the hour they had spent together, with deep sharing drawing them so much closer together.

When Timothy calls on her a few nights later, he says, "It's a beautiful evening with the nip of frost in the air. Let's climb up on the sentry walk and look out at the countryside. It's still light enough to see the fall colours."

"Look at all the reds, yellows and oranges with the green evergreens as well; trees as far as the eye can see. That looks like water with sun sparkling on it," Beth exclaims enthusiastically.

"The sun is nearing the horizon. Look at the colours beginning to appear in the sky. Feel the cool breeze on your cheeks. Can you smell the trees Beth? "

"You love it out here don't you Tim? Would you ever consider moving back East to live, say in Boston?"

"I do love it here, the freedom to roam in God's country, the wide-open spaces, and the natural beauty. It takes strong people to be pioneers. I wouldn't like to give all this up."

Tim takes her hand, helps her down the ladder and as they continue the walk he forgets to let go. At Mary's cabin he is reluctant to let her go. Beth is coming to mean a whole lot to him, far more than he ever thought possible for him to like a woman. He always thought he would spend his life on his own.

Meanwhile Beth is smiling and humming softly as she enters the main room of the cabin. Tomorrow night she might ask Tim in for coffee and some dessert she will make, perhaps peach cobbler from the peaches picked from the trees last fall and preserved.

Each evening Beth eagerly looks forward to the time Tim will knock on the door for their evening outing. The weather is cooperating with no rain and there hasn't been any snow yet but it is noticeably colder requiring a heavier coat. She has a navy blue one that is lovely and warm and brings out her beauty. Tim is awed when he sees her in it for the first time that evening. He takes her hand and off they go. They spend a long time talking but there are quiet companionable times as well.

"The day after tomorrow, Daniel has asked me to go with a group on a hunting expedition for our winter supply of meat. We will likely be gone for a few days."

"We can certainly use some meat for the settlement. Everyone is running low," Beth comments.

"What meat do you like best? We will try to get some deer, maybe moose, buffalo and even bear," Tim says.

"Mary has taught me how to cook deer and moose. Bear is tougher and has to be cooked much longer. Deer is my favourite," Beth shares.

"We will see how successful we are. We will be walking many miles from the settlement," Tim comments.

"I'll miss our evening walks and talks while you are away, Tim."

"I'll miss you too," Tim assures her. The stars are out in full array once again tonight after a gorgeous sunset. Tim draws her into his arms and holds her close. She doesn't resist but seems to melt against him. He kisses her long and deep and she responds and the kiss deepens. Then Tim holds her close once more. All of a sudden Beth starts to cry.

"Will you take me home now, Tim?"

"Did I do something wrong? I have wanted to kiss you for days now."

"You didn't do anything wrong. I'd just like to go now."

He holds her hand all the way to the door and draws her into his arms once more but doesn't try to kiss her again. "I'll see you in a few days when we bring back meat. Take care of yourself."

Beth goes to the room she shares with the children and the tears are streaming down her face; she tries to hold the sobs back but a few slip out. Why hasn't she seen this coming? She has been deceiving herself, enjoying each minute she spends with Tim, playing with fire, courting the forbidden, for her.

Chapter 8 – Surprise

"Aunt Beth is sad today. She was crying during the night and I almost got up to rub her back like you do for me when I am sad, but I thought she might not want me to know that I heard her crying. Is she sad because Uncle Tim is going away hunting?" James asks his Mom.

"Maybe. How can we cheer her up? Maybe some material for a new dress. What colour do you think?"

"She looks really beautiful in blue."

"Yes, let's go to the General Store and see what we can find. Let's keep it our secret for now."

"Beth, would you mind watching Sarah and Isaac for an hour? James and I have an errand to do."

"Sure, we will have fun with their toys and whatever else I can find to amuse them."

Mary and James put on their coats and mittens and head for the General Store. They want a nice warm material for the winter and it has to be just the right colour. After much looking, they find the most beautiful royal blue. Rather than going straight home, Mary and James stroll around Boonesborough greeting the neighbours who are outside. James is excited and runs ahead to see a friend for a few minutes before rejoining his mom who is walking slowly as soon she will have her baby.

"That's enough walking. Let's head back to the cabin."

"When can we give Aunt Beth her present? Should we wait until Dad is home after supper? Or should we give it to her now?"

"Let's keep it a secret all day and then it will be a big surprise tonight," Mary suggests.

James plays with his horse and wagon, but every so often he pauses and looks to where his Mom has put the package and he breaks out into a smile. Aunt Beth is so sad she doesn't even notice.

Suppertime arrives and then it is time. Mary gets the package down and hands it to James. He walks over to Aunt Beth and says, "We noticed how sad you were with Tim going off hunting and we decided to get you something to cheer you up."

Beth reaches for James and hugs him close fighting hard not to cry. She knows she is going to have to put on a very brave front in the next few minutes to show joy that she is having a hard time with today.

"Open it. Open it." James is jumping up and down in excitement.

She takes a deep breath and begins to undo the string around the brown paper. The most beautiful soft blue material is exposed and the tears want to fall again but she holds them back and forces a smile on her face and enthusiasm into her voice.

"Oh, that's lovely James. You have made Aunt Beth very happy."

"I'm glad. I don't like you to be sad. And Uncle Tim will be back soon."

If only he knew, Beth thinks, but she can't think of that now. It is time for dessert, then dishes and getting the children to bed. Then maybe she will have a chance for a talk with Mary.

A little while later, Beth says, "What am I going to do, Mary?"

"How do you feel about Tim?"

"I care for him way more than I should, or can."

"You will have to clear up your situation back east before you can be happy. It's really dragging you down," Mary consoles her.

"I'll have to wait until the spring. But I'm not sure it can be cleared up. I should have stopped myself from enjoying time with Tim. I was deceiving myself that we were just friends. When he kissed me last night it was like the stars were exploding all around me and I responded with all of my being. It was afterwards that I realized what I had done and that I wasn't free to love Tim."

Mary gets up to hold Beth to her. But at that moment a pain grips her and she clutches her stomach. "I think it may be time for this baby to be born."

Beth, along with Eliza Calloway, is busy helping Mary throughout the night and at 5:00 a.m. baby Ellie is born, a spunky seven pound girl ready to take on the world. Mike takes James, Isaac and Sarah out for a walk and wishes the hunters well which gives Beth a chance to get a little sleep. Rebecca Boone offers to take the children for the rest of the day and Mike helps with the newborn until Beth wakes up.

It isn't until after supper and the evening chores are completed that Beth remembers Tim and realizes he has gone off hunting before she had a chance to talk to him again. The next few days will give her time to figure out how to tell Tim of her dilemma.

With Mary resting in bed, there are lots of extra things to do, as Sarah and Isaac still need a lot of care. The baby is feeding well and Mary is recovering quickly. In the evenings, Beth ponders on her life back East. *When I return in the spring, what decisions will I make? What can I do? Is there a way to have a happy ending to everything? Will I win and find true happiness here in the West? Or am I destined to live in the East?* Tim willingly shared his trauma with her; now Beth needs to unburden to him. Maybe that will solve the western dilemma if Tim no longer wishes to be her friend and perhaps someday something more. But, she hopes that won't be the case.

The hunters have been away for five days and are expected back that day or the next. But what greets Beth's eyes in the morning is the sun glistening on a sea of white, a foot of freshly-fallen snow. James and Isaac can't wait to go outside and play in it. Sarah enjoys it as well, sitting in the snow and moving her arms quickly through the snow to see it fly around.

"Let's build a snowman," Aunt Beth suggests. "Let's start rolling a ball for the bottom of the snowman."

Beth and James get the ball started. "Come on, Isaac. Help us roll the snow ball."

A second ball that is a little smaller for the middle section is rolled next. "That is big enough now. James and Isaac, help me lift it and carry it over to place on top of the other ball. It is heavy isn't it? There it is in place. Sarah, come and help to pat some extra snow between the two balls so that the top one won't topple over.

"Now it is time to roll a much smaller one for the head. Isaac ask your Mom for a hat for his head, a carrot for his nose, and a scarf for around his neck." Isaac runs to the door of the cabin and calls out to his mom who quickly finds the required items. He returns with them and Beth lifts him up to put the hat on the snowman's head. Beth winds the scarf around the neck.

In the meantime, James found small stones and even a few pieces of charcoal for the eyes, mouth and for buttons down the front.

"Should we put a broom in his right hand? Did we make arms for the broomstick? Let's use a stick for the broom and place it beside the snowman and pretend he is holding it." They all stand back to admire their creation. The children's cheeks are rosy and their mittens are soaking wet. It is time to head inside for dry clothes and to warm up by the fireside. Hot chocolate will be a delicious treat.

Chapter 9 – The Capture

The next morning Beth exclaims, “There’s the alarm bell! Is it another Indian attack?”

“Probably the hunters returning,” Mary smiles. She is up and dressed today and ready to resume her duties in the household. Beth is a little reluctant to go to meet the group, not knowing how Tim will react to her, but she puts on her coat and boots and hurries with the rest of the townsfolk towards the gate of Boonesborough. Sure enough there is the wagon with meat and the hunters returning. But the hunters look grim. Something is wrong.

The wagon is driven inside and once all the hunters are inside, the gates are closed.

Daniel Boone calls to the sentries, “Stay alert!”

Beth is near the back of the crowd and can’t see what is happening but everyone has stopped talking. Daniel says, “We have been successful in getting meat to last us all for awhile. We’ll get started on smoking and salting it for storage.” There is a pause before he continues. “We have some bad news. Tim was captured by a small band of Indians. We tried to follow but had to turn back, deciding it made sense to get the wagonload of meat back to the fort. David and I will go out later today and see if we can rescue him, or at least find out where he is being held.” Beth blanches in total shock.

"Let's get to work on the meat." The wagon is driven towards the smokehouse.

Daniel makes his way towards Beth. "We will do all we can to get Tim back. We know he was captured alive. He got separated from the rest of us and it was awhile before we realized he was missing. He was able to get off a shot which alerted the group that Tim wasn't with the rest of us. We headed in the direction of the shot, found no fresh kill, but Indian tracks indicating a skirmish and Tim's footprints amongst the group heading off. There were five horse tracks, one indicating from the depth of the hooves in the dirt that there were two riders. We noted the direction they had taken and then rejoined the men guarding our belongings and headed back to the fort with the meat. David and I will take supplies with us and head out to follow the tracks later today." Daniel has been leading Beth back to Mary's cabin and at this point they arrive at the door. Daniel knocks and opens the door, speaks softly to Mary saying, "Look after her; she has had quite a shock."

"Tim has been captured by Indians," Beth sobs as Mary holds her tightly, soothing her with calming words and gently rubbing her shoulders. Beth calms down and tells Mary what has happened. Mary assures her, "Daniel will do everything he possibly can for Tim. He is an excellent tracker and has a good rapport with many of the Indian tribes in Kentucky. It seems strange they took Tim – there must have been some special reason. We will have to wait to hear Tim's story when he returns."

Life carries on in Boonesborough although for some there are constant thoughts of those who are out in the wilderness, the one captured and the two trying to locate him and hopefully rescue him. Beth and Rebecca Boone are drawn closer together in their mutual concern for two of the men absent from the fort. As they work together preserving the meat, they converse together.

"I remember when we left North Carolina and headed out in 1773 to settle in Kentucky. After our son James and five others were killed by the Indians, we turned back. Daniel was willing to return with me and the children but he had such a wonderful dream for us in Kentucky, with his face beaming and eyes glowing as he talked about the beauty of the land. I decided then to give up my fears and help Daniel realize his dreams."

"Were you never afraid again? I guess that's an unfair question when we are both unsure of the future of our men at this time," Beth comments.

"I have often had to fight fear and have often been called upon to be courageous and encourage the other women. We pioneer women are a strong bunch. Indians are a big threat, but so is sickness, and the cold is also something to contend with during the winters, although it is much better now that Boonesborough is completed. A big challenge is trying to grow some of our own food for variety of meals. We can grow some vegetables beside our cabin. Maybe next spring we'll grow some wheat on the other side of the blockhouse – no one is doing anything with that piece of ground. That's a dream of mine for next year."

"I have to go back East in the spring. I'm not sure at this point whether I will be returning. But I would like to help you with your dream if things work out for me to return."

"I have been alone for long periods of our married life as Daniel thrives on exploring and hunting. It is great to have friends to be able to talk to and sometimes to help bear the burdens. We were staying with David and Sarah Gass when I lost our son William in early 1775, just before Daniel and David left to build the road to this place," Rebecca continued. "Sarah, along with your sister Mary, was a big help at that time, as well as my grandmother, Martha Strode Bryan."

"What were your feelings when you lost the baby? Where was your mother at this time?" Beth asks.

"I never knew my mother as she died soon after I was born. My grandparents helped to raise me until my father remarried. My sister Martha was two years older than me and later we had six younger sisters and three brothers. As to my feelings when I lost William, I was devastated. After carrying the baby for nine months, it was very sad to lose another son. It made me think of our first son, James, a handsome young man, just about to turn sixteen. What a shock to have him killed and scalped by Indians when we first tried to settle in this area. Now here was another son who was gone from me. I sobbed so hard. Daniel tried to be a real comfort to me but he was at a loss of how to help me. I blamed myself at first. Maybe I had been working too hard, maybe I didn't eat the right foods, maybe it was that mug of ale I had. I tried to come up with a reason. Even though I had several other children who needed my attention, I had looked forward to this one as the fruit of Daniel's and my love."

"That was quite an emotional time for you, Rebecca," Beth sympathizes. "How did you get over it? How long did it take?"

"At times my heart still cries out for my two sons who are gone. My arms ache to hold William. For several months, Daniel and I had talked about the baby. Would it be a girl, or another son? We expected the baby to be healthy and live a good life. The baby was a reality to us before I gave birth." A few tears drop from her eyes and roll down her cheeks. Beth reaches for her to give her a warm hug.

"Rebecca, it is okay to cry and let it all out. Sometimes it helps in the healing process," Beth states.

"Thanks Beth. I don't often get weepy but I guess talking about last year has brought it all to the surface," Rebecca is almost apologizing. "I felt less than whole, something was missing. Oh to smell the newborn baby smell! Oh to hold that small weight in my arms! I understood in my mind that the baby wasn't healthy and it was better that he died quickly, but my heart ached and said why?"

"I have never lost any close relative and certainly not a child. You have made the experience real to me Rebecca. Thanks for sharing it with me. It must have been hard to do."

"I decided I had to get through one day at a time and that I must not neglect the other children. Susanna was the biggest help as she was sixteen and she had been helping with the younger children for many years. We had a wedding to prepare for as Susanna was to marry in the summer, as soon as the men returned. Jemima is two years younger and you have met her on your fateful walk to see the summer flowers. My other two daughters and two sons were younger and needed a mother's attention. I try to spend at least a few minutes each day with each of them on an individual basis although this is not always possible especially with all the chores out here in the wilderness. Jesse was two years old, walking all over the place, but he got extra cuddling and hugs. Even my five year old Danny and seven year old Israel had to endure their mother hugging and holding them. It was especially difficult for Israel as he felt he was too grown up for a lot of hugging. My four girls were a big help around the cabin with six year old Becky helping to set the table and do other small things."

"It must have helped to ease your sorrow by thinking about a wedding. I always enjoy weddings as they are such happy times," Beth smiles.

"Yes, that certainly helped. I turned to my grandmother for comfort and words of encouragement as she knew the sorrow of losing children shortly after birth. Your sister, Mary, and Sarah Gass were very good at keeping me busy to take my mind in more pleasant directions. We all worked together to get ready for our move further west. We had clothes to sew, food to preserve, trunks to pack. We did as much as we could while the men were gone for four months working on the road," Rebecca continues. "That's enough reminiscing. Have you ever worked with animal skins? We have buffalo and deer skins to make use of. Let's organize some of the women tomorrow. We can use the empty cabin which becomes a meeting room for many different occasions. All of the meat is being smoked or has been salted. In a week's time we will be able to divide the meat up so that it isn't all in one location."

"I never thought of that. I've learned a lot in the five months I have been here. It's time for me to get back to Mary's to help out. See you tomorrow Rebecca."

Tim, I hope you are keeping well. I wonder why the Indians took you with them? Did you have a special skill they wanted you for? Beth thinks as she walks back to the cabin.

"Hi, Mary. I'm back, how can I help you?"

"Little Ellie has just fallen asleep, Sarah and Isaac are both napping, and James is with Israel. We have time to sit down for a cup of coffee and then we can start on our supper. What have you been up to this morning?" The aroma of coffee can already be smelled in the cabin.

"That coffee sure smells wonderful. We have been so busy all morning that we only stopped for a quick cold lunch that one of the women brought over. We got all the meat looked after, either salted or in the smokehouse. We organized a rotation of the men to keep the fire going in the smokehouse so that everything will be preserved."

"That's good news. We live in an area where the game used to be very plentiful but now they have to go many miles for it. It's always good to have a few weeks' supply of meat for the times when it isn't possible to get out and hunt. During a blizzard is not the time to go hunting."

"I had a really good visit with Rebecca. Tomorrow she wants to show some of the women what to do with the animal skins. The local friendly Indians have been of great help to teach Rebecca and others some of the Indian methods."

"I'll join you for awhile. The children will be able to play quietly while we work. The more hands, the quicker the work moves along."

"Please tell me if you need me to do more for you, Mary. I seem to be spending several hours a day away from you," Beth says.

"I'm feeling strong again; Ellie is a contented baby so I am managing quite well. Sarah is becoming quite mobile but as long as I keep an eye on her and keep her away from the fire she is fine. Isaac is growing up and able to amuse himself part of the time. James has been spending time each day with his friends Israel Boone and George and Johnny Wallace."

"When I see James with Israel when I am visiting with Rebecca, it helps me to feel that I am not totally neglecting you."

"You don't need to feel bad. I want you to enjoy yourself while you are with us too. For the first month you were here you didn't have much free time as I wasn't any help to you at all."

"I sure miss Tim. He was becoming a good friend and I looked forward to our evening walks together, even if I did get spooked on our last evening when we kissed."

Chapter 10 – The Rescue

Later that day, Daniel and David return with Tim. "Help me get Tim into bed. Get the doctor. He is probably half starved. We couldn't risk stopping anywhere; we wanted to get back to the fort. He's been with the Indians for three days, and then we spent today travelling back. Some broth will likely be good for him."

"He doesn't seem to be injured. Other than chafing around his ankles and wrists where they had him tied up, I can't see any other wounds," sad Doc Watson after thoroughly checking him over. "We have to get this fever down and when he wakes up we will try to get some liquid into him. Where's Beth? She did a fine job looking after Tim when I removed an arrow from his shoulder. I could stand listening to her voice singing again. I think Tim would like that too."

"Here's Beth now," says Daniel. "News travels fast around the town. He's not hurt, but he has a fever. Would you like to help the doctor?"

Beth nods and moves towards Tim, touching his forehead and immediately gets a cool cloth to wipe his brow. "Would someone get me some snow? That will help to cool him down."

"Cool him down slowly though, a little at a time," advises the doctor. "A little snow on the tongue might feel good as it's quite swollen from lack of nourishment."

"I'll head home now Beth. I'll have Rebecca bring over some broth."

"Thanks Daniel for bringing him home. Go and get some rest yourself now," Beth urges.

Doctor Watson turns to Beth, "I'll come and check on him again in an hour or so but be sure to ring the bell outside if you need me sooner."

"Thanks Doc. I'll be fine now," Beth smiles, then turns back to Tim.

Beth wipes his forehead and leaves a cool cloth. She takes another cool cloth to wipe his hands, to clean them as well as to help cool them. She tries a little snow on his lips but there is no response at this time. He is restless so music is the remedy that comes to mind. Her voice floats around him and seeps into his pores sending healing waves of sound, a sound he hadn't been sure he would ever hear again.

Rebecca arrives and asks, "How's he doing Beth? I brought some broth for him. Here's the Doc now. Maybe he can help us lift him so that we can get a little into his mouth."

"Thanks for coming over Rebecca. Daniel must need you, too."

"Daniel has fallen into an exhausted sleep. He'll be as right as rain in the morning."

With Doc's help they manage to get a spoonful of broth into him but it seems best to let him rest a little longer before trying again. He is sleeping better and isn't as feverish.

"Beth, try to give him a spoonful every hour. If he will take more give him a little more. Try to space it out over the night. Do you want me to stay and help or can you manage?"

"With that extra blanket you brought for me to slip under his head, I'll be able to manage. You go and get your sleep Doc. You too, Rebecca."

"See you in the morning, or earlier if you need me. If he seems worse during the night, call for me right away," Doctor Watson says before ushering Rebecca out and closing the cabin door.

Beth is so happy that Tim is back. She will willingly, lovingly nurse him back to health. To help pass the night, in between the spoonfuls of broth, and to keep herself awake, Beth starts to sing the songs she knows, one after another. They are soothing songs as well as hymns that she sings. She adds a log to the fire, covers Tim with the blanket as his fever has subsided, gives him another spoonful of broth, each time he responds a little better to the nourishment.

Chapter 11 – Recovery

“Why is Aunt Beth still sleeping, Mummy?” says James when he gets up the next morning.

“She just went to bed, James. Uncle Daniel brought Tim home last night and Beth has been looking after him all night. He is sick.”

“Sick like after he got hit by the arrow?” James asks

“Yes, something like that.”

“Did he get hit by another arrow?”

“Not this time.”

“Why is he sick then?” puzzles James.

“He is tired and hungry.”

“Can we make a cake to cele…?”

“To celebrate?”

“Yes, to cel-e-brate,” James says with a beaming smile on his face. He is so proud that he can say that big word.

“That sounds like a great idea.”

“When can I see Uncle Tim?” James asks as Isaac comes into the room. Isaac says, “I want to see Uncle Tim too.”

“When he is a little better you can go to see him.”

"Okay Mummy."

"Now it's time for breakfast. Daddy will be dressed soon and Sarah will be awake. Ellie just finished having her milk."

Beth sleeps until noon. When she wakes up, she feels alive and smiles as she hugs herself. Tim's home! She washes and dresses and heads for the kitchen for something to eat. Mary has heard her and has bacon, eggs, toast and coffee ready for her.

"Tim's fever broke during the night and he was swallowing a little broth."

"That's good to hear. Before long he will be up and regaining his strength. This is the second time you have looked after him in two months. He gets around."

"Nothing boring about his life. Are you okay on your own with the children today Mary? I would like to spend time with Tim."

"I will be fine with the children. You get back to your man," Mary responds.

"Thanks Mary." Beth gives her a quick hug, gives each of the children a hug and a kiss, before donning her coat and mittens and heading to see Tim. She no longer has any reticence about seeing him. She is convinced that everything will work out.

Tim is awake when she arrives and able to take more broth. He gives her a smile but isn't able to talk.

Doc peers up at her from beside the bed and says, "You can feed him as much as he can take today. I'm sure Rebecca will be around with some more broth before long. By evening he might be ready for some soft vegetables. Give him water to drink as well. Don't let him talk – I don't think he can yet. I'll check back in awhile. I have a few other patients to see." He waves as he leaves the cabin with a smile on his face.

"Thanks Doc. See you later," Beth calls after him.

Moments later Rebecca opens the door, holding a bowl of steaming broth in her hands and Beth greets her warmly.

"How's the patient doing today?"

"I just arrived and got my instructions from Doc Watson. Tim isn't to talk but he is ready to eat now. He can have soft vegetables for supper."

"I'll be sure to bring some over," Rebecca responds.

"Thanks Rebecca for your help. How's Daniel feeling today?"

"He's still a little tired but up and about town." Tim looks dreamily at the two ladies as they approach his bedside. "Good afternoon Tim. You're making a habit of needing Beth to nurse you," Rebecca teases.

He smiles a little with a twinkle in his eyes. He starts to say something but Beth hushes him. "You can talk tomorrow once your tongue is less swollen and you are stronger. Just rest today."

"Tim, you are in good hands," says Rebecca cheerfully. He nods in agreement. "I'll leave you now and bring some vegetables over for supper."

Now Tim and Beth are alone. She talks to him about her life in Boston and their home. Tim is eager to hear all the details.

"There is a wrap-around verandah on the front and two sides, with wide wooden steps leading up to the front door."

"Colour?" asked Tim.

"The house is white with green trim and a brown roof.

"As you walk inside through the front door, a long hallway leads back to the large kitchen and pantry where Mrs. Oliver reigns. She is a great cook and her desserts are a real treat. She makes delicious butter tarts and fresh berry pies." Tim smiles and nods.

"Off the entranceway to the left is the parlour with two wing chairs, two love seats grouped around the fireplace which is adorned with a hand-carved mantle. The walls are a soft cream colour with dark wood baseboards and trim. There is an oil painting of an outdoor scene above the fireplace. During the spring and summer each day fresh flowers are cut from the garden and placed in the parlour to enjoy. I can see the yellows, oranges, browns and pinks now. I never thought to bring flower seeds with me on my trip, but we have been able to enjoy all the wildflowers this summer. There was a little damper on the beauty we were enjoying in July with our capture by the Shawnee and Cherokee braves."

"We found you," Tim croaks.

"Yes, we were thrilled at your arrival to rescue us," Beth says in reflection.

"House?" Tim questions Beth, wanting to hear more details of the home that means so much to her.

"Across the hall is a dining room large enough to seat twenty-four adults. We often had groups of people over for dinner and to play cards or charades or for a musical evening with me playing the piano and we would have a sing-along. Have I talked enough?"

"More," Tim smiles.

"Between the parlour and the kitchen is Father's study with book cases on three walls and a big desk by the windows and sliding door leading to the gardens, gardens that are lovingly cared for by Mr. Oliver, along with two assistants. Mr. and Mrs. Oliver have a cottage just a short distance from the main house. Mrs. Miller is the housekeeper and is in charge of two maids who assist with cleaning the house and taking care of the clothes for the family. The maids and the housekeeper have rooms on the third floor of the house.

"In the basement is a well-stocked wine cellar from which the butler chooses a bottle of wine for each evening meal. A root cellar has storage for potatoes, carrots, turnips, squash, and onions, preserves of fruit and pickles, as well as jams from the berry bushes on the grounds around the house.

"On the second floor are the main bedrooms, dressing rooms and washrooms. There are four set aside for the family, although two of them haven't been used for awhile since Mary married and Robert moved away from home. Father and Mother's room has maroon furnishings, Mary's old room is yellow, Robert's room is brown, and my room is pink and white. The six guest rooms are all elegantly furnished, each in a different colour, one is green, one is navy, another is powder blue, then there are light green, peach, and gray décor with matching drapes, bedspreads and area rugs."

"Outside?" asks Tim.

"The front yard is surrounded by a white picket fence and has a cherry tree and two maple trees. There is a wishing well to the left of the large circular driveway. In the backyard, there is a swimming pool, a tennis court and lots of flower beds full of beautiful blooms throughout the seasons beginning with crocuses, daffodils and tulips in the spring, followed by a wide array of summer flowers with the roses in many hues showing off their beauty, and then the oranges, browns and yellows of the mums. There are several fruit trees, the fruit being preserved for use on the table throughout the year. The garden provides many vegetables for us to eat, although the town market provides additional produce to supplement our meals."

Beth can see that Tim is tired so she tells him to close his eyes and get some sleep. Within minutes he is sound asleep. Beth gets up to walk around, feeling lighter in spirit than she has in quite awhile. It felt good to share with Tim about her home in Boston.

Beth has her knitting with her so decides to work on the sweater she is in the process of making. If she wants a change, she also brought along some embroidery. Soon the afternoon is coming to an end and it is getting dark in the cabin. Beth lights the lantern, adds more wood to the fire, and while checking on Tim sees that he is awake. "You had a good long sleep. You are probably hungry by now. Supper will be along soon."

Rebecca arrives and offers to feed Tim while Beth goes to her sister's for a couple of hours. It is good to get out and stretch her legs in the cold, crisp evening air, spending a few extra minutes outside before joining her family for supper.

"You look really happy tonight, Aunt Beth. I'm glad Tim is home. Is he feeling better now?" asks James when Beth arrives back at the O'Neill cabin.

"Tim is feeling a lot better but he is still very weak and not able to talk yet – at least, we aren't allowing him to talk today, giving his body time to heal and take in the nourishment that we are giving him. He finished his broth and now he is having some vegetables which Rebecca offered to feed him while I joined my family for supper. I have been neglecting you today."

"I think Tim needed you more today, Aunt Beth. We had fun with Mummy today. We made a…surprise. I almost said it, but I stopped myself in time, didn't I Mummy?"

"You did well, James. You have been helpful today." James beams at his mother's praise.

"Everyone is finished eating, Mummy. It must be time for the surprise." James can't wait any longer.

"Yes, James," Mary says as she ruffles his hair, "I'll go get it."

"Aunt Beth, you have to close your eyes while Mummy gets it."

"Okay, my eyes are closed."

"No peeking," chorus James and Isaac together.

"Now you can open them. Surprise!" the family chimes in.

"What a beautiful cake! Did you help Mummy make it, James?"

"I sure did! Do you think Tim would like some?"

"I think so. I'll take some to him after supper. If he can't eat it tonight, I am sure he will enjoy it tomorrow. Thanks for the lovely surprise," Beth smiles warmly at him.

"Beth, you are excused from cleanup duties tonight. Mike is going to help me with the dishes and getting the children to bed. You go and spend a couple of hours with Tim. Then I suggest you come home and get a good night's sleep. By tomorrow Tim might even be up for awhile. Then he will be impatient that he isn't strong enough to get back to work yet."

Beth eagerly heads back to spend time with Tim. He has enjoyed the vegetables and is thrilled with the cake that Beth brings.

The next day Beth stays with Mary and the children until mid-morning the following day and then Mary shoos her out. This time with Tim continues the bonding process, drawing them closer to one another. Beth talks about lots of things. Tim is able to sit up for a couple of hours and is able to feed himself, even able to talk a little but not for long, not yet able to talk about his experiences with the Indians.

Even though a letter is not a good way to explain feelings of the heart, Beth has been adding some of her feelings to her weekly letters to her parents. This morning the stagecoach arrives with the mail and she has a long letter from her parents. They have read a lot between the lines that Beth hasn't said outright and it is encouraging that everything will work out well in the spring. It seems like her younger brother will be stepping in to fill the void left by Beth's long absence from home.

Although Beth is not needed as much by Mary now and is able to spend much time away from the cabin, she thoroughly enjoys each moment spent with her nephews and nieces, and Mary and Mike.

Beth shares her letter with Tim and they talk about it. He says he would like to see her home one day as she has described it so lovingly. Beth tells Tim about her parents. "My parents, Jacob and Sally Worthington, have been friends with John and Catherine Brownley for a long time. John is a lawyer and has a good practice. It has always been hoped, even planned, that one of the Worthington girls would marry their son, Samuel. With Mary already married to Mike that left me as the only choice. Samuel and I grew up like cousins, with both families celebrating the yearly holidays of Easter, Thanksgiving and Christmas together, alternating between the Brownleys' and

Worthingtons' homes. The Fulton, Smiley and Townsend families were part of the festive group. Vacations were shared events by the five families, spending time at Martha's Vineyard each summer. Samuel is twenty-five now and expected to settle down, take over more responsibilities in the family business, marry and start a family. I have been pondering this for some time, expecting Samuel to ask me to marry him, but he hasn't done so yet." Tim nods in understanding.

Tim slept in the afternoon and since he did not require constant care, Beth was able to have a visit with Rebecca and several of the other women who gathered at the Boone cabin for coffee.

In the last few days, Daniel and David have been visiting the friendly Indian tribes and everything is peaceful with them. As long as there is respect on both sides, there is harmony. There is to be a big Thanksgiving celebration the next weekend at Boonesborough and several of the Indian chiefs and a few braves have been invited to come for a meal sponsored by the pioneers.

Daniel came to see Tim to have him tell about his experiences. Tim had been so preoccupied with his thoughts or he never would have become separated from his own hunting party. He apologized for causing everyone so much concern and thanked Daniel for bringing him home.

"I was taken by horseback, with my hands tied behind me, about four hours away, to a lovely valley where there was an Indian encampment. There were dozens of teepees in the camp with lots of women and children and old men observed going about their lives, but only the five young braves who had captured me were seen." Were the braves away? Had they been killed or died in an epidemic? Tim was not able to determine which.

"I was tied by one leg to a pole in the ground, guarded by two older men, and directed to chop the wood piled nearby by the guards pointing to my strong muscles. Trees had been cut down but had not been made into firewood." Tim was a strong man and was able to make short work of the trees and soon had a pile of kindling and a stack of firewood.

"After awhile I asked for water by using sign language but the guards shook their heads. At this point, I wasn't worried as I figured water and food would be provided later. At dusk, my other leg and two arms were also tied to the pole. It was an awkward position to sleep, but I knew I needed to rest."

"The next morning in the crisp air, I was nudged awake and shown a new pile of trees to chop. My hands and one leg were untied and I was told to chop. My motions were only a little slower. I was thirsty and hungry but not faring too badly so far. The axe had been sharpened and I was able to do the job. At noon, my hands and second leg were retied to the pole. Still no food or water was offered. It seemed like that was the intention, to make me work but not feed me.

"I knew I could survive for only so long under those conditions and the sooner I escaped the better for me, and the better my chances at being successful. The second night I tried to untie my hands but they were tightly bound. Quite by accident, I noticed there was some movement in the post to which I was tied. I worked away at rocking that post to loosen it completely, not an easy feat. Next I used my hands and feet to lift the pole out of its hole. Inch by inch it came out. No one guarded me at night so I could work away at this project undisturbed, but it took hours and I had to rest frequently. Finally the pole was out of the hole, then I was able to slip both feet off, then slowly, knowing this was the crucial moment, not wanting to make any noise by dropping the pole on the ground, I gently lowered the pole and then slipped my hands off, the rawhide being loose enough now for it to drop off easily. I had to rub my wrists and ankles to get the circulation going. I figured I had to get moving as I had about three hours to get as far away from this camp as possible before they would be coming after me."

Tim knew the direction to go from having used his woodsman skills and being observant while he had been working. He headed out of the camp. Even though hungry and thirsty, he still had strength to walk and once a little ways away he managed to run for a short piece, but soon he had to slow down. He kept walking as long as he could, but he had to rest often. Survival drove him to keep moving forward. The rising of the sun was both his friend and enemy. It would provide him with warmth, but also would alert the Indians of his escape. He pushed on as long as he could this time, using an extra spurt of energy, but then he had to rest.

"I guess that's where you and David found me."

Daniel took up the story at this point to fill Tim in on the return to Boonesborough. "We gently nudged you awake – initially you thought it was the Indians and started to fight us off, but you soon realized who we were. We gave you a small drink of water and then said we must get moving. I helped you onto one of the two horses and then climbed on behind you. David led the way and we made good progress. By late afternoon, we were just a few miles from Boonesborough. We succeeded in keeping ahead of the Indians and had not met any others to deter us. We were concerned for you because you were feverish by this time and a little delirious. But we didn't want to risk stopping to care for you along the way, wanting to make the safety of the fort. We pressed on and called to the sentries, announcing our presence just as darkness set in. The gate was opened to let us inside, and closed behind us. I directed the men to double the sentries."

The next day Tim is able to do several short walks around the cabin, followed the next day by a short walk outside. Beth is thrilled to see him improving. He is ready to move back to the bunkhouse.

That afternoon she joins a group of women for a quilting bee at one of the cabins with little ones asleep in the other room. The tiny stitches are made to join the scraps of material together into a beautiful pattern. With a dozen women working on it, it is soon ready for covering someone's bed and to provide warmth during the winter days. These are fun times for the women, laughing and sharing together, usually light-hearted conversations, sharing funny things the children have done or said, sharing silly things that occur in their own lives. When times of trouble come, the women are a cohesive group, willing to do their part right alongside of the men, willing and eager to fight for the rights of themselves and their families. Without the women working together many a battle would have been lost. The older children do their part, fetching needed items, putting out fires, watching younger siblings, and other chores they are capable of performing.

Beth makes a point of conversing with the young women and older ones whom she meets at the General Store, trying to learn a little more about them, delving into their needs and strengths, how she might be able to help them, or how they might be able to help her. The path to the spring becomes trodden down quickly after a storm with the many people going back and forth, most settlers taking the opportunity daily for the chance to walk outside the walls, an opportunity only available when the natives are peaceful.

A few days later Tim calls on Beth, "Let's go for a walk down to the river today. Daniel says it's safe to go outside the fort. We'll take a couple of men along as lookouts."

"It will be nice to stretch our legs outside the fort. The snow is quite deep – I didn't realize it had snowed this much already. This is fun to be out in the open."

"The sun is sparkling on the snow today like a sea of glistening diamonds. It's good to be alive."

Chapter 12 – Thanksgiving

By Thanksgiving, the people in the town of Boonesborough have many things to be thankful for, including safety with recovery from the Indian attack, the safe return of the girls in July, the wedding in August, and Tim's capture and subsequent escape and rescue. With the snows having arrived, peace is expected from the Indians as they usually do not go out fighting in the cold weather.

When the men first arrived in Kentucky, there were many game animals, including deer, moose, elk, rabbits, squirrels, bears and buffalo. Fruits, such as mulberries, cherries, grapes and walnuts were available in abundance. America was a land of plenty. With the help of the Indians who live on the land, the settlers learned how to survive. The Indians introduced lima beans, peppers, pumpkins, squash, and sweet potatoes into the settlers' diet of cabbage, parsnips and herbs. Corn was an important vegetable and could be roasted, boiled, and made into pudding and bread. Indians taught the settlers to grow beans up cornstalks.

Turkeys were wild birds often travelling in flocks numbering over a hundred. The wild turkey has a beautiful purple and bronze coloured plumage and each could weigh over thirty pounds. White potatoes were introduced from overseas in the 1700's.

A bonfire and feast are planned after a service of thanksgiving. The food includes wild turkey with onion and bread stuffing, corn, cabbage, and parsnips. Pumpkins and apples are plentiful and the pies are mouth-watering. The fiddlers are tempted to play a few tunes and the people kick up their heels in a few dances. Tim enjoys dancing with Beth.

Shortly after Thanksgiving, a blizzard strikes the area. Everyone stays close to home or within the fort. The snow blows and the wind howls outside, while the fire glows throwing off its welcoming heat and light inside, as the blizzard rages day after day. They are well-protected in the fort, but it is cold with blowing snow. It gives the women a chance to get caught up with mending, candle-making, and sewing. Hot soups and stews go down well. There is also time to do some reading. Mike had built a lean-to shelter beside the cabin for the cow, pigs and chickens. There is always a good wood supply, with Mike carrying enough inside each day for the family's use.

Beth is happy to let Mike take care of the animals while she looks after the children and helps Mary with the indoor chores. Tim stopped by for a short visit on the second afternoon to see if they needed anything. A few men are checking on the families to see if anyone is running short on food or water. Mike assures Tim they are fine but invites him back for a longer visit in the evening, an invitation he is happy to accept, an invitation that causes joy and anticipation for Beth, as she and Tim always have lots to talk about.

Tim stops by for a visit by the fireside each evening. Mike and Mary join them for coffee. Sometimes the four of them have a sing-along as Mary and Mike both have lovely voices, and Tim can carry a tune, although every so often everyone else will stop singing and let Beth carry on solo, such a rich sound, pleasing to the ears and the rest of the senses, filling the occupants of the room with awe and wonder, bringing peace to the home. Other times, Mary and Mike will leave Tim and Beth alone to talk about anything and everything. Still other times, the chess and checker boards come out with Tim being quite the chess strategist. Beth and Mary fare better at checkers. There are many pleasant ways to pass an evening when all the days' chores are done.

During the fifth night of the blizzard, Beth wakes up to total silence, the wind has stopped blowing, the storm is over. After quickly checking on the children to make sure they are all snug under their blankets, Beth snuggles down and falls into a deep sleep until morning.

Soon after awakening and getting dressed for the day, there is a knock on the door. It is Tim come to see if Beth is free to go for a walk as the blizzard has now ended. "I want to show you how different the countryside looks now." They climb up the ladder to the sentry walk and look over the stockade.

"There is white everywhere! Some of the trees are almost buried. What a beautiful world. No steps yet in the snow, untouched by man or beast," Beth exclaims with wonder in her eyes.

"After your morning chores, let's put on snowshoes and go for a walk. Have you tried them before?" Tim questions.

"No, I haven't, but I am eager to give it a try."

When Tim returns, he helps her fasten on a pair of snowshoes, gets his own pair on and they start out. It is slow going as Beth first steps on the opposite snowshoe and almost tumbles into the snow – it requires stepping a little wider apart. Soon she has the knack of it but it is tiring, using some different muscles. They go down the hill to the river, most of which is frozen over. When it is time to climb back up the hill, that is a bit tricky, but Tim's strong muscles provide assistance for Beth to make it up the hill and they return to the fort. Beth invites Tim into the cabin for a hot drink before he heads off to work in the blacksmith shop.

Ice skating on the river is an outing Beth looks forward to, as it was a pastime she had enjoyed in Boston. Just this week, Mike has fashioned blades for attaching to her boots and Beth is anxious to try them out. Tim is calling for her at two o'clock. There he is now. Tim helps her put her coat on and waits for her to put her boots on. Beth picks up her blades and they head for the river to the area a little further downstream where the bank isn't as steep. They have a broom and shovel to clear the snow and soon are pushing off for a glide down the ice. Beth even tries a few twirls, but Tim is a bit more cautious, not having used skates more than a few times many years before.

Jemima Boone and Flanders Calloway join Beth and Tim on the ice. They are dating now and have just announced their wedding date in the summer. Beth and Tim were asked if they wanted to make it a double wedding, but Tim and Beth are "only friends." They continue to enjoy spending time together doing all kinds of activities, both inside and outside, depending on the weather.

Soon they have rosy cheeks and Beth's eyes are sparkling. All too soon it seems to her, it is time to head back as there are chores needing to be done.

Tim regularly goes on hunting and exploring expeditions with Daniel Boone, always staying close together, no longer allowing themselves to be distracted, paying constant attention to their surroundings. As well as meat, firewood has to be brought back to the fort, since fires burn constantly during the winter months for warmth and cooking and laundry, with hardwood being the best choice as it burns longer.

Mike has a busy day tomorrow and requires Tim's help as an army detachment are expected and all of their horses need new shoes. When the soldiers arrive, it gives the people a chance to learn about the world outside their own little place, a time to learn about the Indian situation in a wider area, a time to hear news from farther east, sometimes they even bring mail, a welcome sight as it is always good to have links to other family members.

"I sure live a different life here in Boonesborough than I did in Boston," Beth says to Mary as they relax with a coffee and their knitting one afternoon.

"You have done very well learning so many new things. You likely never did any cooking at home – I know I didn't until after I was married," Mary said. "Mike had some strange meals in our early marriage, some burned, some raw, tough meat. Even to make his coffee took awhile – he taught me how to do that. He's been a wonderful husband."

"He has been very patient with me as I have burned a few things," Beth reminisces.

"What's the best thing for you since you have been with us?" Mary questions.

"I have enjoyed spending time with you, Mary. I always adored you as my older sister. I missed you after you got married and moved out to North Carolina first and then out to Kentucky. It sure is a beautiful country out here, but far from civilization as I have always known it. I guess I have really grown up a lot since I have been here."

"Yes, you have. Life keeps changing. Look at Ellie how much she has grown. It seems like just last week that I gave birth to her. She's almost three months old."

"Since Tim's capture in early October we haven't had any further trouble with the Indians. We have had three incidents of trouble since I came in July."

"Yes, you got a taste of frontier life in a hurry after only being with us for a couple of weeks and me only just starting to feel better after a rough few months of my pregnancy."

"I didn't see any of the action that time as I was busy helping the doctor with Tim. I sure heard the noise of the cracking of the guns."

"It was a blessing to have the soldiers arrive to help us fend off the attack."

Chapter 13 – Christmas

It is nearly Christmas time. Each night after the children are in bed, the parents are busy working on making each child something special. James is eight and Mike is making him a model of the blacksmith shop. Isaac has turned four and will like the horse and wagon that Mike has fashioned. The women are busy knitting and sewing and cooking some special treats for everyone to enjoy. The perishable food will be cooked closer to Christmas.

"Mary, what are some ideas for a gift for Beth? She's been a good friend this year," Tim asks Mary when he finds her alone. Mary gives him a couple of ideas and he makes his plans accordingly.

"Mike, what do you think I could give Tim for Christmas?" Beth asks when Tim is off on an errand. Beth asks Mike to make something for her to give.

For two days, Mary, Beth and Dorothy get together to make pies, cookies and tarts. Christmas pudding was made several weeks before and is aging nicely, keeping cool in the underground pantry that Mike had dug for keeping the milk, eggs and preserves cool. Mary enjoys working with Beth and Dorothy, the time passing quickly as they chat, in-between looking after the children. Mike took bread and meat with him for lunch so that the women can continue uninterrupted with their cooking. Mary had learned how to do things the year before with Rebecca Boone's help and now she can pass this on to Beth and Dorothy.

"We have learned so much in the past few months, haven't we Dorothy? Remember our first night on the trail?" Beth smiles.

"I was quite grumpy, not one bit happy being on the trip. I was plenty miserable to you for a few days. Gradually I got to enjoy the trip and your company. Sam and Paul were patient with us as we learned to cook over the fire," Dorothy adds.

"Remember that first meal we tried to make? The biscuits were burned, the coffee was awful, and the meat was tough."

"I'll bet it didn't take too many days before you caught on," Mary enters the conversation.

"You're right, Mary, but we burned our fingers as well as the food a few times at first."

"The sunburn on the first day of travel was certainly painful. Even with our bonnets on, our skin was red and sore. Remember how I complained at the smell of the bear grease that Paul wanted to put on my face?" Dorothy reminisces.

"Yes, but it was only moments before your mouth closed as the grease worked right away to cool your skin and make it feel better. After a week on the trail, we didn't need the bear grease anymore as our skin tanned and toughened with exposure to the sun and wind."

"Then when you arrived in Boonesborough I was no help to you at all for the first week. I sure was sick with Ellie," Mary adds.

"Ellie is a sweet little thing," Dorothy says. "I would like a little girl this time."

"I remember the first time Mike tried to show me how to milk the cow. I couldn't get the hang of it. It took him a lot longer to get the milking done that day. But the next day he had me try again and I had a little success."

"Now it's as though you have done it all your life. You don't even have to think about it," Mary says.

"What else have we learned, Dorothy?"

"How to make candles and tallow lamps, how to make quilts, and I even learned something about working with animal skins to make buckskin shirts and moccasins."

"I missed the lessons on the deer skins as I was nursing Tim at the time," Beth comments.

"Tim's becoming quite a leader among the men. He is well-liked and respected," Dorothy says and Mary nods in agreement.

"I agree with you, Dorothy. Tim and I have some animated talks together on our walks."

"Do I hear wedding bells?"

"No, Dorothy. Tim and I are good friends only."

Dorothy and Mary look at each other and smile knowingly.

"It's time to put the children down for a nap. We're finished here for now. Dorothy, can you stay for coffee?"

"I'd love to Mary, but I think I'd better check on George and Johnny; Rebecca Boone has had them most of the day now. She will be ready for a break. How about I look after your children tomorrow, Mary, and you and Beth can finish up your baking. I'm going to have Rebecca's youngest, as I think she is planning to come here tomorrow."

"That's right. It's always a treat to work together on some special projects and then share whatever we make. Thanks for all your help today, Dorothy."

"You're welcome. We'll do it again," Dorothy says as she waves goodbye and closes the door behind her.

The next day is sunny but cold. Rebecca arrives in the early morning. Betsey Calloway Henderson has offered to help Dorothy with the children, so Rebecca has several hours free.

"We'll have time to get everything done today, without having to stop to care for little ones. Then in the afternoon I want to go to the store for a few things before I relieve Betsey and Dorothy," Rebecca informs them.

The Christmas Eve church service is held in the common meeting room. There is great enjoyment as the singing of the familiar hymns fills the room with music. Mabel plays the harpsichord, picking out the notes for "The First Noel" to start the singing. This carol is followed by others, "While Shepherds Watched Their Flocks by Night", "Hark the Herald Angels Sing", "God Rest Ye Merry Gentlemen," and "Christians Awake Salute the Happy Morn." Squire Boone reads the Christmas story from the Bible and presents some reflections on it. There is more singing to follow with "Ding, Dong Merrily on High" and then the service closes with "We Wish You a Merry Christmas." Tea, coffee and milk are provided along with some sweet treats as the people mingle and share afterwards. Then it is time to head to their homes and put the children to bed. There are still a few last minute things to prepare for the morning and the gifts to put out under the tree.

Christmas morning is a special family time. It is wonderful to see the delight on the children's faces when they open their gifts. James loves his blacksmith shop with a working miniature bellows and wood for a fire, a hammer, and horseshoes hanging on the wall. Isaac loves his horse and wagon with sacks of flour, cornmeal and sugar and stacks of hay to load and unload. Sarah hugs her doll and enjoys changing her into the new outfits. Later in the day the children put on their new mitts and scarves to play in the snow. Beth made a new dress for Mary and knitted a blanket for Ellie. There is dress material for Beth from Mary and Mike.

Since there are so many young single men living in town, the families each invite a few of them to join them for the Christmas meal. Beth has invited Tim, and Mary and Mike invited four others, making for a full table to sit down for the meal the women have been preparing for the past three days. Joseph Combs and Joseph House continue to live in the bunkhouse behind Richard`s Café and have been helping out on some of the outlying farms in between their hunting and trapping expeditions, taking on a lot of the day to day work for the Wallaces on their farm as Jack is so busy with his carpentry work. David McPhee and John Martin also stay in the bunkhouse and together they carry on a freighting business bringing in most of the supplies for the store and the tavern by pack mules. They also make deliveries to outlying farms by wagon.

The dinner consists of buffalo roast, and venison along with home-grown potatoes, carrots and beets. What a wonderful smell greets the guests as they arrive, licking their lips in anticipation of the feast to be enjoyed soon, and breathing deeply of the pleasing aromas. The Christmas pudding with a caramel sauce along with cookies and squares are tasty sweets to be savoured.

It is a lively group around the table. After the meal is over and the cleanup complete, Beth and Tim slip out for a walk and to exchange their own gifts chosen with special thought for each other. Mike has fashioned a belt buckle with a "T" in the centre which Beth gives to Tim along with new socks, scarf and gloves that she has knitted. Tim has purchased a string of beads for Beth and a length of cloth in a deep mauve with a bonnet to match. Beth is thrilled and gives Tim a hug of thanks which Tim returns, holding on tight for just a little longer.

New Years' Day of 1777 is celebrated in Kentucky by several hundred settlers. Amid the frolic of this day are uplifted the cheery voices of wives and mothers and the romping noise of children, as well as the loud laughs of hunters and pioneers. In the cabins, huge fires burn in large fireplaces where meat is roasting and cornbread is cooking to a rich brown colour. In the wild loneliness of their lives the brave people remember the holidays which they were used to celebrating in their eastern homes and make the holidays bright, joyous and happy. The air is crisp with a clear sky. There has been a heavy snowfall and the weather is very cold. Beth has been out on snowshoes several times by now and is becoming quite proficient at it. Tim calls for her today to go for a walk and they are out enjoying the winter countryside for an hour.

In the evenings, Beth and Mary often have knitting or sewing in their hands while the conversation flows. It is a special time for Tim and Beth to be alone, but it isn't always desired as they enjoy spending time with the others, deepening their relationships.

Other evenings Beth and Tim are invited to Rebecca and Daniel Boone's to share events of their lives, building the friendship. Jack and Dorothy are also part of the circuit, opening their hearts and life's experiences to the others as they build rapport working together to make Boonesborough a better place for all of their families.

When Beth first came to Boonesborough she often mentioned returning in a few months, in the spring at the latest, to Boston. As she grows, her attachment to the frontier also grows and Boston is only spoken of on the rare occasions when they receive a letter or parcel from her parents.

Chapter 14 – The Pattersons and Ruth Hancock Arrive

In late March when most of the snow has gone Tim suggests, "Let's go for a canoe ride, Beth."

"We haven't been out on the water yet. That's a great idea, Tim."

"Have you ever paddled before?"

"No. That's one more thing you can teach me," and Tim proceeds to do so.

"It's a beautiful day with a lovely breeze. It's been wonderful to have peace with the Indians. The English and French sure rile them up."

"Do you feel your muscles working as you pull the paddle through the water? Be careful not to splash yourself," Tim chuckles as she turns a dripping face towards him for a moment.

"It's tougher than I thought it would be. I'm getting the knack better of dipping the paddle into the water without splashing quite as much but I'm making a lot of noise."

"We will make this first outing a short one and gradually build up to longer ones. We have had a lovely time out. Your new bonnet suits you well, a cheerful splash of colour. We are almost back to shore." After beaching the canoe, Timothy takes her hand as they climb up the bank and walk back to the fort.

This year the British officials open a new front in the war with the American colonists by recruiting and arming Indian war parties to raid Kentucky settlements. Henry Hamilton, the British Lieutenant Governor of Canada at Fort Detroit, finds willing allies in leaders such as Chief Blackfish of the Shawnees, who hope to drive the Americans out of Kentucky and reclaim their hunting grounds. As the raids intensify, Americans who stray from fortified settlements are likely to be killed or captured. The British pay the Indians for scalps and prisoners, with more than two hundred losing their lives or being captured in this year.

On April 24, Shawnees led by Chief Blackfish are outside Boonesborough, in hiding, waiting for small numbers of men to leave the fort. Daniel Goodman and a companion leave the fort to bring in some horses when they are fired upon by four Indians. They aren't wounded so they flee towards the fort. With deadly accuracy one of the Indians throws his tomahawk and kills Goodman. Simon Kenton, a recent arrival at Boonesborough, and two others are at the fort gate ready to go hunting and they run to the relief of their friends and chase the Indians to the edge of the field. Daniel Boone hears the gunshots and heads out with a dozen men to join Kenton and the others in the lane. About one hundred Indians have been in hiding and are successful in drawing the whites into an ambush. A large number of Indians jump into the lane and cut off the groups' line of retreat. Daniel quickly grasps the desperate situation they are in and directs the men to fight hard and charge through the Indians. They fire upon the enemy and then beat with clubbed guns those that stand in their way. Boone is shot in the ankle which breaks the bone and throws him to the ground; Kenton kills the first Indian who comes to take Daniel's scalp, and clubs the second with his gun and knocks him down. Then he runs with Boone in his arms towards the fort. Jemima sees that her father is wounded and rushes out to assist Simon for the last several yards. As a result of this incident, Kenton becomes Boone's close friend as well as a legendary frontiersman in his own right; they are often seen together in hunting parties. These raids are nerve wracking and deadly but life must go on. The fear of death is always present but the zest for life and the desire to make a better life is much stronger.

At the end of April, Richard Patterson arrives in Boonesborough with his wife Lydia, and four children, Linda age 14, Lucy 13, David 12, and Johnny 8. Upon their arrival, the travelers are directed to the Holt Campbell Inn and Tavern where they can rest, have some home-cooked food and present their plans. After they finish eating, the discussion begins.

"My wife, Lydia, is a seamstress and would like to open a shop in Boonesborough. We have four children and would also need a place to live." The faces of the women light up because it has been awhile for most of them since they have been to a city and had a dress made for them.

"I have been working with dyeing cloth and would like to pursue that interest here. I would require an outside area for this." The men are thinking and talking among themselves. Where would be a suitable place?

"What about across the way next to the Hart blockhouse?" Tom suggests.

"There is that open area between the cabin and the blockhouse," Paul says.

"And the cabin is wider than most which might be helpful," Dorothy mentions.

"Isn't the cabin next to it available as well?" David pipes up.

"There is one more thing," Lydia speaks for the first time. "Our son Johnny loves to work with fragrances. He would like to grow fragrant flowers and make perfume. Do you have an area for him to grow flowers?"

"The Harts live on the corner. On each side of it there is an open space. It should be just about the right size."

"Let's take them over to see it. There will likely be some cleaning up to do in the cabins as they have been vacant for a few months."

"We'll be happy to help," Dorothy says eagerly.

Richard Patterson puts up his hand to slow everyone down. "Now that the Patterson situation has been presented, we have one more. Ruth Hancock travelled with us from Philadelphia to try to find her niece. She hasn't heard from her sister for six years, since her niece was born. Ruth has had people searching for months and she thinks Naomi Anderson came to Boonesborough and her brothers may be in the area." There is a gasp from the assembled group.

Tim hears Ruth's last name and he has an inspiration and heads out to follow it up.

Dorothy slips out of the Tavern and hurries over to the Anderson cabin. "Naomi," she calls as she knocks loudly on the door. Naomi answers and invites her inside. "Naomi you must come right now to the Inn. I think your sister is here."

"My sister? You mean Ruth?" she asks in unbelieving wonder.

"Yes, Ruth has just arrived and is looking for her niece."

"Dorothy, would you mind staying with the children while I go see?"

"Take as long as you need. I'll wait here," Dorothy agrees.

Naomi can hardly believe it. Ruth here? She rushes over to the Inn and quickly opens the door. "Ruth?"

Ruth turns around and looks almost unbelievingly at her sister. "Naomi, you look so much like mother," Ruth says as she rushes into her sister's arms. What a reunion this is for the sisters after all these years!

"Where's my niece Esther?"

"I have a surprise for you. There are three nieces and two nephews!" Naomi responds with a smile and a twinkle in her eyes.

"Wow! Where are they? I can't wait to see them. I have been trying to find you for several months. I sure was hoping to find you here after all the searching. I was fearful that it would be another dead end."

They hug each other again and the tears of happiness are flowing down their cheeks.

"How is Ben? Mother talked about you sometimes. You left home when I was ten, that's eleven years ago," Ruth continues.

"That is a long time not to have seen you. I have so much to tell you. How long can you stay?" Naomi questions.

"I have no definite plans. Mother asked me to try to find you. She missed you so much at times. As she approached her end, she really pressured me to promise to try and find you."

"Come on to the cabin and I'll catch you up on all the news," Naomi says as she links arms with her and they head out the door, giving a wave and smile to Paul, the innkeeper.

At the cabin, Naomi thanks Dorothy for watching the children and then introduces Aunt Ruth to the children. Esther is seven, James and Nicholas are five year old twins, Aletha is almost four, and Mary is three. Naomi puts some coffee on and then sits down on the rug with Ruth and the children.

"Where to begin, that's the question. Ben and I moved first to North Carolina where Esther was born in 1770. Ben wanted to go further west and he heard about plans for Boonesborough. We got in touch with Daniel and Rebecca Boone as they were organizing settlers for Kentucky. We arrived here in the fall of 1775, one of the first families here. All of our supplies were brought in by pack mule including a good store of staple food to last us over the winter, things like flour, oats, and corn. Ben hoped to hunt for meat to eat. We have made our cabin into a home. But then Ben got sick and died about two months ago. I have been concerned about how I was going to manage on my own with the small children. The people in the settlement have been very helpful, but I do have to make some decisions soon."

"I'm sorry to hear about Ben. You must really miss him," Ruth sympathizes.

"Yes, I do."

"What ideas have you had about what you can do?" Ruth asks.

"Well, I know how to look after the cabin and the children and I know how to bake, but I haven't been able to figure out how I can support myself and the family on my own," Naomi says as she shakes her head in discouragement.

"Is there a bakeshop in Boonesborough?" Ruth asks.

"No there isn't."

"I wonder if that would be a way for you to continue living here. You talk lovingly of the place so I guess you would like to stay here," Ruth continues.

"I like it here but until you came up with the idea of a bakeshop, I had not figured out how I could stay. That's a big commitment and I will need to have help to make it worthwhile."

"I could help you. Mother taught me how to bake and I even brought some of her recipes."

"Dorothy might like to help too. The three of us could supply bread and baked goods for the Inn and for Richard's Café. It might work," Naomi says thoughtfully as she continues to think about the idea.

"Why don't you check with the innkeeper and with Richard to see if they would be interested?" Ruth suggests.

"If they agree, I can then ask Dorothy if she would join us. Maybe you and I could do it on our own but with the children it would be tough to do. Dorothy is a lovely woman. She has two boys and in a couple of months she will have another baby. If she can give us a couple of hours two or three times a week that would help." Naomi is starting to getting excited about the idea. "That's enough of those plans for now. What about you? You indicated Mother died. When was that? What about Father? Have you heard from our older brothers, Stephen and William?"

"Mother died in November after a long illness. It was sad to see her go but she was in a lot of pain near the end so it was a relief for her. Father and our youngest brother Robert are doing fine in the home town. I haven't seen or heard from our older brothers, but in searching for you I had some feelers out for them as well. There was an indication they might be in this area too."

"Wouldn't that be something to find them too?"

"I'm hopeful, especially since I found you here. I was almost afraid to believe I might actually find you here. After everyone else left the Inn to look at the cabin for the Pattersons, I stood there a little discouraged doubting that I had come to the right place," Ruth muses.

"You had your back to the door when I came in. I asked Paul who I was supposed to see and he pointed to you. The Ruth I remembered was ten years old so it took me a moment to realize who was standing in front of me when you turned around. Your cry of "Naomi!" caused an immediate response of "Ruth?" from me."

"What an unbelievable day!" Ruth says as she beams at her sister and the children.

"We never know what will happen from one day to the next. You must have brought things with you. Where are they?" Naomi asks.

"I'll go and find the Pattersons and have everything brought over here." Ruth finds them in great excitement about the cabins assigned to them. They are busy unpacking but they stop what they are doing when they see Ruth.

"I can tell from your face that you found you sister," Lydia says.

"You are right. We have just had a good time together. I have come to get my belongings."

"I'll have Johnny help you right now. Most of your things are on the one pack mule. Anything else we find we'll bring up later. Johnny, please help Ruth with her things," Richard calls.

"Are you staying for awhile Ruth?" Lydia asks.

"It looks like I will be staying."

"I'm happy for you. It will be great to see you about town. We got to know each other well on our trip out here," Richard adds.

As she was ready to leave with Johnny, Ruth called out, "Have fun getting settled in. It will be a little like camping out for awhile."

"Yes, we have to get beds and furniture made. We've met the local carpenter already and Jack will have some chairs for us later today."

"See you soon. Bye for now," Ruth waves as she heads to her sister's cabin.

"I'm not sure where I'm going to put all my stuff – it didn't seem like much when I left home. I'll check with Naomi." Ruth returns a moment later and says, "Johnny, if you will help me, we can just pile it inside and then my sister and I will move it from there." After everything is unloaded from the mule, Ruth thanks Johnny for his help.

"You are welcome Ruth. Have fun settling in," he says as he heads back to his new home.

In the meantime Tim heads out along the Kentucky River to the saw mill. "Steve and Will, how are you? It's Timothy from the fort."

"Good to see you Tim. Will you join us for some supper? We were just about to sit down."

"I would be happy to join you. I imagine you don't have too many visitors out here."

"No, not many people come by. So far the Indians have left us alone too. What brings you out so late in the day? Does Jack need some special lumber?" Steve asks.

"Jack didn't say he needed anything. I'm here on a personal mission."

"What do you want to know?"

"What can you tell me about your family?" Tim questions them as they begin eating.

"It's been many years since we saw any of them. Once we left

Philadelphia, we never went back."

"What family do you have?" Tim persists.

"Naomi would be over thirty by now, probably married and with a kid or two."

"Ruth would be twenty or so. I wonder if she is as beautiful as Ma," Steve comments.

"Steve, maybe we should seriously think of making a trip back home," Will adds.

"We also had a baby brother Bobby. He's probably still at home with Ma and Pa," the brothers agree.

"From what you have just told me, I have what I hope is happy news for you," Tim says.

"What do you know about our family, Tim?" they ask in unison.

"Ruth just arrived in Boonesborough today looking for her sister Naomi Anderson and her niece. She found Naomi living in a cabin in the fort and a whole family of nieces and nephews."

Momentarily Steve and Will are speechless; then they both start talking at once.

"Naomi and Ruth are in Boonesborough? Are you sure it's them?"

"What are we waiting for? Can we go and see them now or should we wait until tomorrow?" Steve wonders.

"I'll never sleep tonight now knowing our sisters are so close."

"Let's bank the fire, close up the cabin and head to the fort."

"I wonder if we will recognize either of our sisters."

"I wonder if they will recognize us," says practical Steve.

"Maybe we should have washed up first."

"I'm too excited to wait."

The three of them make the trek in a little over an hour. Tim leads the brothers to the Anderson cabin. He knocks on the door and calls out, "Naomi, it's Timothy Eadon. I have a couple of visitors to see you."

Naomi opens the door and looks out. "Come on in Tim. Who do you have with you?"

"Naomi? Is it really you?" Will asks as he looks at his sister. It has been so long since he has seen her.

"Will? And Stephen too? Let me sit down. This is quite a shock. I was all alone with five small children. Five hours ago my little sister arrived and now my two older brothers. It is just simply amazing." She jumps up and throws herself into Will's arms and he holds her close. Then Steve has his turn.

"How long have you been in Boonesborough Naomi?" the brothers ask.

"Ben and I were one of the first families to come here in the fall of 1775. How long have you been in the area? You don't live inside the fort do you?" says Naomi in wonder.

"We have a saw mill about five miles from here. We built the saw mill almost a year ago," Steve begins the story.

"We deliver lumber to Jack Wallace and bring in firewood but we don't know everyone in town," Will continues the conversation.

"We never expected that our sister lived here."

"It's a wonder you didn't run into Ben around town," Naomi says.

"We knew Ben Anderson well, but we didn't know he was married to our sister. I guess we never asked who his wife was."

"Where is Ben? I haven't seen him since before the winter," Steve questions.

"Ben got real sick over the winter and died two months ago," is Naomi's sad response.

"You have been on your own for two months? How have you been managing?"

"It hasn't been easy, but the people in the settlement have been really helpful. Tim has been cutting firewood for me and bringing me some meat. I have been trying to decide what to do."

"Now that we know you are here, we will look out for you, won't we Will?"

"We sure will, Steve. It's great to see you, sis. For months on end we don't really think about our family. It's been so many years since we saw any of you. When Tim started asking us about our family, it built up a real yearning in us."

"It was a yearning that was so soon able to be satisfied. We were so eager to see you, we didn't stop to wash up or change our clothes."

"We didn't walk here either. We were in such a hurry we set a very fast pace."

"You said Ruth was here. Where is she?"

"She is putting the children to bed. She should be back anytime now." Just then Ruth comes down the ladder from the loft and Naomi calls her over. "Ruth, guess who Tim just brought home?"

Ruth looks at all three men, puzzled, having no idea who she is looking at.

"Wow, she's a beauty!" whistles Will.

"Ruth, meet your brothers William and Stephen."

"Will and Steve? Is it really you? How did you find me so quickly? I just arrived today."

"Good news travels fast around here. Tim heard you say your last name was Hancock and he came out to talk to us. He fished information out of us about our family and then sprang the news on us that both of our sisters were close by."

"I almost despaired of even finding Naomi and my niece. Now my two brothers are here as well, and there are several nieces and nephews. Do you have families as well?"

"We are both still bachelors but we have our eyes on two young women."

"Can you stay the night Will and Steve? I would sure like to visit longer with you and introduce you to my children. It has been so long."

"Tim, do you think Paul has room at the Inn for us? It might be a good idea to have a bath too."

"I think Paul has a room available. I'll leave now, let him know you are coming and ask him to heat some water for baths."

"Thanks Timothy for everything. You have been a real friend."

"I'm glad you have family now," he says as he gives Naomi a quick hug goodnight.

"It looks like we will stay the night and spend the day with you tomorrow."

"Come early and have breakfast with us. Ruth and I can talk over our plans with you."

"Have a good sleep. See you in the morning," Will says as he holds each sister tightly in his arms. Steve is right in line behind him to hug his sisters. "See you tomorrow."

"Good night," they call to each other.

"What a blessed day!" Naomi and Ruth agree as they head for bed.

The next morning Tim heads over to Beth's early in the morning. "Good morning Beth. How are you today? Have you got time for a half hour walk this morning?"

"Sure Tim. It will make a good start to the day."

"I missed seeing you last night but wait until I tell you what happened," Tim says as he reaches for Beth's hand. "You know that a new family arrived yesterday, the Pattersons."

"Yes, Lydia is a seamstress which interests all the women. I'm interested in working with her even a few hours a week if she wants an assistant."

"That will be good for you, Beth. Give them time to settle in and then see if that is an option for you. Jack is busy making furniture for the new family. I think I will offer my services to him in the shop."

"That will be something different for you than blacksmithing."

"Mike doesn't have enough work for me to do full time. I'll still continue to work with him as needed. Now for the other exciting news. The Pattersons had a young woman with them, Ruth Hancock. It turns out she is Naomi Anderson's sister."

"How wonderful for Naomi! Is she going to stay for awhile?"

"We'll have to see what her plans are. I know the sisters are happy to have found each other after many years."

"It was only a few years since I had seen Mary when I came here and we always knew where she was. I gathered that Naomi had not been in touch with any of her family for years."

"There is more news. Ruth mentioned her last name was Hancock and that got me thinking. I put two and two together and headed out to the saw mill. It turns out Will and Steve Hancock are the older twin brothers of Ruth and Naomi."

"Amazing! Naomi has been struggling since Ben died, not sure what to do. I sometimes take the older children for a walk or take them something to eat that I have made. I know other women do the same."

"We always try to help others out," Tim agreed.

"It must be a relief not to be on her own in the world anymore, to have a whole family of help now."

"Will and Steve stayed at the Inn last night and will spend the day with their sisters and the children," Tim informs Beth.

"What a story to lift our spirits today. Thanks for sharing it with me. Now duty calls for both of us."

"I'll come and see you later for a longer time together. Enjoy your day," Tim says as he hugs her warmly.

Beth enters the cabin and begins to help Mary with the daily chores and fills her in on the wonderful news in Boonesborough.

Will and Steve arrive at their sister's cabin for breakfast making it quite a festive occasion. After the meal, the brothers play with the children, getting to know them a little while Naomi and Ruth do the dishes and tidy up. Being twins themselves, they are especially intrigued with their twin nephews, Jimmy and Nicky. Esther is quite shy at first. Aletha takes to Ruth and tries to wiggle in close to her. Mary, the youngest, is a real charmer. The children set about playing while the adults have a serious talk.

"Yesterday Ruth suggested that we open a bakeshop in Boonesborough as a means of revenue. It was my first ray of hope for a way to stay here."

"Yum-yum, I can already taste a delicious treat. I would encourage you to do some baking," Will beams.

"There will be lots of young men who will be eager to have your treats. It will be a lot of work for you though," says Steve.

"We talked about that too, with the five children to care for as well. I thought I would check with Paul at the Inn and Richard Henderson for his café to see what kind of interest there is. If they are agreeable, I suggested we could ask Dorothy Wallace if she would like to help us a few hours a week. Her boys are older but soon she will have another baby and won't have a lot of free time. She has a special knack with pastry."

"How can we help you out?" the brothers ask.

"Just having you here is a wonderful treat. Come for a visit whenever you can."

"You will need lots of wood to keep your fires going. We can supply you with as much as you need. At least one of us comes into town every week with a wagonload of lumber and firewood. We will try to arrange our trips so that we can both come and stay to spend some time with you," the brothers agree.

"Would a large outdoor oven be helpful for you? We could build one a few yards in front of your cabin with a roof over top and a table so you could bake a dozen loaves of bread at a time. In the summer the bread baking would not overheat the cabin." Steve adds his thoughts.

"That would be a great addition for us. I must go and see Paul and Richard on Monday. I'm excited about getting started. We will start slowly and build the business from there. We will use the small oven in the cabin that Ben made for me until you have the larger one built. We can make cakes and pies to begin with. There is only room to make bread for our family needs in the cabin oven. I have tried some cookies. Ruth what recipes did you bring from Ma?"

"Cookies, muffins, loaf cakes and cupcakes as well as some bread recipes."

"It will be fun trying them out in our pioneer oven. It will be different than what you are used to Ruth."

"We get to eat the things that aren't perfect to sell. I hope you have lots of flops," teases Will.

"We'll be sure to have some treats for you when you are in town," the sisters smilingly agree.

"We are heading out to our cabin now. We'll get some material together to make your oven. There is a nice section of clay to make bricks not far from the saw mill. We'll check with Mike at the blacksmith shop about some sheets of metal for inside the oven."

"We'll see you in about a week. We have lumber to prepare and firewood to cut. We may bring two wagons in next Saturday."

"Have a great week. We will look forward to seeing you next week."

Chapter 15 – A Seamstress in Boonesborough

There is a large double cabin available for the Patterson family; the larger side is converted into Lydia's seamstress shop and the smaller side is for cooking, eating and sleeping, with a loft up the ladder for the children to sleep. There is a shed beside the cabin along the stockade wall that Richard will use for dyeing cloth. There is a good size room behind the main room where Johnny will be able to experiment with perfume.

Lydia is tall and willowy, soft-spoken, but when discussing dressmaking, she gets quite animated and her hazel eyes glow and warmth radiates from her whole being. It has been tough for several years only working with rough homespun material. She is in her element now working with the beautiful brightly coloured cottons and satins. The many shades of greens, blues, and reds can be mixed and matched for a single coloured garment, or two colours used to complement each other. Pale yellows and oranges are lovely spring shades, while the deep royal blue and royal purple are fall and winter shades. Lydia and Richard have a full store of these materials that they brought with them and now that the British blockade of Boston has been removed and French fleets are able to also make shipments, there is a ready supply. However, it is a long, rough journey to Boonesborough to bring in supplies.

Richard Patterson makes arrangements with Richard Henderson to bring in a shipment of material every time he brings in supplies.

Lydia has plans to expand as a milliner, making hats, gloves and purses, knowing how wonderful it feels to dress up for a barbecue and dance. She has the latest sewing machine with her, quite a feat to pack it in on a mule but it has arrived intact. She also brought a few looms for weaving which her oldest children are learning to use. Four pack mules were loaded with cloth, thread, yarn and all the tools of the trade. Next year Richard plans to go along to Salem to choose material and sometimes he will take Lydia with him and she will have quite a thrill stocking up on colours and designs in different materials.

In the meantime Richard is asking around about local plants used for dyeing cloth. He shows his keen interest and picks up valuable information from the friendly Indians; he also learns about herbs and roots for healing. When anyone has an eager student who is like a sponge to soak up information, this makes you eager to share as much as you can with them. Richard has a few things to share in return to teach others. He and the medicine man of the nearby village become regular companions. Richard is respected for his knowledge and eagerness to learn and teach. Remembering that his son Johnny is interested in fragrances, Richard learns about local plants that can be used for making perfumes.

Johnny has always enjoyed planting and watching things grow, following in the footsteps of his father. Richard used to read whatever he could get his hands on about plants and how they grew and what would grow in a particular climate. He has a collection of seeds with him and is eager to start growing them. It is early spring when they arrive so they can soon begin planting. There is a nice sunny spot beside their cabin to grow some vegetables. He is eager to grow tomatoes, the newest thing he has been reading up about. Johnny is as eager as his Dad to try out some of the new seeds they have with them. He loves flowers as they give so much joy to the eyes for everyone who sees them. He wants to experiment with a collection of seeds for flowers that have various fragrances. He read several books on the process for making perfume, with his father explaining some of the technical details that were strange to him. Johnny has some equipment with him that he will use. The lilacs are almost ready to bloom when they arrive. The air is soon full of their smell. Johnny decides to give it a try making perfume from these fragrant trees. He cuts some cedar and boils it down to use as a base, adds a couple of drops of his mother's vanilla to help the fragrance of the perfume last and then boils the blossoms in a small amount of water to capture the aroma.

The women of Boonesborough make a special effort to welcome the family to the fort by bringing them food to eat for the first couple of days until they get settled in. Jack has some chairs ready for sale and is happy to make whatever other furniture they want. Jack has built up quite a reputation with his fine workmanship. After he set up his woodworking shop in the cabin next to the rear gate, it wasn't long before Flanders Calloway wandered in to watch him work. Jack carried on a conversation as he worked and Flanders paid close attention. On other days, Flanders would wander around touching the finished products and the pieces in progress. At night he would talk a little about it to Tim. Tim was very busy with blacksmithing and had little time to consider any other occupation.

Soon Jack had Flanders helping him with little jobs and as his business picked up, he offered Flanders a job helping him in the shop. Flanders shows real promise for woodworking. Nathaniel Hart, the other assistant, is eager to do the mundane jobs but has no artistic skill, making for good teamwork so that everything needed is done in a cooperative way, together moving the projects forward to completion. Tim Eadon walks with Flanders to the shop some days and stops to watch Jack at work, listen to him talk, and to touch the wood. Jack still has more work than he can handle and often has Tim hold a board or get a board for him.

In his spare time Jack makes wooden toys. He has hired two men to work his land so that he has more time to carry on his craft of woodworking. Dorothy and the boys are thriving in the fresh country air. Soon they will have another child in their home. Dorothy has settled in well in her life in Kentucky. It was a rough start for her, not her idea to leave civilization in the east, but willing to follow Jack in his quest for adventure. Jack has grown in confidence and is a very happy, contented man when he has wood to work with. Dorothy planted flowers at the front of their cabin, some that will bloom year after year. Soon the first flowers will be out. The days are getting warmer and longer.

Lydia's sewing machine whirrs along sewing the seams together, speeding up part of the process, but there is still much of the finishing work to do by hand. She has some samples of her work on display.

"Jack, can you make a long narrow work table for me?" Lydia asks. "We also need a kitchen table and four more chairs. You know about the four beds for the children in the loft and a double bed in the back room of our living quarters."

Dishes and cutlery and pans are purchased from the general store. With the addition of curtains at the windows and a couple of paintings on the walls the cabin is soon beginning to look like a home. The woven table runner made on the loom by Linda and Lucy is very attractive. Richard soon has his own loom set up for making plain cloth that he will experiment with dyeing. David meets other boys around his age such as Israel Boone, James O'Neill and George and Johnny Wallace.

In a week Jack has the table ready for Lydia so she can lay her material to cut out a pattern and use it as a work space for performing her craft. Jack makes shelves to hold the bolts of cloth. The room is starting to take shape as a functioning work area. Jack has been using the services of Stephen and William Hancock, after they set up their sawmill, for the past year. They prepare the trees into lumber, a great service for Jack to cut his time in half for doing the creative work of making the wooden furniture. The men also provide firewood for those not able to cut their own. Many settlers come to the area and trees have to be cut to build cabins and plant crops. The brothers offer to chop the wood, reserving the straightest pieces for lumber and the remainder for firewood. Fires are used for cooking all year round and for warmth for a good portion of the year. A large amount of firewood is always required.

"Hi, Jack. How are you today?" Tim asks as he walks into the shop one day.

"I'm fine Tim but I have more work than I can handle at the moment."

"That's what I have come to see you about. I would like to offer my services on a part time basis. I haven't worked with wood before but I would like to give it a try." Jack and Tim talk further and Tim agrees to come back the next day.

Although sewing was taught to girls at a young age, there are some who never quite get the knack of it. When Dorothy saw the dresses on display she wondered how she could afford one. Dorothy can sew after a fashion but her stitches are never as small and neat as Lydia's. Dorothy observes and decides she has something to offer as she makes delicious butter in moulds, churning it to just the right consistency. She sells some of her extra butter at the General Store as well as extra eggs. She also makes jams from the berry bushes around their cabin. Jack made her an oven last year and she has developed quite a knack for baking. Wednesdays are baking days and the pastry for her butter tarts is flaky and light and the filling mouth-wateringly satisfying. She makes delicious berry and fruit pies when the ingredients are available and visitors seem to appear at her door shortly after the pies are baked with the aroma spreading out around the area. Dorothy is glad that she brought with her the collection of recipes from her mother and aunts, recipes which she almost left behind but something made her bring them along, a bit of her ancestry that she held onto, having had to leave everything else behind when they moved west.

***

"Hello, Lydia. I'm here to help you and learn from you."

"Welcome Beth. I'll explain the layout of the room first and then show you what I am working on and where I can use your help. Let's get started."

The afternoon files by and Beth is in her glory. She enjoys all the things she is doing but most of all she enjoys the feel of the material in her hands. Richard came in to stop their work to say it was time for supper. Beth hurries home to help Mary put the finishing touches on their meal.

Beth arranges to work a couple of hours a day with Lydia. Beth is able to sew very neatly, but working with Lydia adds a whole new dimension. Lydia is able to teach her how to work the loom and the treadle sewing machine. Beth is soon able to make several yards of cloth in a week. Lydia teaches Beth how to make a pattern for people of different sizes. Beth finds it fascinating and is eager to learn everything Lydia can show her. Sewing on lace trim, buttons, whatever is required, is a joy for Beth to do. She feels alive for those few hours each afternoon. When Tim calls for her in the evening for a walk, she is quite talkative about all she has learned that day. Tim is just as eager to share about his woodworking projects.

It didn't take Jack long to realize that Tim has a real knack for woodworking. Tim finds he likes making things with his hands. He is very surprised how good it feels to fashion a piece of wood into a chair or table, making a beautifully shaped leg on the lathe. Mike only has work for Tim for half days. Now Tim is spending a few hours daily with Jack in the carpenter shop.

James Ellis, the local artist and his wife Sally live next door to Naomi Anderson. He likes to sketch and will often set up his easel in the sunshine outside his cabin and sketch whatever is taking place around him. From his cabin he can watch Ching building a fire to begin the laundry for the day, and has his sketch pencil busy creating the scene. He sketches the arrival of newcomers to Boonesborough, the daily trips to the spring for water, the blacksmith hard at work with the army horses waiting to be shoed. What he enjoys doing the most is painting in water colours. He paints a few scenes from town life with the women in their colourful bonnets. He enjoys a walk in the woods to see the flowers and eagerly sets about to capture their beauty on canvas.

Chapter 16 – A Bakeshop in Boonesborough

Naomi woke on Monday morning with her mind whirring with plans. She quickly begins preparations for breakfast and Ruth joins her a few minutes later. By the time breakfast is ready the children are up and settle at the table.

"Aunt Ruth is going to look after you for awhile this morning children. I want you to listen to her."

"Yes, Mommy," they all chorus with smiles on their faces.

Naomi is eager but also very nervous. Richard's cabin is the closest and he is usually in the General Store first thing in the morning so that is her first destination.

"Good morning Richard. How are you on this beautiful morning?" Naomi calls as she enters the store.

"I'm doing well, Naomi. You look extra cheerful this morning."

"I have a proposition for you."

"Okay, I'm listening."

"I need a way to provide for myself and the children in order to stay here. I have been blessed this past weekend with the arrival of my sister and on top of that the discovery of my older twin brothers living only a few miles away."

"That is wonderful for you. I'm so happy for you to have family near. That is certainly a treasure."

"This is my proposition. I have no desire to sit back and let my brothers bear all the responsibility for looking after me although I will be glad of some help from them. Ruth came up with an idea and Steve and Will have added to it. I would like to start a bakeshop. Would you be interested in having me supply you with bread and baked goods for your café?"

"That would be a real treat. I can almost taste a fresh baked pie. Naomi, let's go and discuss your idea with Dan." He calls to his wife Pleasant, "Honey, can you mind the store for a half hour? I'm heading over to the café."

"I'll be right down Rick." As she arrives, he gives her a quick kiss and leaves with Naomi.

Dan pours coffee for the two of them and is invited to sit with them for a few minutes. "Naomi has an idea of how to support herself now that Ben is gone. Go ahead and tell Dan your plans."

"My sister Ruth suggested we start a bakeshop. I am offering to make bread, rolls, pastries and desserts for the Café. Would this be a help to you?"

"I love to cook, but baking has never been what I do best. I am very interested in what you are offering."

They talk further about their needs. Naomi cautions that it will take a little time to get organized and figure out how much they can provide. Dan discusses how many customers he has on a daily basis to give Naomi an idea of what quantities would be required, or could be used in the Café and she takes careful notes. Naomi and Richard talk about the supplies she will need and places an order.

Naomi stands up, thanks Richard and Dan for their time and encouragement and agrees to get back to them on what the bakeshop will provide them with.

"We'll take whatever you can provide us with," Dan beams. Naomi smiles as she leaves with a lighter heart, beginning to realize a means for her to survive in Boonesborough.

Her next stop is at the Inn and Tavern. "Good morning Paul," she says as she watches the tall, slender man sweeping the wooden plank floor. "You seem to have grown taller. You really enjoy your life as the inn and tavern keeper."

"Good morning Naomi. Yes, it was a good idea for Sam, Tom and I to take over the inn when we came to Boonesborough last year. We have really settled in here and enjoy looking after the citizens and the visitors who come to town."

"You are a welcome sight to newcomers who have been travelling on the trails for weeks."

"What brings you down to this end of town on this sunny day? Are you out for a walk in the spring sunshine? And no children with you either. That's a change for you."

"I'm here on a mission and Ruth is looking after the children." Naomi goes on to explain her plans on how to support herself. Paul is eager to fall in with her plans as neither he nor Tom can bake pastries although they make biscuits and rolls. They talk about types of things he can use and wonders how soon he can have the first delivery.

"I'm planning to get started this week on pastries. Bread will come along once Will and Steve make me a larger oven." They discuss how many people he generally feeds in a week and what they could use. Naomi thanks him and she has a lighter heart and an even quicker step as she heads out of the fort to the Wallace cabin. Jack has already gone to his shop in the fort. He hopes that Tim will come today to help so they can finish some much needed pieces for the Pattersons. When Jack arrived in Boonesborough nine months before, he had no idea that he would have so much work.

Dorothy invites Naomi in for a cup of coffee and they sit down for a visit, her sons eager to leave to play with their friends once their chores are done. Naomi shares her plans and invites Dorothy to join her in the venture. Dorothy stands up and reaches for a wooden box from the cupboard. She brings it to the table and opens it to show to Naomi.

"These are the only things I brought with me when I came here. I will be happy to share these recipes with you and help you in your venture. When can we begin?"

"I know you are going to have a new baby soon. I don't know how much time you will have to help us."

"For the first while the baby will do a lot of sleeping so I'll just bring the little one along and enjoy working with you."

"I put in an order for supplies at the store this morning which Richard promised to deliver this afternoon. Whatever day you want to come over would be great."

"How about I come this afternoon after lunch and we can make more specific plans together with Ruth."

"That sounds great. I'll see you later. I had better get back. I have been gone most of the morning, leaving Ruth with five children. I hope she has made out all right."

"See you later. Enjoy your walk back," Dorothy calls after her.

When Dorothy arrives after lunch, the young children are sleeping and the oldest is playing quietly. The three women look at the recipes they have and decide what to start with and a plan for the week. Naomi's mornings are taken up with caring for the children and taking care of the cabin chores, including laundry. Ruth is willing to work on her own for a couple of hours in the mornings. She will start with muffins as they have several recipes and they are easy to make. After the outside oven is ready, Ruth can try her hand at making bread in the mornings a couple of times a week. In the afternoons when Dorothy is with them they might try some pastry which is Dorothy's specialty. When fruit is available they can make fruit pies and tarts. Dorothy's butter tarts are known to be special around Boonesborough with everyone vying for them at social gatherings.

"We could put up a sign at the General Store with the special of the day, first-come-first-served beginning at 4:00 or have people place orders," Ruth suggests eagerly. "Or are we getting ahead of ourselves?"

"We were going to start slowly," Naomi cautions. "Okay, Ruth, three mornings you can make muffins this week. On the other two days in the afternoons, we will make pastries together."

"Next week Ruth could make cookies one day, maybe loaf cakes on the other two days." Dorothy suggests.

"Ruth, the rest of the time is free time for you. You can spend time with the children, but go out and meet some people in Boonesborough as well," Naomi strongly urges. "When there are berries and fruit to pick, we will need some help with that. Dorothy won't be able to do that for awhile. We might have to slow our baking down at times when Richard is waiting for supplies to arrive. Some weeks we may not have special items, but Richard will try to have flour and sugar available in large quantities. When we want special items, we will have to order them quite a bit in advance."

"Friday afternoons would be a good time to take a break from baking and plan what we will make the next week and what supplies we will need to order," Dorothy makes another practical suggestion as she tosses her hair over her shoulder.

"That's a great idea. This has been a really good planning session. We make a good team, putting all of our ideas together. Thanks for joining me, Dorothy and Ruth."

There is a knock on the door and Beth asks Ruth if she wants to walk to the spring with her. The two of them set out and Ruth shares some of their plans for the bakeshop.

"I'm happy for you and Naomi that things are looking up for you."

"Did you hear about my two brothers being here too?" Ruth exclaims excitedly.

"Yes, that was wonderful news. I was thrilled for you after being apart for so many years that the four of you were together within a few hours."

"What do you like to do around here, Beth? How long have you been here?" Ruth questions her.

"I have been here about a year but it seems longer. I came to help my sister, Mary, with the children before Ellie was born. Now Mary is managing fine. Today I started working with Lydia Patterson."

"Do you like sewing, Beth?" Ruth turns up her nose. "I would rather be baking."

"I have always enjoyed working with material. I am drawn to what Lydia does. I can hardly wait to feast my eyes again on the beautiful cloth and feel the different textures between my fingers," Beth beams.

"It sounds like you are going to really enjoy your time. Will you be working every day?"

"For now I'll go two afternoons a week. We'll see how much business Lydia is able to build up. So far there seems to be a lot of interest."

"Dorothy is going to help us with the baking. She has her eyes on a dress from Lydia. I gather sewing isn't her favourite occupation."

"I travelled here with the Wallaces last spring. Dorothy has changed a lot in these few months. Initially whenever there was trouble with the Indians she would be one of the first to rally the women to go back east. Now she fits right in and helps out wherever she can."

"I've heard that her pastry is delicious so I'm looking forward to a taste later this week," Ruth almost drools.

As they approach the spring, Beth says, "Let's fill our buckets with water. What a beautiful country this is. I was supposed to be going back to Boston this spring but I love it out here and have made many friends. I have no plans to go back yet."

"I'm glad you are here, Beth. We are about the same age and you can teach me some of the things you have learned in the past year."

"Tim has been teaching me many things and so has Rebecca Boone."

"I met Tim the other night. He's the one who brought my brothers to us," Ruth explains.

"He's a great man. We share a lot of good times together as friends."

"Let's try and match our work schedules so that we have some free time together," Ruth suggests.

"I would love that. We have had a good outing this afternoon and I look forward to developing our friendship. I'll call for you in a couple of days. Enjoy your baking tomorrow."

"Enjoy your sewing with Lydia. She is a very loving woman with a lot of drive. I got to know her quite well on the trip out. She made me feel like a part of their family."

"I have spoken with her a few times already and I'm eager to learn whatever I can from her. See you soon," Beth calls as she heads home.

***

"Beth, I spent the most amazing afternoon of my life," Tim beams as they start their evening stroll around Boonesborough.

"What were you doing that so thrilled you?"

"I said I was going to offer my services to Jack Wallace because he was overworked. Flanders has a real flair for working with wood and is a big help in the shop and has often talked to me about what he does. Jack was happy to have my help. He set me to work on some simple sanding after explaining about the grain and I could hardly believe the joy and satisfaction that came over me as the wood smoothed beneath my hands. All my life I have done different things that I have liked doing, such as hunting, exploring and even dancing. Nothing before every lifted me to these heights of satisfaction. After doing sanding, Jack showed me how to use the wood lathe for making chair legs. That was fascinating to do. I could have worked much longer but Jack is wise to close shop at a regular hour each day. Then everyone has time to be with their families for supper and in the evenings. No matter how much work is waiting, Jack values his family. Tell me about your day with Lydia."

"I had a similar day working with the material in Lydia's shop. It's wonderful to find such joy in an activity. Most people go through life in a mediocre fashion, doing what must be done but never finding deep satisfaction in anything." Beth is quite animated as she describes the different colours and textures of the materials, the wide variety of buttons, and the lace for trim. Her eyes sparkle as she tries to describe the exhilaration found in the seamstress trade.

"I went for a walk with Ruth down to the spring today and we had a good time together. We plan to get together later this week. She is quickly becoming a friend in comparison to many acquaintances I have had with other women up to this time, other than Rebecca Boone that is. It feels good to have a friend here my own age. I miss my friends from Boston sometimes."

"I'm happy for you, Beth." As he looks into her hazel eyes he adds, "We also have a special friendship."

"Yes, we can sure cover a lot of subjects. We will always remain friends Tim. But it's a little different with a female friend. It's hard to explain but it feels good to have met Ruth."

"Is she going to stay around for awhile?"

"She and Naomi and Dorothy are going to start a bakeshop."

"Maybe I better drop you and hook up with Ruth," Tim teases, his eyes glowing as he smacks his lips in imitation of enjoying a special sweet treat.

"Don't you dare," Beth challenges. "We have been together a lot in the past months. It's been great learning about the frontier with you, and having fun along the way."

Tim pulls her into his arms and holds her for a moment before placing a kiss on top of her head and saying goodnight.

***

James Ellis comes over in the morning to talk about a sign for their bakeshop. He looks forward to painting a freshly baked pie with steam escaping. The women have to choose a name for their shop. "What about 'Sunshine Bakeshop'?" Ruth suggests. Naomi agrees and James goes off to paint the sign.

Inside the cabin in addition to the small oven, there is a stove and a fireplace. Ruth mixes a batch of muffins and puts them in the oven. She plays with the children expecting them to take about an hour to bake. Ruth's first muffins are burned to a crisp on the outside, but the inside is delicious. The second dozen are raw on the inside. The third batch is delicious, just right. There was nothing wrong with the recipe. The pioneer oven took some getting used to.

The next weekend when Will and Steve come with their weekly lumber and firewood delivery, they have a surprise for Ruth and Naomi. They have the bricks ready for the oven. Together with the metal liner, they assemble the oven in the open area in front of the cabin several yards away from the door and use the wet clay to seal it. The sound of saws and hammers is heard as the men put together a wooden shelter for working beside the oven with a roof for protection from the sun or even a light rain shower. They build a work table and Tim jumps in to sand it smooth, a chore that thrills him to work at until there are no rough spots remaining. It will be another week before they will use the oven, ensuring that it is completely dry and cured.

The week flies by and soon it is time to try out the oven. The first batch of dough is ready; the fire has been built to heat the oven, the loaves are put in and the baking begins. Soon a fragrant odour is escaping and wafting throughout the town, and a crowd begins to gather. Ruth is going by smell on this venture, wanting to make sure the bread is baked but not burned. It is time to take out the first loaf and test it. There is an eager lineup for a sample slice of bread fresh from the oven.

Ruth set aside three loaves for three special people. The Pattersons helped her find her sister and are thanked with this special treat. Beth is a friend and support to her and Ruth thanks her warmly as she hands her a loaf of bread as they are about to start out on their afternoon walk. Beth quickly puts it inside their cabin and then they head to Dorothy's to drop off the third loaf to their partner in the bakeshop.

Beth and Ruth are spending a couple of hours together this afternoon. After leaving Dorothy's cabin, they start off toward the spring for water. The sentries have a clear view of the path and are especially alert when people are making these daily trips. So far no Indians have been seen for awhile. Beth and Ruth are laughing together as Ruth talks about her first pioneer baking experiences.

"The first bread today was a real success. The aroma throughout Boonesborough was wonderful. I could smell it at Lydia's," Beth adds.

"I was making the bread so I didn't realize how far the aroma was travelling. It wasn't long before there was a crowd. Jemima came by in time to whisk three loaves off to the Henderson Café and the crowd followed, lining up for lunch. Fanny Calloway carried three loaves to the Inn. What about you Beth? How has your sewing been going?"

"I have had some frustrations. I still get impatient with myself when everything isn't perfect right away. Sewing on buttons and trim is easy to do, as well as hemming the garments, all the time feeling the beautiful material between my hands. Learning how to use the loom requires a knack that Linda and Lucy have learned really well and they produce some beautiful work."

"Have you tried the sewing machine yet?" Ruth questioned. "Lydia talked about it on the trip here, the newest thing."

"Yesterday I had my first lesson," Beth laughed. "You never saw such a crooked seam."

"I bet it was much straighter by the end of the afternoon."

"You are right, Ruth. I did do better after awhile. Lydia does a fine job. I'm glad she is patiently teaching me. Look at the beautiful flowers; they are cheery today. Soon we should be able to find some berries growing in the woods. That makes me think of last July," Beth continues as she goes on to relate her experiences with the Indian attack shortly after her arrival and then the girls being captured by the braves. "Tim says the Indians are going to attack Boonesborough."

"I don't look forward to that," Ruth shuddered.

"No, neither do I, but it is part of life here on the frontier. The Cherokee want peace but the Shawnee have always wanted us out of Kentucky. Well, Ruth, it's time to head back. We have had a lovely time out in the spring sunshine this afternoon. What are you baking tomorrow?"

"I'm supposed to have the morning off but I want to make another batch of bread since it went over so well today. I'm going to make some rolls as well. The trickiest part is figuring out how long to cook them. After the bread is cooked, the oven will still hold enough heat to bake a batch of cookies, a treat for the children."

"Enjoy your evening with your sister and the children."

"I will. Is Tim coming by tonight?"

"Yes he is. Maybe he will show me more about the stars. Likely he will have some tale to share about his woodworking. He has as many funny things to share about his experiences as we do."

"Bye for now. See you soon." They wave to each other as they head off in different directions.

***

The berries and fruits collected by Ruth and the children provide the ingredients for several kinds of pies. Dorothy has her own berry bushes beside their cabin and brings some of the fruit to the bakeshop. Some of the fruit she reserves to make batches of jam, a delicious treat on the fresh bread. Boonesborough is becoming quite a growing concern. Some people come to visit families living here, but most are coming to settle in the area, with many family members joining those already here.

***

Dorothy has a hard time handling hardships such as Indian attacks and Indian captures, although she does adapt to the day to day activities of pioneer life. Whenever there are troubles, her first spoken thought is to leave and head back to the east, to civilization in a big town. Jack then has his job cut out in persuading her to stay. The boys are happier than they were in the city, there are several boys their ages whom they spend hours with, and they are much healthier as the clean, country air agrees with them. Overall Dorothy is much happier here too, just needing to be reminded of it in times of trouble. She is no longer sour-faced but happy and eager for the start of each new day. Expecting another child has brought her an additional feeling of peace and contentment. Beth and Dorothy enjoy spending time together whenever they have some free time.

A couple of weeks before the end of May, Jack has Dorothy stay at the fort. Since it is her third child, he doesn't want her to go into labour without help nearby. With Johnny, their second son's birth, Dorothy's labour lasted about six hours compared to twenty hours for George. When her labour begins, Jack is just about to leave for work. He calls on Eliza Calloway to request her help before heading to his shop. Eliza says she will go right away to be with Dorothy. Just before lunch time, Eliza sends Jemima Boone to tell Jack the news that he has a daughter. Jack rushes over to see his wife. She is so happy to have a little girl; she is beaming with a grin from ear to ear. Jack is happy to have a healthy baby. They have talked about names and chosen Ellen for a girl's name.

In the early afternoon, Beth heads over to Dorothy's to help out for the next few days. She prepares a supper meal for the Wallace's, taking a plate into the bedroom for Dorothy. After supper she plays some quiet games with George and Johnny and then sings them a couple of songs before settling them into bed. She promises Jack she will be over early in the morning to get breakfast and do the morning chores.

It is a beautiful evening for a walk around town with Tim before heading to her sister's for an early night. In the morning she prepares breakfast for the Wallaces, gets a batch of bread set aside for rising and tidies the cabin. George and Johnny are glad of her company in a walk to the spring for water with a side trip in the woods to search for wild strawberries. The bread is ready to bake by the time they return and tastes delicious with lunch. The boys are able to spend a short time with their Mom and to admire their baby sister. Then they head out to find Johnny Patterson to play a game with the ball that Johnny brought with him from Philadelphia.

Beth prepares the supper meal and enjoys a visit with Dorothy. She looks robust and feels fine, but still tires easily. Beth has time to do some knitting to finish off the baby outfit she is making for Ellen. It feels great to be sharing her time with Dorothy, a woman who has warmed up to her so much in the past year. Although they do not have the same skills or interests, they enjoy conversing together.

On the following day, Beth does the laundry and hangs it on the outdoor line to dry. A similar pattern follows for the next few days. Then it is time for Jack to take the family back to their cabin outside the fort. Dorothy is ready to look after her family, knowing she can ask Beth for help whenever she feels she needs it.

With Dorothy back home, Beth looks forward to her afternoon with Lydia.

Meanwhile in the carpenter shop, Jack speaks to Tim, "You really enjoy your work in the shop and you have a special talent. I could use you full time. Are you interested?"

"I'll seriously consider it. I do love working with wood. I'll talk it over with Mike O'Neill and let you know my decision in a couple of days."

Tim set to work that day with his mind whirring. What an

opportunity for him. I'll see Mike this afternoon. After lunch he heads to the blacksmith shop. "Mike, how are you today?"

"Doing fine Tim. How about you?"

"I'm fine Mike. I have been working with you for the past couple of years. I have enjoyed it but I have been offered the opportunity to do something full time that I love and that is working with wood. What arrangements can you and I make? I can't leave you high and dry."

"Jeremiah Horn was just in here the other day asking if I could use him and teach him about blacksmithing. Can you work two or three half days a week for the next three months while we train Jeremiah? It would mean a lot to him and his wife Elizabeth with their young son Matthew for him to have a steady job."

"That sounds like a good plan. It's good to train someone eager to learn. If it's agreeable with Jack then that's what we will do." After discussing it with Jack, the arrangements are confirmed. Since Mike doesn't always know which days he will need Tim as his business is more sporadic, Tim's time is flexible between the two businesses.

On their evening walk Tim tells Beth. "Jack has asked me to work full time for him in his furniture shop, Beth. I'll work for Mike part time while we train Jeremiah who is eager to learn."

"That will be a wonderful change for you. You are glowing when you work with wood. I have seen you at work a few times."

"Keeping your eyes on me I see."

"Sure, you are a great friend."

"Jack has many furniture orders and I have been working on a cabinet for dishes and linens. It's great to have the opportunity to work on measuring and sawing to make pieces fit together into a cabinet. I have made a few wrong cuts and either had to make a second cut, or even get another board, but Jack is patient with me and I'm learning how to do it better."

"This gives you a purpose for your life, a reason for getting up each day with a smile on your face."

"How about you Beth? What uplifted you today?"

"Ruth and I walked out to Dorothy's cabin and spent a few hours with her and the baby. What a tiny bundle of joy. In the afternoon, Lydia had me helping with cutting out patterns. Lydia has asked me to work more hours but I have reserved two hours three days a week when Ruth has time off for our outings."

"Friendships are important. Jack is becoming a friend to me as well as an employer. We have some good conversations when we break for lunch. Occasionally we take an hour off in an afternoon to walk down to the river for a change of pace and to stretch out the back muscles. Those are special bonding times."

"That is happening for Lydia and I as well."

"Monday mornings we all meet to plan our activities for the week. Jack writes out all the orders he receives. Almost everything ordered is required quickly but he is getting some orders that will take longer and are ordered a few months in advance. Flanders made a suggestion that we get a chalkboard to track everything so that we have something to look at when we come in. It keeps the three of us organized."

"Being organized is good in anything that is attempted."

"I love to do the sanding, but Jack wants me to learn how to do all parts of the projects. The measuring and sawing have been a challenge for me, but I am mastering them. I love to add the finishing touch with either rubbing in beeswax or using linseed oil. There is an art to selecting the right wood for each job with the best wood for furniture being maple and birch, although oak is good too but it is more difficult to work with due to the different grain. The shop assistant carries in the lumber as we need it. As much as possible of the lumber is stored in the back room of the shop so that it stays dry. We are thinking of building a shed in front of the shop for storing lumber. That will give us more room to put the finished pieces until they are picked up or delivered."

"You are learning many things, Tim. Have you seen Johnny's garden lately? Some of the flowers are budding."

"His garden isn't far from the blacksmith shop, but I don't often go to see what's growing. I'll make a point of doing that tomorrow since I'll be down there in the morning. It's time to say goodnight. See you tomorrow," Tim said as he pulls her into a warm lingering hug.

Another evening as they walk, Beth exclaims, "What a beautiful evening after the rain today! The air is so fresh and clear."

"Beth, do you see what's over there in the west?" Tim pointed.

"A rainbow, how beautiful, and look Tim there's a second one starting. Wow! It's been awhile since I saw one. We have quite a nice view from the sentry walk."

"We can see some farm fields in the distance from here," Tim noted. "Let's go for a walk around the inside of the fort to get our blood flowing. I did a lot of sanding today and I'm a little stiff."

"I was doing some of the fine handwork on some dresses today. I'm going to swing my arms as we walk to loosen them up," Beth agrees.

Chapter 17 – The Bryans

The Bryans live about a mile away from the Hancock brothers. They have a large rustic but sturdy cabin on a knoll overlooking the winding Kentucky River. From that vantage point they can see several of the farms in the vicinity. This gave Joseph, James, Morgan and William the idea to build a mill to grind the wheat and corn and other grain. They built a mill with a waterwheel on the banks of Elkhorn Creek. They grow their own wheat, corn, and oats. Sue and Anne tend a large vegetable garden which produces enough for them and provides extra to sell in Boonesborough. Their parents are Joseph and Alice (nicknamed Alyee) Bryan; Joseph`s oldest daughter, Martha is married to Edward 'Neddy' Boone and they have six children. Joseph`s next daughter, Rebecca, was married ten years before to Daniel Boone, brother of Neddy, and has seven children by this time. The Bryans are an enterprising family. It isn't long before other farmers in the area are bringing their grain to the Bryan Mill and the grindstones are turning six days a week. They have a standing order at Henderson's Store for sacks to put the flour and corn meal in after it is ground. Farmers also bring their own sacks to be filled. For every ten sacks of flour or cornmeal, the farmers give one sack to the Bryans in payment. In the harvest season, they often have extra flour to sell to Richard Henderson. Their homestead is not located on a game trail and they have had no trouble with the warring Indians. Friendly Indians also come to trade for flour and cornmeal.

Will and Steve Hancock built their sawmill and soon afterwards met the Bryan family, their closest neighbours. Often on a Saturday evening they have an invitation for coffee and conversation.

"Will, we haven't seen the Bryans the last couple of weekends. Let's ask Sue and Ann to come with us into Boonesborough to meet our two sisters."

"That's a great idea, Steve."

"Let's make it a little mysterious and just say we are going into Boonesborough for the day and invite them to join us."

"They may have some shopping to do. The Pattersons are also new to the town and we could introduce them as well."

Saturday is a beautiful sunny day. Will and Steve load both freight wagons then head over to pick up the girls. They will travel together one behind each other but will be able to have some private conversation as well. The girls have on new spring bonnets and look charming. Will helps Sue onto his wagon seat, climbs up beside her and heads towards the fort. Steve helps Anne onto the other wagon and follows behind his brother.

"How long has it been since you were in town Sue?"

"It has been about a month."

"There are several changes for you to see and some new people to meet," Will informs her.

"We haven't seen you for a couple of weeks. Have you been extra busy?" Sue questions.

"We have a surprise for you." Will's eyes twinkle as he looks at her.

"What is it Will?"

"You'll have to wait until we get to Boonesborough to find out." He changes the subject and asks, "Have you been busy at the mill?"

"Spring is a busy time for planting. We have the vegetables in the garden, the wheat is planted and the corn is nearly all in the ground. It will be another couple of months before we get busy in the mill. We really need a second source of income for a few months of the year when there is no grain to grind. However, we keep busy with the garden and the crops."

"I imagine there are things to catch up on that get left undone when the harvesting is in full swing."

"In the winter we get a lot of sewing done and make our year's supply of candles. There will be weeding in the garden soon. I always enjoy getting out of doors even if it is for weeding," Sue continues.

"Sounds like Steve and Anne are having a good time. It's really special for us to take you out today."

"We were excited about your invitation. We don't get to see many people other than family most of the time."

"Saturday is often a special time at the fort with some families making a trip in for supplies. Sometimes there is some dancing if there are enough interested people."

"When are you going to tell me the surprise?"

"Soon enough," Will smiles. "We'll leave the wagons by Jack's Furniture shop and have someone unload them. We will take the horses to the livery stable and then we'll take you around town."

"You sure are being mysterious Will." He only grins in reply.

Sue turns to Anne after the men help them both down from the wagons, "Is Steve being very secretive to you today?"

"Yes, they have some big secret. We're here in Boonesborough, so I guess we will know soon."

Will and Steve go in to speak to Jack. Jack and his assistants agree to unload the wagons in the afternoon. "We're ready Sue and Anne. Let's walk the horses, and then we'll show you the additions to the town."

At the livery stable, Steve speaks to Thomas Allan. "How are you today? Can you look after our horses for us? We'll be here for a few hours. We're showing Sue and Anne the new additions at the fort."

Thomas is happy to oblige. "It is nice to see you again Sue and Anne," he says as he tips his hat to them. "Enjoy your day. It's a lovely one."

Will and Sue, and Steve and Ann, walk arm in arm as they stroll along the end of the fort.

"Good morning, Johnny. It's a good day to be out in your garden." His hands are covered with dark loam.

"I just finished planting my last seeds."

"Will and I are showing Sue and Anne around and introducing them to the new people. Tell the girls about your plans."

Johnny beams when he tells them about the beautiful flowers that will soon be growing and the smells that will be coming from them.

"I made my first perfume yesterday. Wait here and I'll get a sample for each of you." He returns a minute later with the perfume.

"Lilac!" Sue exclaims. "Thanks Johnny. I'll enjoy wearing it."

"Thanks from me too," smiles Anne.

"Mom and Dad are both in. They would love to meet you."

"Thanks Johnny. That's where we are heading next. Enjoy the sunshine."

James Ellis has been busy designing signs for each of the businesses. For Lydia he has a picture of a dress on one side, and a spool of thread on the other with a needle pulling thread from the spool to the dress under the name "Lydia's Creations."

"A seamstress?" both girls cry out together. "Wow! We are sure lucky in town!"

"Let's go inside and meet the Pattersons." The room has a warm appeal with the colourful bolts of cloth, finished garments hanging to one side, material on the table in the process of being cut out, a real beehive of activity. "Hi, Lydia and Richard. We brought Sue and Anne Bryan to meet you. They are interested in what you have started here."

"Hi, Sue and Anne. Welcome to our shop. I'm experimenting using local plants to dye material that I make on the loom. I am learning from the Cherokee medicine man with whom I have had some interesting talks." Richard is seldom at a loss for words. "But I'm sure you are more interested in what Lydia has to offer you at the moment."

During Richard's talk, their eyes have been wandering to the shelves of cloth. Lydia shows them around and has on display a few outfits.

"We will definitely be back, Lydia. We're happy to have you in town," the sisters enthuse.

They walk on and Will says, "Next door to the shop is where the Pattersons live. There is Jack Wallace's Furniture Shop. He does some fine work. Another day we'll take you inside."

"We are coming up to our surprise," Steve says as he knocks on the door of the next cabin. Naomi answers the door and is immediately gathered into a warm hug. "We brought our girl friends along to meet you. Sue and Anne, this is our sister Naomi."

"Your sister? I didn't know she was living in Boonesborough."

"We didn't know either."

"Is that my brothers at the door?" Ruth calls out as she rushes forward. There is another round of hugs.

"Another sister?" the girls question.

"Sue and Anne come on in, sit down while we get some refreshments and then we'll tell you all about it." A few minutes later everyone has a drink to sip and a cookie to nibble on. Ruth, Naomi, Will and Steve proceed to tell Sue and Anne how they were reunited two weeks ago, thanks to the Pattersons bringing Ruth with them, and Tim Eadon bringing the boys into town. It is a noisy group and the young children are ready for some attention for which there are many eager arms. Lunch time is a merry affair. Then the outdoor oven has to be admired. The men offer to watch the children if the women want to go to the general store. In short order the four women are on their way chatting eagerly together, wanting to pick up a few items and have some time together.

Henderson's Store is full of a wide variety of goods neatly arranged on the shelves and tables on each side of the aisles. There are items to use in the home such as blankets, washboards, dishes, candles, candle holders, glass jars, pots and pans, brooms. With the embargo on tea following the Boston Tea Party, many people have switched to drinking coffee and coffee grinders are a new item now available. There is brown sugar and molasses, spices, raisins and rice to be weighed out and wrapped in brown paper. When families have extra milk, butter and cheese they bring it to the store and trade it for other items. As the farms prosper, vegetables are provided for sale, as well as jams and preserves.

There are bolts of cloth with much of it being homespun material made by the women of the colonies. Richard Patterson is now selling some of his dyed material in the store and is beginning to sell some of his dyes for those who want to do the work themselves. There is thread in an array of colours, lace, ribbon and buttons to decorate garments, needles and pins for the sewing that needs to be done on a regular basis for a busy home. For the men there are overalls, leather gloves, boots, hats and shoes. Not to be outdone, there are bonnets for the women to add splashes of colour around town. Many women knit items for Richard to sell.

On the wall at the back one can see the ornately crafted pendulum clocks. On a table next to the stove are a few books available to read, as well as some newspapers that are weeks old. News from outside the area is slow to arrive but when it comes it is treasured and the newspapers are read page by page. For those who can read, often they will be asked to read the news at the tavern where people gather to enjoy a drink or a meal. Paper, pens and ink are of interest to the women who want to keep in touch with their families back east. It is tough having left their loved ones behind when they moved to Kentucky.

Lanterns, lamps and kerosene are available to provide light in the early evening hours during the winter. All the needs of the men for hunting, trapping and building are available with several guns hanging on the walls with ammunition on the shelves below. It is hard for Richard to keep enough ammunition on hand, especially when the Indians are raiding. There are animal traps for those who want to trap for animal furs to sell in exchange for other items the people need. Ropes and hammers are hanging above the bins of wooden pegs.

For the farmers there are hoes, shovels and axes stored upright in barrels. For the children there are jars of candy, and licorice for special treats. There are toys, dolls, marbles and balls. With scrap lumber, Jack Wallace makes toy wagons, horses, cows, chickens and pigs. Timothy Eadon is turning out some beautiful animal toys such as buffalo, deer and rabbits.

The women wander up and down the aisles to look at the variety of items and select their purchases. After the women return to the cabin, it is time to continue the tour as it is nearing the supper hour. Their walk continues past the store. "The first cabin is where Mike, the blacksmith, his wife Mary and her sister Beth live." They pop in to say hello to Mary and Beth.

"Hello, Mary. It has been sometime since we saw you last. Beth, it is nice to meet you. We don't get to town very often. Will and Steve are showing us the additions in Boonesborough and introducing us to many people. They kept the surprise of their two sisters until we reached the door of Naomi's cabin," Anne explains.

"Men aren't always good at keeping secrets," Beth smiles.

"They sure kept us in suspense today. We are getting signals from the men that it is time to move. We'll see you again when we are in town. Bye for now," Sue says as they depart.

Will takes Sue's arm as they continue the tour. Sue and Anne pass the cabin where their sister Rebecca Boone lives, but she is not at home today. They pass several more cabins without stopping. Their walk leads them to the Inn where Will and Steve have reserved a table for dinner. Paul Holt and Sam Campbell have a table set for them and provide a fine meal.

After supper, Steve goes to the livery stable for the horses and Thomas returns with him to the wagons and helps hitch the horses up for the journey back home. Steve and Will aim to make it back to the Bryans before dark. They stop the wagons just out of sight of the Bryans cabin so they can say their good nights and enjoy a long, satisfying kiss in private. It has been a very good day.

Both men discuss it when they get back to their cabin about asking the women to be their life's partners. Maybe they will plan for a double wedding in Boonesborough. Everything is looking promising for them, but the summer seems to fly by before they get a chance, and the nerve, to pop the question.

Chapter 18 – Big Surprise

From the 23rd to the 25th of May 1777, Indians attack Boonesborough and attempt to set it on fire but are unsuccessful in their attempts. By the middle of June of 1777, it is safe enough for Tim and Beth to take a canoe trip to visit the Calloways. Their settlement across the Kentucky River is a growing enterprise. They have settled in well after more than a year of the families working together on their farms. Lydia is the first to see Beth and Tim arrive and sends the signal out to the others that they have visitors. Everyone is glad of a break from routine and plans to enjoy a visit.

Zechariah is to marry Amelia later this month and a new cabin is built for them. The wood frames for houses are made out of heavy timbers a foot or more thick which are joined together by cutting notches in the logs to fit them together; at stress points, a wooden peg is driven through auger holes. The cracks between the logs are filled with small wedges of wood, moss, and mud to keep the cold and damp weather out. They use greased paper for windows or cover the window openings with plain wood shutters or greased animal skins. Doors are hinged with wooden pegs. Tim brought his blacksmithing tools along to shoe some horses and make some latches and hinges for the cabin doors.

Isham and Caleb have no immediate plans for marriage. Betsey Henderson has just given birth to their first child, Fanny and Beth is happy to hold her for awhile until it is time for her next feed.

The next day, Beth and Tim are off to try their hands at catching some fish. Neither is very patient and both find it hard to sit still or keep quiet, often thinking of something to share. In spite of all that, they do manage to catch a few fish which they will bribe someone to clean in order to enjoy them for supper.

At Zechariah Calloway's wedding, Flanders asks Beth for a dance and they talk about his upcoming wedding to Jemima Boone. He is getting excited about it as it is only three weeks away. Today Beth is dressed in a powder blue gown and she is putting the finishing touches on an apple green dress for Flanders' wedding. It feels good to wear a more brightly coloured dress than those worn for daily chores. It is a lift to the spirits, both for her and for the men who admire her.

On Monday afternoon two days before the wedding, Beth has the biggest surprise of her life when her four friends arrive for a visit. Mary and Mike knew the visit was planned, but they kept it a secret from Beth. She can't believe her eyes when she sees Katie, Brenda, Barbara, and Patricia ride through the gates of Boonesborough. She thinks for a moment that she is dreaming, blinking her eyes to clear the apparition, but the sight remains. She rushes forward and hugs them all as they step off the mules they were riding. They have been writing letters back and forth for more than a year, sometimes getting several letters at once and then a long stretch without hearing from each other. Now they are together and the girls can see the things Beth has tried to describe in her letters.

"I can't believe you are here! This is a wonderful surprise. How long are you staying?" Beth questions as soon as she can get the words out.

"We hope to stay for a month, depending on when we can get transportation back east," Barbara informs her.

Mike and Mary come up to welcome them. Beth turns to them and says, "Where will the girls be able to stay? We don't have room in our cabin."

"You have been getting the cabin ready for the past two weeks,"

Mary says with a twinkle in her eyes.

"You mean you knew the girls were coming? You never said who I was getting the cabin ready for. What a surprise to see them. I am so excited."

"You have worked so hard helping us and others in the town that when Father first mentioned the possibility, Mike and I decided to keep it a surprise. When we wrote to Father, we suggested that he tell the girls not to breathe a word of their coming. This was a little something we could do for you," Mary explains.

"It's not a little something, this is a huge surprise and a most welcome sight," Beth gushes as she hugs Mary tightly.

"Come on Katie, Brenda, Patricia and Barbara. Let's get you settled into the cabin. It's all ready for you, although I didn't know I was preparing it for my best friends." They lead their mules towards the cabin and begin unloading their possessions.

"How was your trip? Did it seem like you were never going to get here?" Beth questions.

"It was a long trip, but we had the four of us to converse with, laugh with, and we had the sight of your face to look forward to seeing. There was a large group we travelled with and we had a good time. The trail is rough but perhaps a little better than when you came through. It is a little later in the year and we didn't have to swim through any of the rivers as they were shallow enough for the mules to splash through," Barbara spoke for the group.

"How long have you been planning this trip?" Beth asks.

"Around the beginning of April, your father heard about a large group travelling out. He checked with our parents to see if they would permit their daughters to go with the group to visit you. Our parents agreed and when we were asked we were initially surprised, but this followed very soon with great enthusiasm," Brenda explains.

"We have been using homespun material for most of our clothes in the past year with the British shipping blockades and with the colonists' decision to boycott British made goods. When you wrote about how much easier it was to get around without hoops, we experimented and found out you were right and it has been much easier getting through doorways," Patricia says laughingly.

"The homespun dresses are easier to keep in shape; our housekeepers have been commenting on how much easier it is to iron them without all the lace and ruffles and frills," Katie adds. "The clothing was easier to assemble than when you were getting ready to leave Elizabeth, although each of us had to do a lot on our own as all four of us were coming on the trip." They each had two pack mules, one to ride and one to pack their belongings on.

"You will be here for my friend's wedding. It is in two days. What good timing!" Beth informs them.

"I notice that people in Boonesborough call you Beth," Katie remarks.

"Mrs. Worthington wouldn't let any of us call you anything but Elizabeth," continues Patricia.

"It started with Johnny and George Wallace on my trip west. Within hours they were calling me Beth and the name stuck after that," Beth explains.

"It's wonderful to actually see where you have been living for the past year," Brenda comments.

"It's so good to see all of you. I didn't know when I would see you again. My time has just stretched out and I have no plans for returning home. If you are settled in, let's go see what Mary has for us to eat for supper. She has been cooking up a storm, preparing several dishes and larger amounts than usual. I thought she was cooking for two days so that she could have a day off. It's only now I am realizing that Mary has been planning for your arrival."

"I adored Mary when I was young. She was pretty, always smiling and willing to give a helping hand when I dropped some stitches in my knitting. She was very patient," Barbara replies dreamily thinking back on those many special times.

"I remember her helping me with my drawing when I had trouble with arms and legs," Katie remembers. "She wasn't very interested in painting but she did some beautiful ink sketches."

"I'll introduce you to Mr. Ellis," Beth promises. "He does some lovely drawing and painting."

As they arrive at the O'Neills' cabin, Beth opens the door and calls hello to Mary. She welcomes the girls and introduces the children. James, Isaac and Sarah shake hands with each of them, and Ellie reaches up her arms to be picked up. Brenda laughs as she bends down to oblige. It is a merry group around the table for supper that evening. After the cleanup, Mary shoos them all off to their cabin and suggests Beth stay with them that night as she knows they have lots to talk about. It is a noisy group who enters the cabin a few minutes later.

"Tell us about your friend's wedding, Elizabeth…I mean Beth. It is difficult to think of you as Beth after calling you Elizabeth for close to twenty years," Barbara states and the others nod in agreement.

"I will answer to Elizabeth or Beth. You can call me either one. Jemima Boone is to marry Flanders Calloway and his cousin Fanny Calloway is to marry Captain John Holder in a double wedding ceremony," Beth begins.

"I seem to remember that you were with Jemima when you were captured by Indians last year. Is that the same person?"

"Both Jemima and Fanny were with me along with Betsey, Fanny's older sister. That was quite a frightening experience and what a relief to be rescued on the morning of the third day."

"You played the experience down in your letters, but we did a little imagining about it. We all decided that none of us would want that to happen to us!" Katie comments.

"Beth, do you get much chance to sing out here?" Barbara asks. "You have such a beautiful voice and we always love to hear it."

"Just about every night I sing a couple of songs to the children before they go to sleep. Sometimes Mike, Mary, Tim and I have a sing-along in the evening. At our community barbecues there is usually a sing-along. Often I hum or sing as I am doing my daily chores."

"Back to the wedding…what are you wearing Beth?"

"I have just about finished making an apple green gown."

The four friends look at each other, amazed by what they have just heard. They had decided to make similar dresses so that all four of them could wear the same colour once or twice during their stay. They made dresses in pink for one occasion and in pale green for another. Now all five of them can wear apple green dresses to the wedding.

The next day Beth takes her friends for a walk to the spring to get water and to show them a little of the area, but they don't stray from the path as there has been recent Indian trouble. They content themselves with a walk around the fort, greeting those they see outside, planning longer visits with some of the folks in the days to come. Johnnie Patterson's flowers are in full bloom this beautiful summer day and Katie has a few packages of seeds for him in response to Beth's information in a letter about his perfume making. They end their walk at the General Store where the friends are amazed at the variety of goods that can be purchased. Much of the day is spent talking and catching up on the past year with no shortage of topics to be covered. The girls came to Boonesborough with the idea of doing something to improve themselves and to help someone else during their time here.

The following day is quite a colourful affair as Daniel Boone walks his daughter Jemima down the aisle, followed by Richard Calloway walking his daughter Fanny arm-in-arm to stand beside her man. Both brides are dressed in the palest powder blue gowns, Jemima's with deep navy trim, and Fanny's with a softer blue trim. Daniel has changed out of his normal buckskins and is dressed in gentleman's attire that he wears when he goes to Salem, making quite a striking figure. Richard is dressed in a black suit. Rebecca has on a deep pink dress while Rachel Calloway has on a sunshine yellow gown. Flanders Calloway and John Holder are both dressed in navy suits. Squire Boone performs the wedding ceremony in the fort square under the large chestnut tree as all the guests gather round. People from all the farms in the area have come to town for the celebration, all dressed in their cheeriest clothes with the women sporting brightly coloured bonnets. Each family brought along food to add to the table for the meal following the afternoon ceremony.

Charlie brings out his fiddle, Ben has his accordion, Mike O'Neill gets out his harmonica, Mabel sits at the harpsichord and the music begins for the first dance. The bachelors have noticed the five girls dressed in green dresses and they all have partners for the first dance and every dance from then on, dancing long into the evening. Some of the men are elegant dancers, but some are rough and the girls have to watch their toes; Joseph Kennedy hasn't improved much over the past year and many a foot is stomped on but his partners quickly learn to avoid his boots. Tim Eadon met the girls on their first evening and he doesn't hesitate to ask each of them for a dance, with each of them commenting on how fine a dancer he is, especially after some of the stomping they have experienced. Tim is especially impressed with Brenda Smiley and Katie Brownley's dancing as it is plain to see that they have taken advanced training. When a waltz is played, they glide over the ground; when a polka begins, they elegantly perform the steps.

The next day begins a little later than usual after the late night before, but it is with great cheering that all of the townspeople greet Colonel Bowman on his arrival in Boonesborough on August 1 with one hundred soldiers with the orders to protect the people of Kentucky.

The girls chat about the wonderful time they had the day before and are soon ready for the adventures of the coming day. Beth has arranged for them to visit James and Sally Ellis. The walls of the main room of their cabin have many examples of James's work on display. There are sketches in charcoal of common scenes around the town. There are water colours of the countryside, a field of flowers, and many paintings of individual plants found in the area outside the fort. The five girls admire the pictures, with Katie spending extra time noting the details that James has included. Sally serves them refreshments and then James sets up his easel outside the cabin to draw a picture. Initially he has the girls sit in a semi-circle in front of him and he quickly sketches each of their faces. Then he has each of them stand and draws a quick picture of each. With his water colours he adds colour to their dresses. Soon there is a picture of the five friends with the fort in the background. Katie begins to question him on technique and supplies he uses. She says she would like to learn more from him while she is in Boonesborough. He invites her to come and visit him the next day.

In the afternoon, the women gather together for a quilting bee. Barney and Helen Stagner are in town today and Helen has her three youngest children with her, Benjy age three, Mary six, and Margaret eight. Jane Pogue has her three year old twins with her, Suzie and Mellie. Laura Pogue has her two children with her, Sarah four, and Will six. The Stagners and Pogues moved back into the fort when there was Indian trouble earlier in July. Pleasant Henderson and Mary O'Neill join the happy group. Nancy Benton is a niece of Thomas Hart and has her son Tommy with her. Everyone is happy to meet Beth's four friends, Katie Brownley, Barbara Townsend, Brenda Smiley and Patricia Fulton. Just before they are ready to begin, Nancy Benton and Patricia Ballard arrive. There is lots of lively conversation, sharing some of the joys of their days, exchanging news, recipes and quilt patterns. Nancy and Patricia have with them a couple of the blankets they made from their own sheep, carding, spinning, dyeing and weaving the wool. They plan to spend some time with Richard Patterson today to share their experiences with dyeing wool. Helen Stagner, and Jane and Laura Pogue are neighbours and try to find time each week to do rug hooking. Patricia's ears perk up when this is mentioned as it intrigues her. She admires the samples the women have with them and asks some questions. Patricia is invited to the Pogue cabin the next morning to learn more. Barbara really gets into the quilting; she is eager to apply her sewing skills for they are the neatest of the five girls. Sally Ellis has prepared the individual squares for this quilt and is willing to teach Barbara how it is done.

Brenda sticks at the quilting for awhile, but it is not something that holds her interest long. She soon wanders over to where the children are playing quietly together. She has an idea for the girls ages 6 to 10. She would like to teach them spool corking to make scatter rugs and table mats. She shows Mary and Margaret Stagner the spool project she is working on and let's them try it out. They are both eager to have their own. Brenda says she will get supplies together and get them started. That evening she has a chat with Tim before he takes Beth for a walk. Brenda shows him her spool and asks if he is able to make a few for her; Tim agrees to give it a try.

Beth and Tim have really settled into work that they have a passion for. Beth cut out her first dress all by herself today. That was quite an accomplishment from taking measurements for Mrs. Ellis, to making the pattern and preparing the fabric. Lydia watched from a distance but let her do it. The next step is to begin piecing it together, making the seams on the machine and then the trim, hem and buttons. "I did it Tim." Beth beams as she tells him about it that evening. "For the first time I made a pattern for a dress for someone other than myself."

Tim congratulates her, smiling warmly in his encouragement of her efforts.

"What about you Tim? You looked plenty pleased with yourself when you came to the cabin door."

"I made my first chair from start to finish today. The legs are all the same length, the wood is smooth to the touch and the pieces fit perfectly together. It's a thrill to be able to create."

"A good thing Jack insisted you do more than sanding. Lydia encouraged me to do more as I was quite happy to do hems and sew on buttons and trim."

"Once you have done it the first time, there is eagerness to repeat it."

The next morning Katie and Barbara head to the Ellis cabin, Katie to learn from James, and Barbara from Sally. James soon has Katie drawing with charcoal, starting with a simple still life of a bowl of fruit on the table. Then they each take an easel and go outside to see what is going on. Ruth is baking bread, and Ching is doing the laundry. Katie begins sketching Ruth, and James works on a drawing of Ching. James keeps an eye on Katie's progress and gives her tips when she seems to be struggling with an angle. Two hours quickly pass and it is time to end the lesson.

Barbara and Sally work on piecing together quilt squares. The pieces of material are gathered by all the women and then Sally decides on a design to use the various materials collected. The cloth comes in the form of scraps leftover from making garments as well as pieces from clothing that is too ragged to wear any longer. Some common designs are "Double Wedding Ring", and "Log Cabin", and a new name for an old design is called "Wanderer's Path". Sally explains the importance of contrasting colours and contrasting squares, some with solid colours, some with patterns. Sometimes an appliqué is sewn onto a square such as for a baby quilt with a block in one square, a doll in another, a wagon in another, and some solid colour squares in between.

Patricia goes to the Pogue cabin to learn about rug hooking. Thomas Hart makes the burlap for the backing. Susanna Hart joins Helen Stagner and the Pogue sisters as she wants to learn about rug hooking as well. Jane and Laura have been hooking rugs for many years. They started with simple designs and have progressed to some very detailed rugs. They have several designs to show, with the first one being a picture of a bear, a pine tree, and rolling hills, with the sun just beginning to rise against a blue sky. Another is a picture of a rose, while a whole arrangement of flowers is a much more detailed and complex project to work on. A favourite is a picture of a cabin reminiscent of their homes on the frontier. The first task is to draw the design on the burlap, then choose what colours of wool to use. The wool cloth is cut in narrow strips and a hook is used to pull the strips of wool through the burlap to fill in the picture. Helen, Jane and Laura have prepared a sample for Patricia and Susanna to work on. One is a single rose, the other is a cabin. The wool has already been cut in strips. Now Patricia and Susanna have to choose the colours they would like to use. Patricia chooses the rose design and picks several shades of pink and red strips of cloth. Susanna uses brown, beige and green for her cabin with grass in the foreground; she may add some blue for the sky. Helen is working on an arrangement of flowers for her next rug. Jane and Laura want warm scatter rugs for their cabins and are using coloured wool in stripes of colours. Jane is following the colours of the rainbow from violet to deep blue, to lighter blue, blending to green, yellow, orange and red. Laura is making a square rug with one colour all around the edge, followed by another band of colour, until the whole area has been hooked.

Beth and Brenda head to the Andersons to help in the bakeshop. Naomi greets the girls warmly and gives them each a job to do. Ruth is making bread and rolls today and Beth offers to help her. It is a beautiful morning and they are both happy to be outside in the fresh air. Patricia is set to work mixing the ingredients for several raisin loaves and zucchini loaves. Then she tries her hand at some pastry with the help of Dorothy; they have an order for both the Café and the Inn for butter tarts today. There is lots of interest in the settlement for the wonderful treats that come from the Sunshine Bakery.

In the afternoon, Ruth joins the girls for a walk to the spring to enjoy the summer weather and to bring back water for the cabins. Ruth shares the story with them about finding her sister and older brothers in Boonesborough after searching for them for months. Her face beams as she fills in the details. All too soon it is time to head back to the fort to help Mary prepare the supper meal. They wave to Ruth as they part company.

"I have a special treat for all of you tomorrow. At least I think it will be," Beth tells them as they peel potatoes freshly dug from the ground.

"We have already done so many interesting things," Katie says. "While we were getting ready for our trip, we talked about some of the things we would do and some of the people we would meet."

"I never expected to learn about rug hooking. That was not something you mentioned in any of your letters," Patricia adds.

"I thought we might do some quilting, but I am thrilled with what I was able to learn with Sally this morning," Barbara beams.

"What are we doing tomorrow?" Brenda asks.

"Should I keep it a surprise?" Beth teases. "We are going to Lydia's seamstress shop. I love working with the cloth and making gowns for the women."

"I wonder if any of us will be taken with the same passion that you have expressed in your letters about dressmaking," Katie ponders.

The next morning, the girls are chatting excitedly as they walk to Lydia's shop. They all learned the art of sewing from a young age, some made finer stitches and were more patient than others. Since their parents are all well-to-do, the girls did not have to make all of their own clothes. It was always fun to go downtown to the shops in Boston to be measured for a new gown and choose the fabric for the next soirée.

Many of the women who live in the fort and on the surrounding farms have not had the luxury of having a dress made for them in several years. Saturdays are often busy days for Lydia with more women dropping in to be measured for a dress. Usually these are dresses for special occasions, such as weddings or dances, but Lydia has even had requests for homespun work dresses. Lydia has planned for this day in advance, deciding how to give each of the girls the opportunity to experience much of what the seamstress trade involves. There is the treadle sewing machine which she wants each of the girls to try, as well as the loom. She decides to start with the loom and shows all of them how it works. Brenda and Katie then sit behind two of the looms and begin producing cloth. Patricia and Barbara are shown how to work the sewing machine and Patricia gives it a try first. Their first customer arrives and Brenda joins Lydia to take the measurements for a gown. Helen Stagner chooses a soft peach material and asks for it to be ready in three weeks time when she will be back at the fort.

Beth comes up with an idea. "Lydia, you could use a chalkboard to write your orders on. Jack uses one at his furniture shop and it helps to keep everyone on track. In the morning they know what projects they have to work on."

"That's a great idea Beth. The orders have been growing and I need a better way to keep track of them so that everything is ready when promised. Will you check with Jack on where he got his chalkboard?" Beth agrees to do just that.

Laura and Jane Pogue arrive a little later and Lydia has Brenda take the measurements for one, and she draws Patricia over to show her how to take Jane's. After the Pogues leave, Lydia has Barbara and Patricia move to the looms and shows Brenda and Katie how to work the sewing machine. Beth is able to assist when anyone runs into a problem. They stop for a quick lunch which Richard brings to them from the Inn. They carry on in the afternoon to learn more. Lydia explains about the different types of material, and has Richard show them some of the homespun material that he has been dyeing. Patricia is drawn back to the loom; she is hooked, being amazed at what happens as she works the shuttle and sees the cloth form. Barbara gets a real thrill out of working the sewing machine. Although her first seam is quite crooked, it doesn't take her long before she is able to move the cloth along in a straight line. This is the neatest invention she has ever seen and she has a chance to make a seam on the dress that Lydia is making for Pleasant Henderson. After a mid-afternoon coffee break, Lydia has all the girls gather around the cutting table to show them how to make a pattern from the measurements and how to lay the pattern on the material to cut it out. This is an area where Beth especially likes to work as an outfit begins to take shape.

It has been a great day for the girls to spend with Lydia and they all thank her warmly as they head back to their cabin to freshen up before supper with the O'Neills. All the talk that evening is about their visit to the seamstress shop.

Sunday arrives and the girls are spending the day with Mike and Mary and the children. After the church service, they enjoy a special meal of roast buffalo, corn and carrots. The afternoon is sunny and warm and they decide to stretch their legs with a family walk around the outside walls of the fort. It gives a different perspective to look at the fort from the outside. There are no windows on the outside walls as they are for protection. There are some gaps in the stockade walls that should be fixed. Ellie isn't walking yet but she has lots of arms eager to carry her and gets passed around from one to another as they take a leisurely stroll. Sarah and Isaac have lots of energy and often run on ahead a short distance, with Mike and Mary cautioning them to stay close to the group. James walks beside Katie and Brenda and tells them about searching for frogs with Israel Boone the day before. When they arrive back at the cabin, it is time for Ellie and Sally to have a nap. Isaac and James are off to play with some of their friends within the fort; no wandering in the woods these days.

Beth has invited Tim for supper. He takes Brenda aside soon after his arrival to show her the spools he has crafted. She figures they will work just great. She will try to get several girls together on Tuesday morning to teach them how to do the corking. After supper Beth and Tim go for their evening walk and share the events of the day. Tim is happy for Beth to have her friends visiting her.

On Monday morning, it is a busy day at the bakeshop and all the girls are helping out. They arrive early so that Katie can help Ruth make the bread; then it has to rise before it can be baked. The other girls are making the dough for cookies. They are trying out a new recipe where the dough is rolled and then cut in shapes. At his blacksmith shop, Mike made metal cookie cutters in simple shapes: circle, square, and triangle. Oatmeal raisin cookies are another favourite and Beth measures and stirs the ingredients for a large batch. They will use the indoor oven and the outdoor oven to cook them and Naomi, Dorothy and Ruth have conquered their use and know just how long to leave the cookies in. When the first four trays are ready to bake, Brenda takes them out to Ruth to put in the outside oven. They have the dough rising by this time and are just in the process of cleaning up the work area making it the perfect time to switch to baking the cookies. Soon there are dozens of cookies cooling on the table. Meanwhile Dorothy is in charge of baking the sugar cookies in the cabin oven. The last of the dough is cut out just before noon. Dorothy is joining Jack at Richard's Café for lunch.

Tuesday morning is the time for the girls to split up and carry out their own specific pursuits. Brenda arrives at the Stagner cabin to find a very large gathering. Mary and Margaret are so excited about the corking they are going to learn how to do that they have invited several of their friends to join them. Everyone was instructed to bring along a knitting needle and they are eager to start. Some of them even brought along some wool yarn to use and that will be a big help because Brenda was not expecting so many people. Brenda explains how it is done with her own project then she starts each spool. Mary has chosen blue yarn and is soon working way.

"Don't get discouraged as you work," Brenda cautions. "It seems to take a long time before you see the first of the knitting come through the bottom of the spool."

Margaret chooses green yarn and is soon ready to begin, concentrating with her tongue sticking out. Jemima Boone Calloway and Fanny Calloway Holder are part of the eager group, always interested in learning something new. Even four year old Sarah Pogue receives her own spool and is able to perform the simple craft. The morning flies by and the girls thank Brenda for teaching them. Brenda says goodbye to Helen and heads to Mary O'Neill's for lunch.

Katie has another drawing lesson and is even given the opportunity to add some water colour to her picture. Katie says to James, "You should make a sign for your home like you have for several ventures in the town. You have quite a business going here with many people stopping by to purchase a drawing or painting."

"I never thought of it, Katie," James replies. "I enjoy drawing and painting so much that I don't think of it as work. What would I call my business?"

"Pioneer Pictures? Life in Pictures?" Katie suggests.

"They don't sound quite right. I will have to think more about it," James responds.

Barbara and Sally are getting along well as Barbara learns more about quilting. It takes creativity to decide on a design, and then a lot of patience to piece material together for each block. Barbara is a quick learner and has always had lots of patience for fine work.

"Sally have you seen Lydia's sewing machine? I think it would really save some time to sew some of the seams on the machine. Maybe I will try it one day when Lydia isn't using it."

Patricia spends the morning at the Pogue cabin working on her rug hooking project. The rose is beginning to take shape on the canvas. Beth works with Lydia making good progress on the current projects. The afternoon is unstructured time with a walk to the spring, a visit to the General Store, a visit to the Holt Campbell Inn and Tavern with Ruth joining them.

Dorothy has invited the girls to her cabin about a mile outside the fort to pick berries and make jam on Wednesday. There are strawberries, raspberries and currants to pick from the bushes outside her cabin, and blueberries in the clearings in the woods. The girls set out on the walk after breakfast, bringing along their berry picking buckets and some containers for the jam. There are enough bushes by the cabin for all the girls to pick the raspberries and currants first. While Dorothy gets Katie and Brenda started making the raspberry jam, the other girls pick the strawberries from the patch. Once this chore is completed, the berries have to be hulled and then it is time to make them into jam. The black currants are the easiest to do, only requiring a quick wash before cooking them. It is a full morning of activity but the table is soon full of cooling jam. At lunch time, they enjoy sampling the jams on fresh bread made at the bakery the day before.

They now head for the clearing in the woods where the blueberries are ripening. They all spread out to search for berries, bending down to search for the delicious treats on the trailing vines. Then it's back to the cabin for afternoon coffee break before making the blueberry jam. Some of the blueberries, strawberries and raspberries are set aside to take to the bakeshop for blueberry muffins and berry pies. Some of the berries are preserved for use during the winter.

After supper that evening when the girls are back in their cabin, they talk about all the things they have been doing. Katie puts forward a suggestion. "I would like to stay for at least another month. What about the rest of you? I have lots to learn from James Ellis that will take longer than two more lessons."

"It will take me more time to finish hooking my first rug and I have plans for my next one that I will need Laura and Jane to help me with. I also want to spend more time on the loom at Lydia's," Patricia adds her comments.

"I am enjoying working with the young girls with their corking. I am trying to think of other things I can do with the children. Does anyone have any suggestions?" Brenda asks.

"You could teach the younger ones to knit as probably the older ones already know how to do it. I could help you teach them how to crochet. Maybe Tim will be able to make us some wooden crochet hooks. We could start with thin wool yarn and progress to fine cotton thread. I haven't seen anyone crocheting," Barbara suggests.

"Those are great ideas, Barbara. I will be happy to have your help. We will likely have to choose a separate day during the week to work with the children as you are already busy on Tuesday mornings," Brenda continues.

"We could all work with the children to teach them how to print and write. None of the children have been to school and have only been learning from what their parents can teach them. Mother taught all of us to write beautifully. That would be a real bonus for the children," Beth suggests.

"Mrs. Worthington was a strict task master when it came to handwriting. She made us stick at the task until she was satisfied," Patricia smiles as she remembers how she struggled to form the letters.

"Maybe James Ellis could be encouraged to teach the children some drawing and painting," Katie suggests.

"There are several other girls that I can think of who have not been included yet. The two Patterson girls, Lydia and Linda, are very proficient on the loom, but they might enjoy corking, knitting or crocheting as well. Naomi's daughter, Esther is a good age to teach as well. The Harts next to Johnny's flower garden have a very shy girl named Eliza," Beth adds.

"When we start putting our minds to it, there are many things we could teach the girls. I always wanted to be a teacher," Barbara comments. "When we were planning our trip, we decided we wanted to be a help here as well as enjoy the environment. We were eager to see all the things you wrote about and we wanted to learn a new skill. We have all started to learn something and have had several great experiences along the way. It wouldn't be fair to start anything too involved with the children and then stop it almost as soon as we begin it if we are going to leave in about two weeks."

"To really do it right, we would need to stay until the spring. That would give us time to teach Jemima, Fanny and maybe her sister Betsey how to continue teaching the children when we leave," Brenda suggests.

Patricia has been listening to all the suggestions and now adds her practical side, "I have been listening to everything that has been said and there are many good thoughts. Ruth commented the other day that when they were thinking about beginning a bakeshop she had to be cautioned to take it slowly and build from there. It is easy to get caught up in plans and forget about the rest of life that must carry on. First of all, what about our commitments back in Boston?"

"You are right to slow us down Patricia," adds Katie. "It is easy to talk about doing something but it takes real effort to follow through.

The first thing we will have to do is decide if we all want to stay either for a month or until the spring. What do you all say?"

All the girls eagerly agree on a spring date. "Secondly, where will we be able to stay? This cabin was given to us for a month. Will it be available for six months? What will it cost us to rent it?" Beth says she will look into it for them.

"The bigger hurdle will be getting our parents to agree to let us stay until the spring," Brenda cautions. "I think my parents were won over by Katie's parents. They may have a hard time with us remaining away for close to a year."

"For the moment, let's assume that our parents all agree to our staying, what are definite plans we can make right now? If we have firm plans rather than just talk, it will better clarify our reasons for wanting to stay. How much time each week do we want to give to this venture? In other words, how committed are we?" Katie, the planner in the group, questions.

"Tuesday mornings we all have our projects we are working on, except Brenda who has been teaching corking to the girls. Brenda, what project are you going to take on to improve your skills?"

Brenda scratches her head and shakes it, "I don't know yet. Maybe my project will present itself over the next few days. Maybe my drive will be to teach the children. But I have a goal to improve myself in one area as well. I am still staying open for what that will be."

"I am thrilled that you are thinking of staying longer," Beth smiles. "I certainly missed you for the year I was out here although I have been able to do so many things I never would have experienced in Boston. I usually work for Lydia five mornings a week, but I can arrange to work a couple of afternoons and have some mornings free as my schedule is very flexible. I will be glad to help wherever I can."

"Let's start with two half days a week is my suggestion," Brenda begins the plans. "I will continue working with the girls on Tuesday mornings with corking and add knitting. And we will invite more girls to join us as Beth indicated there are some who have not been invited."

"The rest of us could take turns working with Brenda on Thursday afternoons. Barbara could teach crocheting after we get some hooks made. Beth, will you ask Tim or Mike to see what they can do? Barbara has her crocheting with her. Remember though that we will need larger hooks to start with," Katie continues.

"Another afternoon we could teach printing for an hour and then a craft, or continue working on a project begun the week before. We can ask around to see if any of the women or men would be willing to work with the children for an hour on an occasional basis," Patricia adds.

"That's a good start for the plans. Let's sleep on what we have thought about tonight and continue the discussion tomorrow afternoon," Beth suggests.

The next afternoon the girls are still of the same mind and set down to write letters to their parents indicating their desire to stay in Boonesborough until the spring and share an outline of their plans for this extended visit.

Chapter 19 – An Upcoming Visit

Their month is almost up when a packet of letters arrives, one for each of the girls from their parents, a letter for Beth from her parents, and a separate private letter to Mary from her dad. The girls eagerly open their letters to discover that their parents have agreed to allow them to stay until the spring. Mary slips away from the noisy group to quickly read the letter from her Dad. As a result, she asks the girls if they will look after the children after supper and put the children to bed so that she and Mike can go out for a couple of hours. They are happy to oblige as it will give them some special time with the children. James is quite the talker as he shares about some of his adventures with Israel Boone.

"George and Johnnie Walker are fun to be with too, and so is Johnny Patterson when we can pull him away from his flowers," James pulls a face.

"Flowers are beautiful to look at," Brenda responds, "And Johnny is already starting his own business. What an enterprising young man he is becoming."

"What would you like to be when you grow up?" Katie questions.

"Sometimes I think I would like to be a soldier like Colonel Calloway, or a trapper and hunter like Daniel Boone, or a blacksmith like my dad, or even a furniture maker like Uncle Tim. I like to draw – maybe I'll be an artist like Mr. Ellis."

"Maybe you could spend a day with each of them to see if you really like what they do," Barbara suggests.

"For now, I just want to be me and go out and explore with the other boys."

"Time to wash hands and faces and get into pajamas," Katie directs. James and Isaac do a quick wash, while Brenda helps Sally. Barbara fixes a bottle of milk for Ellie and proceeds to feed her. Patricia reads a story and then Beth sings two songs. The boys ask for another one and Aunt Beth obliges with Barbara joining in with her complementary voice.

Meanwhile Mary and Mike find a quiet table at Richard's Café and are enjoying a fresh cup of coffee and a butter tart while Mary shares her letter from her dad with Mike. All ten parents have come to the conclusion that there must be something worthwhile in Kentucky that all of their daughters want to stay. The parents have decided they want to come and check it out for themselves. They would like to come out in the spring and stay for six weeks.

"Dad has asked me to check around and see if there are places for the five couples to stay in the spring. They have tentative plans to leave at the end of April to arrive in Boonesborough a month later. They need to be home by the middle of August as their oldest sons have militia duty coming up at that time," Mary shares with Mike.

"I can see you are very excited about seeing your parents. It has been many years since we left Boston. James and Sally Ellis might have room for one couple," Mike suggests.

"I thought of Jemima and Flanders, and Fanny and John."

"That takes care of three couples. What about the other two? Unfortunately we don't have room for your parents with us."

"The Pogues and Stagners are often not using their cabins in the fort. Maybe they would agree to rent them out for six weeks. They are in town this week. Why don't we go and see them now."

"That sounds like a good idea. Thanks for the coffee and tarts,

Dan. It was great to be here," Mike calls as they head towards the door. Mike takes Mary's hand and squeezes it lightly as they stroll across the square. "We have too few opportunities to be alone together, Mary. We should do this a little more often," he says as he draws her against his side.

"Beth and her friends enjoy spending time with the children. Beth never minds me asking her to help."

"She has really grown up in the past year. She is no longer shy and unsure of herself but has become quite confident and a valuable member of the town."

"She would be happy to hear you say that Mike. She still needs praise and encouragement at times."

"I'll try to remember that, Mary. Have I told you lately that I love you? It's dark enough," he says as he pulls her into a hug and gives her a deep kiss. Mary sighs in contentment.

They walk on and knock on the door of William and Laura Pogue, where John and Jane have joined them for an evening visit at the end of the day. Mike and Mary are invited in and offered coffee which they decline saying they have just come from Richard's Café. "The children are in bed so it's a perfect time for visitors. The days are so busy with Sarah and Will, and the twins, Suzie and Mellie that we welcome this peaceful time. They have lots of energy and create lots of noise. I'm sure you have some lively times in your cabin as well, Mike and Mary," Laura comments.

"James is quite a talker, while Isaac is very rambunctious and really gets excited with his play and often gets Sarah exited too. Ellie just takes it all in," Mary adds.

"We have been getting to know your sister better. It is wonderful for Beth to have her friends visiting from Boston," Jane continues the conversation. "When do they leave?"

"They all received letters today from their parents giving them permission to stay until the spring. They are all thrilled as they have projects they are working on and plans for the next several months of people they would like to help," Mary informs them.

"Which brings us to a special reason for calling on you tonight," Mike says. "Mary received a confidential letter from her father and we are following up on it. Mary, do you want to share what we discussed?"

Mary smiles as she looks at Laura and Jane, "My father would like to come out for a visit. I am excited as it has been several years since I have seen him. And here is why we have come to speak with you, he would like to bring Mother," she pauses for a moment before continuing, "And the parents of Beth's four friends."

"That's ten people who will need a place to stay for six weeks from about the end of May until the middle of July, so we are looking for places for them," Mikes continues.

William and John look at each other and nod their heads in agreement. "Our cabin will likely be empty as we will be busy on our farms at that time. We would have room for two couples here. Would that help out?"

"That sure would help. We also thought of asking the Ellis', Jemima and Flanders, and Fanny and John," Mike adds.

"That's settled then. When we come into town for a few days, we can share the space or find a spot to bed down with the Stagners next door," Laura and Jane agree to the arrangements.

"Beth and her friends are all wonderful young women and we look forward to meeting their parents when they visit. Encourage them to come and see us on our farms while they are here. We have more room there to have them stay overnight," Laura adds and the others agree.

"Thanks so much. We have time to see Jemima and Flanders before it gets too late. We will head there now. See you soon," Mike and Mary say as they bid their goodbyes.

Mike and Mary chatter away as they head on down the street,

past the Inn and Tavern, past the Luttrell blockhouse, past the Livery Stable, to the young Calloway cabin. They knock on the door and Flanders invites them in. Upon entering they notice that Flanders already has company as Fanny and John Holder are visiting. Mike and Mary look at each other and realize they will be able to present their request to both families this evening. This time they do accept a cup of coffee as it has been awhile since they left the café. While the water is heating, there is light conversation. The two young couples look very happy.

"Beth and her friends are minding our children this evening and we have been out visiting. We just came from spending time with the Pogues," Mike adds to the conversation.

"Beth's friends will be leaving soon as they have been here for about a month. Beth will sure miss them," Jemima comments.

"All the girls got letters from their parents today giving them permission to stay on until spring. They are all thrilled as they are working on projects for their own improvement and have plans for working further with the young girls," Mary says.

"Brenda has been helping us to learn corking. She has also been trying to teach us some printing but we haven't had enough time to get far yet. Hopefully she will be able to teach us a lot more as she is staying longer," Fanny says eagerly.

"That is one of the things that the girls are hoping to expand on while they remain here," Mike states. "We have some confidential information to share with you. You must not breathe a word of this to any of the girls."

"We can keep a secret. What is it?" Jemima and Fanny chorus.

"Father has written to me that he would like to come to visit, and bring mother along. That puts a song in my heart as it has been years since I have seen either of them. We moved from Boston to North Carolina, and then later to Boonesborough and there has been no opportunity to return home in those years," Mary continues.

“That will be wonderful for you Mary. I am glad my mother lives close by,” Jemima says and Fanny nods in agreement.

“Father would like to bring the parents of the other girls with them to spend six weeks here. We are looking for places they can stay during that time. Would you be willing to share your cabins with one of the couples?” Mike asks.

Jemima looks at Flanders, Fanny looks at John and they all nod in agreement. “That takes care of four couples as the Pogues will be able to have two couples stay in their cabin since they will be out at their farms in the spring. Thanks for your help. Remember, not a word to any of the girls.”

“We will keep the secret,” they all agree. Mike and Mary stand up to say their goodnights and head back to their cabin. They wander past the seamstress shop, the carpenter shop, and as they are about to pass the Ellis cabin they notice that the lights are still on. “Shall we call on them, Mike?”

“Sure,” Mike says as he knocks on the door. James opens the door and welcomes them in. “You are out late visiting tonight. Is Beth watching the children?”

“Beth and her friends are all at the cabin. Hopefully they have the children all settled down for the night. They enjoy spending time with the children and often increase the noise level,” Mary informs them.

“We are enjoying the evening on our own and we have been visiting several people tonight. We have a request to ask of you.”

“What is it? We will be happy to help you out if we can,” Sally says.

“Beth and her friends have received permission to stay in Boonesborough until the spring. My father is planning a surprise for them in the spring. He wants to come with Mother and bring the parents of the other girls with them to find out what is so special out here that none of the girls are in a hurry to go home. We have lodging arranged for four couples and we wondered if you would have room for my parents to stay with you for about six weeks until the middle of July."

James and Sally agree and Mary cautions them to keep this quiet and not say anything to the girls. It is with a much lighter heart that Mary heads home with Mike. The arrangements are falling into place nicely. Mary will be able to write home and tell her parents that all the living arrangements are in place for the end of May.

***

At the end of the summer, Will and Steve Hancock ask Sue and Anne Bryan out for an early evening walk, each couple taking a different path. They ask the women to be their wives. The two couples meet up and discuss wedding plans, plans that are shared with the rest of the Bryans on their return to their home for coffee. It is a happy evening. The women agree to have Naomi and Ruth as their bridesmaids, and will ask their sister Rebecca to be their matron of honour. Steve and Will will ask Tim Eadon, Jack Wallace and Daniel Boone to stand up for them. They set the date for the end of June the following year.

"Maybe Lydia will make our wedding gowns. We'll have to make a trip into town to ask her and discuss our plans. We can ask the women to be part of the wedding party while we are there."

"I have a special order to deliver on Wednesday and I'll be able to take you in to the fort then," Will says.

Wednesday arrives and the trip into town is quickly made. While Will unloads the wagon and carries out his business, the women talk with Lydia who agrees to make their dresses. Beth happens to be there at the time and Lydia asks her if she will be able to help seven half days a week. Beth agrees to be the extra pair of hands to help make the dresses and work on the many other orders that have been coming in. The women choose the material, Sue's is a pale apple green, and Anne's is a pale sky blue.

Will meets up with them as they are heading to Naomi's. Both

Naomi and Ruth are thrilled to be their bridesmaids. Will says he saw Tim Eadon in Jack's shop and both he and Jack agreed to stand up for them. They head to their sister Rebecca Boone's for coffee and to share their happy news; Rebecca is happy for her sisters and looks forward to their wedding. Daniel is happy to stand up with the men. The next stop is to see Squire Boone to book his services to perform the ceremony. Plans are falling into place.

Chapter 20 – Making Plans

The following Monday afternoon, Beth sits down with Katie, Brenda, Barbara and Patricia to make plans. “Let’s make detailed plans for the next three months. In December we can plan for the following four months.”

“On Tuesday mornings we will continue our learning activities. Tomorrow will be my last session with Laura and Jane as they are heading out to their farms later in the week. I plan to discuss my second rug hooking project with them and hopefully get started on it so that I can continue on my own,” Patricia tells them. “I would like to keep Tuesday mornings as a dedicated space of time to continue rug hooking. If I don’t set aside a specific time, I likely will find other things to fill in the time and then be disappointed that I have not finished my projects.”

“That is very wise, Patricia,” Katie agrees. “I hope to be able to continue working with James on Tuesday mornings throughout the fall and I would like to add a second session each week as well.”

“The purpose of our planning session is to bring out those feelings, Katie. All of us need to feel free to share our desires for the next few months. When we have a passion for something, it will drive us to fulfillment. I encourage you to pursue your artistic skills,” Beth comments. “Barbara, what are your thoughts?”

“I am enjoying my time with Sally as she knows so much about quilting and has lots of tips and suggestions to share. I would like to try doing some of the sewing of the cloth pieces on Lydia's sewing machine. That will require an extra slot of time during the week for me as well. I enjoy spending time with all of you and didn't want to suggest it before, but this is something that really excites me. What do the rest of you think?" Barbara asks.

The others are in agreement with her ideas and add that there are still many hours each day and week that they can be together. Now is her opportunity to expand her skills and be innovative.

"As you know, I am a working girl and I have seven half days to fit in at Lydia's each week. It is flexible time so I am able to plan my time around other activities that we might wish to do," Beth adds. "I also enjoy spending time with Ruth and we try to get together at least twice a week. The rest of you are always welcome to join us as you have done several times already."

"It is great that you have developed a good friendship. You have made friends with others as well since you have been here. I encourage you to continue building those friendships. Don't hesitate to spend time with Rebecca Boone, Dorothy Wallace, Jemima, Fanny or anyone else you have become friendly with. We want to share your time but not restrict it," Katie advises. "I forgot to mention Tim. He is a special friend of yours too. Don't neglect him while we are here. He means a lot to you."

"Yes, Tim is a great guy. Most evenings we spend some time together and we like to go on some outings for half a day or even a whole day, depending on our work schedules. I must take you to Jack's Furniture Shop where you will be able to see some of the fine work the men do. It is wonderful to have you here in Boonesborough. It is a special treat to share my experiences here with you. I want to continue including you in as many of my activities as possible as we can all learn from others."

"We have enjoyed all we have done so far," Barbara comments and the others nod vigorously in agreement. "We haven't been horseback riding or canoeing yet. You mentioned those activities in your letters."

"We have stuck close to the fort as the Indian situation is unstable this year. I will check with Tim and see if we can go canoeing down the river on Saturday," Beth suggests. "I'll also check about horseback riding to see if that is possible. Maybe we can go along with the Pogues and Stagners when they head back to their farms. If Tim and a couple of other men can join us we would then have an escort back to the fort. We can check it out this afternoon and see the on-going woodworking projects at the same time."

"Before you ask, we all took riding lessons soon after you mentioned that you were learning that skill. We can all stay in the saddle and have been on trips of four hours at a time. It may be a little rougher territory out here but we will make out fine," Katie informs Beth.

"You never cease to amaze me! You have all grown so much over the past year, even as I have. It is wonderful to share our lives again," Beth says.

Just then there is a knock on the door which Beth goes to answer. It is Rebecca Boone and she draws Beth outside to make a suggestion. Beth is eager and agrees to check with the girls.

"We haven't finished making our plans yet, but here is an opportunity for Wednesday. Daniel and several of the men have just returned from a hunting trip. They brought back meat and two deer skins. Rebecca asked if we would like to join her on Wednesday to learn how to make moccasins or a buckskin shirt. What do you say?" Beth questions.

"We remember you saying in one of your letters that you missed the opportunity to work with deer and bear skins because something else had your attention," Barbara says with a twinkle in her eyes. "I wonder what that something was." Beth only smiles realizing that Barbara is teasing her.

"Did you ever have the chance to work with animal skins?" Brenda asks.

"No, I have never had the opportunity. I would love to go on Wednesday to Rebecca's. Are the rest of you interested?"

They all chorus their agreement with smiles and nods of eagerness. "That's settled then; I'll let Rebecca know later this afternoon."

"Now back to our plans. For the sake of organizing, let's say that Barbara, Patricia and I will be busy on Tuesday and Friday mornings," Katie gets the girls back on track. "Brenda will continue working with the young people on Tuesday mornings with corking and introduce knitting. On Thursday afternoons we can rotate activities. For the first hour we can teach them how to print. Whoever is helping Brenda that week can use her special talents for a project. If no one is available to help, the children can continue working on the project begun the week before."

"The first week, I will start the children on crocheting," Barbara offers. "Beth did you talk to Mike and Tim about hooks?"

"Yes, both of them will have something for us in the next day or so. That should work for Thursday."

"It will likely take two weeks to really get going with how to work the hook, so I will plan to be with Brenda the second week as well."

"Week three we can check with Dorothy to see if we can teach the girls how to make pastry. That is Dorothy's special skill and it will be great to include her," Beth suggests.

"Here is a completely different suggestion for week four. How about we ask Tim to help the children design their own butter mould and have Tim work with them to create them?"

"Tim might be a little shy, but we can ask him and I can gently nudge him along," Beth agrees. "I have three weeks to work on him," she laughs.

"Now we are into the month of October. Some of the girls may have enough corking done to make a hot pad and we can teach them how to sew it together," Brenda suggests. "That will require a few extra hands. If everyone is available that week it would be a real help."

"For the rest of October, perhaps we could each take a week to teach the girls the craft we have been learning. I can teach them about quilting first. Who will take the second week?" Barbara asks.

"Rug hooking isn't a difficult task. Perhaps I can have Jane and Laura prepare very simple children's pictures on burlap. I can teach the older girls how to cut narrow strips of cloth. For the younger girls, I can already have narrow strips of cloth ready in several colours. Brenda your extra set of hands will be needed. You will get to learn about rug hooking at the same time. Maybe it will become your passion too!" Patricia inserts herself into the schedule. "It may take two weeks for the children to become comfortable with their project.

"The last week of October I will try to have James come and show some of his art work and allow the girls to try some drawing and painting. Perhaps James will come once a month to provide an opportunity for the children to learn this skill. Some may show real talent and James may be able to begin working with them on a more regular basis. I am speaking for James, but I will have to talk further with him. In our sessions he has indicated a desire to teach others what he has learned over the years; I'm just not sure how comfortable he will be working with children or whether he was thinking more about working with adults. I'll talk to him and see what he says." Katie continues. "That brings us to the end of October. That is a real good start to our plans."

"Some of the girls will be real eager beavers and will be doing a lot of extra work on their projects. We may have to have a second project ready for them to begin on while the others are more slowly working on theirs," Beth suggests. "If Laura and Jane are willing, perhaps they could prepare several designs on burlap so that we would have a supply. There could be half a dozen of each design. There could be a large number of simple designs and a few of each of the more difficult ones. Perhaps in the future Katie will be able to prepare some of the designs once she sees what Laura and Jane start with. Patricia, are you already able to do this yourself?"

"Laura and Jane have been working with me on this and I know the tools to use. Perhaps if Laura and Jane provide me with one of each design, then I can make more of the same design," Patricia agrees. "Just because the children are using the same design doesn't mean the finished projects will all be identical. They will choose their own colours."

"Good point Patricia. That will take us into November. Perhaps some of the projects the children will want to use for Christmas presents for their parents. We may have to be careful what we say so that we don't spoil any of the children's surprises," Katie adds.

"Now we have some detailed plans, what are our next steps? Brenda you can tell the girls tomorrow about plans for Thursday afternoons. Beth, will you invite the Patterson girls to join the group? I will ask Naomi on my way to James' if Esther would like to join us. Look around town and see if there are any other girls that we have left out," Katie continues.

"Where are we going to meet? Should we do it at our cabin since Beth has finalized arrangements for us to stay here?" That seems like a logical place to everyone. They will have to have the main room of the cabin extra tidy on Tuesday mornings and Thursday afternoons.

"That's enough plans for one day. It is a beautiful sunny afternoon. Let's call on Ruth and go for a walk down to the spring," Beth suggests. Everyone jumps up, picks up a pail and they head out. Ruth is ready to get out and enjoy the fresh air as well. The sentries assure them that they will keep a sharp lookout but everything seems to be peaceful.

Chapter 21 – Learning Skills And Helping Others

The following morning the girls eagerly set out on their individual pursuits. Linda and Lucy Patterson are eager to join the group of girls getting together on Tuesday mornings and Thursday afternoons. The same response is received from Esther Anderson and Eliza Hart.

The pumpkins are ready and everyone helps in the afternoon to make two dozen pies. It is a sunny, warm afternoon and half the group is able to work at the outdoor table while the others work in the cabin. Jemima and Fanny are recruited to help deliver the pies with eight of them going to Richard's Café and twelve going to the Holt Campbell Inn and Tavern. Ruth ensures that she is part of the group taking the pies to the Tavern and then she and Paul are off to spend an hour together before supper time. Their romance is moving along quietly, but the town's people notice the courtship blossoming. Paul has been thinking about how to redesign the Inn so that there is a separate room for himself. Perhaps the bunkhouse can be converted to his own space. Ruth has already added a few female touches to the Inn. Johnny Patterson regularly brings flowers to put on the tables for centerpieces, an additional way for him to earn a few cents. He has made perfume from Bergamot flowers growing wild all around Boonesborough, as well as from lavender, sweet alyssum and sweet peas that he grew from seeds. He is now experimenting with mixing scents to see which ones are especially pleasing to the senses.

After breakfast on Wednesday morning, the girls head eagerly to

Rebecca Boone's cabin. Jemima is watching her young four-year-old brother Jesse this morning so that Rebecca is able to dedicate her attention to the job at hand. After removing the skins from the animals, the men rubbed the skins with salt. Rebecca has had the skins soaking in ash water for the past few days. It is now time to scrape the hair off the hides which Rebecca shows them how to do. They are working outside the cabin to give them enough room to work. Conversation flows as the scraping continues. The hides are then turned over to scrape off any remaining flesh, sinew and fat.

The skins are then washed and stretched tautly over a frame. Rebecca had boiled and mashed the brains of the deer before the girls arrived. It is now time to spread this mixture over the skins with the use of moss.

"In a couple of days, the skins will be removed from the frames, washed, wrung out and then stretched and left to dry. The washing, wringing and stretching are done a few times to make the skin soft and supple," Rebecca explains. "I have several skins ready for us to use this afternoon. Let's wash up and go to Richard's Café for lunch and then we can start work on making moccasins from the skins."

The girls are glad to get up and stretch as they have been using some different muscles this morning. They quickly wash up and remove the aprons they have used to cover their dresses and are soon ready for lunch. Dan gives them a friendly greeting and ushers them to a table where food is soon provided. To top off the meal, they have pumpkin pie which they helped to make yesterday at the bakeshop.

Back at the cabin, Rebecca shows the girls samples of buckskin shirts, leggings and moccasins that she has made. "I thought we would make moccasins today as they are the simplest to do. They can be plain, or decorated with dyed porcupine quills and moose hair. You can decide now what you would like to do. Brenda, let's make a pattern for your feet." While Rebecca is drawing around her feet, Brenda has several questions to ask which Rebecca patiently answers. Brenda is glowing from working with the leather and the possibilities of items that can be made. Each of the girls has patterns of their feet made. Then Rebecca shows them how to lay the pattern on the skin, trace around it with charcoal, flip it over for the opposite foot, trace around it and then cut both out with a sharp knife. The patterns are placed close together on the skin so that there is as little waste as possible.

"If you plan to decorate the moccasins, it is easier to do it before you sew them together. The patterns can be fairly simple or more elaborate. What are your thoughts girls?" Rebecca asks.

"I would like to decorate mine," Brenda eagerly says and the other girls smile and chorus their agreement.

"For this first project, let's choose something simple so that we can begin sewing the moccasin together today. Caribou sinew is strong and used for the sewing with needles made out of bone. We use as many parts of an animal as we possibly can. The local Indians have shared their knowledge with us and now we are able to make several items from the skins. Deer skin is the softest, but we use moose skin as well," Rebecca instructs as the decorating begins.

"How the day has flown by!" Beth announces. "We are not going to get these moccasins finished today. We will have to plan on another session. What day works for you Rebecca?"

"Next Wednesday morning works for me. Is that suitable to everyone?" Everyone agrees. They pack up their items and leave them with Rebecca in order to continue with the instructions the following week. Four of the girls are ready to head out the door, but Brenda is lagging behind as she looks again at the items Rebecca has made, and feels the soft leather. She has found her passion! During supper with Mary, Mike and the children, Brenda beams as she talks about their day, her face is glowing as she shares her excitement. Everyone is happy to see that she has found the area where she will learn a new skill.

That evening when Tim calls on Beth for their evening walk, she shares about their day working with the deerskins and starting to make a pair of moccasins. "Brenda took to it like a duck to water. It was great to see her excitement."

"That's just the way Jeremiah Horn is with the blacksmithing. He was a natural with it from the start. He is turning into a great assistant for Mike."

"Mike often comments on how Jeremiah is doing. That is, whenever he can get a word in edgewise with five extra young women sharing meals. I wonder if we should make different plans for our meals now that the girls are staying until the spring. What do you think, Tim?"

"As long as Mary is happy with the arrangements, there is no need to make any changes. I am sure all of you pitch in helping with the meals, and you are an extra pair of hands to help with the children. I would expect that Mary would miss you if you weren't there. You can always talk to Mary about it when the two of you have a few minutes on your own. I hope you still do find time to be sisters."

"You are wise, Tim. You always help me to see further into a situation than I think of myself. I will have a chat with Mary in the next day or so."

"We have a cabin raising in three days' time for the Hancocks."

"That will be a festive time with many men in the area joining together to build a second cabin next to Will and Steve's so that each married couple will have their own space."

"It is great for the guys how everything is working out for them. They are two men of strong character, good workers and lots of fun to be around."

The cabin raising is a day of hard work for the men with the women helping where they can. The women provide water and food to nourish the men with the main meal being at two o'clock in the afternoon to allow the group to leave at four for the five mile trip in the wagons and on horseback to be back in town for supper. It is quite a festive time for everyone in Boonesborough and all the settlers in the outlying regions. Jack is busy making furniture for the young couples with Tim proving to be a real skilled helper in the job. Tim is working full days all week now with only a rare day being needed at the blacksmith shop. He is working on a cabinet for dishes and linens and he is enjoying adding some carving and smoothing the surface and rounding the edges.

Sunday is a quiet day for family time and Beth enjoys spending time with her nephews and nieces. James has become quite independent and enjoys his exploring times with other boys in Boonesborough. Isaac is four and always active and often boisterous; he enjoys a romp with his dad at the end of each day. Sarah is two and loves to play quietly with her dolls whenever Isaac will leave her alone. Isaac likes to be the centre of attention and wants the others to do whatever he decides. Mary has her job cut out to redirect his energies from time to time. Ellie is nearly a year old. Beth thinks back to that time and is amazed how quickly the time has flown.

"The children have really grown a lot in the last year and a half, Mary," Beth comments as they work together preparing lunch. Mary looks at each one of them, smiles and nods her agreement. "I enjoy spending time with them but I have become quite busy with my job, and having my friends here. Are we too much of a burden for you, Mary? Now that the girls are staying for another six months, should we make other arrangements for meals? Should be start doing our own cooking at the other cabin?"

"Beth, you have been such a help to me in so many ways. Your friends will always be welcome to share their meals with us. All of you are a joy to have around. You bring so much life into our home. All the time you spend with the children is especially wonderful," Mary smiles.

"We will be happy to continue the arrangements. Never hesitate to ask us to do anything for you Mary. You and Mike should take some extra time for yourselves while we are here. You enjoyed yourselves the other night when you went out. Why not plan that on a more regular basis?"

"That is a wonderful offer, Beth. I will let you know when we would like to have an evening out away from all the chores at home."

"Here come the girls now for lunch. We are almost ready to sit down. Barbara, will you help the children wash their hands? Katie, please call Mike and Tim and see if you can tear them away from their deep conversation. Brenda, please put the potatoes on the table. Patricia, here are the vegetables for the table." Mary turns to Beth and smiles. "See what I mean about all the helpful things you all do?" Beth nods in return.

After lunch, Beth and Tim head out for a longer time together than they have had for awhile. They are planning a walk down to the river. With the gentle rush of the water, it is a peaceful time to talk about their week and share special little things that have occurred. Just to be together is a special time.

"Tim, would it be possible for us to take the girls canoeing? None of them have ever done that before."

"I will see what I can arrange. We will need four or maybe five canoes, and I will need three or four fellows to help. I haven't shown you how to steer yet and it will be enough of a challenge to teach them how to paddle."

"I imagine there will be some major splashing going on…all accidental of course," Beth chuckles.

"I am not so sure about the accidental part. Do any of your friends swim?"

"I don't think so."

"The main thing we will emphasize is how to stay in the canoe. Otherwise we will have a bigger job of fishing them out of the water," Tim laughs. "I will work on plans for next Saturday. Providing the weather is suitable we can spend a couple of hours in the mid-morning on the water."

"If the girls learn quickly, perhaps the following week we can visit the Calloway families down the river."

"That sounds like a good idea. We haven't been across the river for awhile now," Tim agrees.

The week flies by with all of the projects on the go. Soon Saturday is here and the sun is shining. The Indians have not been bothering the settlers around Boonesborough. Tim calls for the girls and they head out to the gate where they meet Flanders Calloway, John Holden, David McPhee, and John Martin waiting beside five canoes. The men lift the canoes onto their shoulders and lead the way to the river.

Tim gives some basic instructions before everyone gets in the canoes. Katie is gung-ho and soon gets the knack of it. Brenda is much more timid and in an attempt to keep from splashing makes very ineffective strokes. David has his job cut out to get her to use more power in her strokes. Barbara and Patricia are eager but seem to be getting themselves and their partners quite wet in the process. There is much laughter and joking as they share this adventure. They travel about a mile downstream and then Tim signals the men that it is time to turn around. The morning has flown by while the girls have learned how to paddle. Several times they had to be cautioned to stay in the middle of the canoe. A fish swimming nearby, or a bird flying low, or a lovely tree with its leaves turning colour would draw their attention and cause the canoes to wobble. They arrive back at their starting location without anyone having fallen into the river.

The men discuss a full day's adventure the following Saturday and suggest inviting Joseph Combs, Joseph Hughes and David and William Robinson. Flanders would like to bring Jemima, and John would like to bring Fanny along as it has been several weeks since they have seen her sister Betsey. Beth suggests that Ruth would enjoy the outing as well. The women plan what food they will take along. It is quite a lively group that heads back to the fort. They wave to Jarrett and Susannah Williams who are just passing by on their way to the General Store.

The girls quickly change out of their wet clothes and arrive a little late for lunch. Mary has their food ready for them and they eat while sharing their morning adventures with Mary. They try to talk quietly as the younger children are asleep. The afternoon is spent quietly at their cabin working on their knitting and crocheting. After their morning's outing, they are feeling sleepy and one by one they head for their beds for an hour of refreshing sleep. They want to be wide awake for the bonfire and dance planned for the evening.

The girls have helped out twice during the week at the bakeshop so that there are extra sweet treats available for the evening. Date squares, cookies and pies have been sending their inviting aromas around Boonesborough. Supper is eaten and cleanup is completed and the girls return to their cabin to put on their pink gowns. Beth has completed hers so the five girls are dressed in the same colour. The dance is to start around sunset and the young people begin to gather for the festivities. Charlie has his fiddle humming, Mabel has her fingers poised over the harpsichord keys, Ben has his accordion ready, and the first song begins with Charlie calling out the square dance instructions. "Partner up and let's start the first dance." All the young women have many men vying for the dance. Joseph Kennedy has made some improvement in his dancing and is a little more cautious about his partner's feet. He even has moccasins on tonight instead of his usual heavy boots. Jemima and Flanders greet each of the girls as they join in for the next dance. Ruth also has on a pink dress which Beth made for her at Lydia's shop. Blue, green and yellow dresses are worn by other women providing lots of colour for the group around the bonfire.

Tim is in his glory tonight as he loves to dance. His first dance is with Beth and then Katie is his partner. Beth never has the opportunity to stand on the sidelines as there are always eager men to partner her. Tim taps on the shoulder of her current partner when he is ready to dance again with Beth. The man reluctantly backs away and looks for another woman to dance with. John Holder steps in for the next dance while Tim finds Brenda for the graceful waltz that is being played. The evening flies by and soon the last dance is being played and it is time to head home. It takes awhile for the girls to unwind and fall asleep.

On Wednesday, the girls each finish their pair of moccasins and try them on. They are very comfortable on the feet. Brenda arranges with Rebecca to get together every Wednesday morning with her so that she can learn how to make a buckskin shirt which she plans as a gift for her father when she returns home in the spring.

Saturday morning there is a large, noisy group gathered by the river to canoe three miles downriver to the Calloway station. They have lots of food along which the men stow in the canoes. Each girl is assigned to a canoe with a man to do the steering. The only instruction given before they start is to remember to stay in the middle of the canoe so they don't tip over and dump the passengers in the water. Tim and Beth take the lead canoe, while Jemima and Flanders bring up the rear. Tim and Beth have a strong stroke and are soon a good piece ahead of the group. Katie has also really taken to canoeing and is able to set a good pace. Brenda is a little less timid than last week but still needs constant coaching by David McPhee who is steering their canoe today. After a mile underway, Tim stops the group in order to allow the last two canoes to catch up, not wanting the group to become separated and provide opportunity for any attack. After the second mile, Barbara and Patricia are starting to tire and there are now three canoes that are given time to catch up. Tim encourages everyone saying they are well past the halfway point. They set a little slower pace for the final mile and arrive at their destination just before noon after two hours of travel on the water.

Betsey hears the commotion and looks out of her cabin and sees the large group arriving. She isn't immediately able to tell who is there but she gives the signal to everyone at the station that company has arrived. She stands by her cabin with her four month old daughter Fanny in her arms. She first notices that there are women amongst the group and as they draw closer she recognizes her sister. She is so excited and rushes towards them eagerly. Fanny runs to meet her sister and hug her tightly, being careful of the baby. Everyone has come in from the fields and is ready for a change of routine to have a visit. It has been a few weeks since anyone has stopped by and only a couple of the men have been back to Boonesborough recently. It is harvest time and they are busy bringing in the grain that will see them through the winter. The women have been busy canning the vegetables they have grown. Next week they will dig up the potatoes, carrots, beets, and onions for storage in their cold cellars. The squash are ready to be taken in from the gardens as well.

The men quickly set up tables using lumber from one of the barns and some sawhorses. Chairs are brought out from the cabins and everyone sits down to enjoy the food that the women brought along as well as what the Calloway women had prepared for the meal. The special treats at the end of the meal are the cookies and squares purchased from the Sunshine Bakeshop. After eating, the men break off into their own group to discuss the political situation, the Indian situation, and to share farming triumphs and struggles. The women are happy to have other women to talk to about their children, share new recipes, and just be together. Betsey and Fanny head to the cabin to put the baby down for a nap and to enjoy some special time as sisters. After awhile, Jemima joins them. Beth is happy to connect with Eliza and her daughter Lydia and to see how much Kezia has grown up.

"Lydia has a beau now and it won't be long before she is married," Eliza proudly shares.

"Who is the lucky man?" Beth asks.

"He is a captain in the militia, Christopher Irvine."

All too soon their visit must end as there is a long canoe trip back home and it is against the current this time. Brenda is placed in the middle of a canoe this time, with David and William Robinson being the main paddlers. This speeds up the progress of the slowest canoe. The others are eager to start and only begin to slow down after the halfway mark. They stop for a short break and then continue on until they arrive back at their starting point. They unload the canoes and help carry everything up the steep bank to Boonesborough. The men store the canoes away and the women head to their cabins to freshen up and head for supper. Richard's Café and the Holt Campbell Inn are much in demand tonight as the men are ready to eat again and Jemima and Fanny are not interested in starting to cook at this late hour of the day. Mary saved supper for Beth, Katie, Brenda, Patricia and Barbara. Naomi has supper for Ruth. It was a lot of fun to be out for the day, but everyone is worn out and glad to find their beds early.

On the following Thursday afternoon, Tim Eadon and James Ellis arrive, both having agreed to help teach the young girls how to design their own butter moulds. "Butter moulds have simple designs of things that you are familiar with in your day-to-day life. What are some things you can think of?" James asks.

"Corn, wheat, leaves, trees, thistle, eagle, wild turkey, snowflake, acorn, pig, cow, horse, flower," are suggestions from the girls.

"Now think for a moment what would have special meaning for you," James continues.

"While you are thinking of what design you would like to use," Tim instructs, "We will talk about the wood that we will use for the moulds. We want to use a hardwood so that you will have it for many years. Who knows what a hardwood is?"

"A hardwood burns longer in the fireplace," Mary Hart, the eleven year old daughter of David and Donna says.

"That is correct Mary. We are going to carve a design into the wood. Do you think it will be easy or difficult to carve?" Tim questions the girls.

"I would say the name suggests that it will be hard," fourteen year old Linda Patterson says.

Tim nods in agreement. "Who can name some trees out in the woods?"

"Maple, oak, cherry, apple, beech, poplar, birch, pine, spruce," are some of the responses.

"Who knows which trees have hardwood?" Tim receives some hesitant answers.

"The best woods for butter moulds are maple, birch and beech. We have samples of them to show you. Look at the different grains on them. Here is a piece of walnut, and another of cherry. What do you notice is different about these woods?"

"The colour is darker," nine year old Chenoa Hart, daughter of David and Donna offers.

"That is correct. Since butter will be moist when it goes into the mould, what do you think might happen if we used walnut wood?"

"Would the butter change colour?" asks ten year old Becky Luttrell, daughter of Thomas and Jane.

"That's right Becky. The butter would turn dark brown. Who wants brown butter to eat?" There are shouts of "No" and noses turned up in disgust.

"We will need to use a very sharp tool to make the pattern. The older girls might want to try it, but we will do the designs for the younger ones. How does that sound to everyone?" There were loud cheers.

James takes over the instructions. "You all have a slate or a piece of paper. Draw your design now."

Jemima and Fanny have given this some thought beforehand and are soon busily drawing a design. Beth is helping out today and she suddenly has an inspiration for her own personal butter mould design. She reaches for a piece of paper and quickly draws the outline of a gown and places the letter "E" near the bottom. When she is finished she sets the design aside. Tim happens to be watching her and when she sets the paper aside, he slyly picks it up, folds it and puts it in his pocket while she is busy with the children.

Linda and Lucy Patterson both draw a length of cloth that they like to create on the loom. Linda decorates hers with six "x"s. Lucy decorates hers with three diamonds; in the bottom diamond she prints her name.

Mary and Chenoa Hart and eight year old cousins Maryanne and

Susie Luttrell are working on leaves. Brenda thought ahead and collected several kinds of leaves and ferns. Oak, chestnut, birch, beach and maple are worked into designs.

Seven year old Esther Anderson draws a pie with steam escaping and prints the initials "E A" to personalize it. James explains that she will have to draw the letters backwards in order for them to show up correctly on the butter. Seven year olds Kezia and Eliza Hart are cousins and enjoy working together, with one drawing a cow and the other a horse. The Stagners and Pogues happen to be in town today so Mary age six, Margaret age eight and four year old Sarah are able to join the group. Mary decides to draw a bear, and Margaret a deer. Sarah is four and needs a little help drawing a sheaf of wheat.

China and Kizia Hart and Polly Luttrell choose a thistle, a tree, and an eagle. China and Polly are both seven while Kizia is a year younger. James is busy helping with the designs wherever he can. "It looks like everyone is ready for the next step which is transferring the design onto the wood. Tim has drawn a rectangle on the blocks of wood that the picture must fit inside. After the designs are carved, sides will be built to form the mould to hold the butter. Use a piece of charcoal and draw your picture on the wood. I will help the younger ones to do this. Katie, I can use your help and anyone else who can draw."

Jemima and Fanny soon have their design drawn on the wood and James shows them how to carefully carve the design out of the wood. He cautions them again that the tool is sharp and requires small taps to chip the design out. Both girls begin on the project. Linda and Lucy are soon ready to give it a try. Mary Hart is eager and proves to be very patient and careful as slowly the design is taking shape.

Kezia Hart is given the opportunity to carve her cow, and Eliza starts work on her horse. Becky Luttrell is ready to begin carving. Susie and Maryanne Luttrell and Margaret Stagner are all eight years old and are eager to carve their own designs. In the meantime, Tim has finished the carving for four year old Sarah Pogue and she is quite pleased with it. He next starts on the bear for Mary Stagner.

"You have five more minutes to work on your projects. Then it is clean up time," Brenda keeps everyone on track. There are several sighs as the projects are not finished yet. "There is always next week to work on the moulds. Mary and Margaret, Tim will finish yours so that you are able to take them with you when you head back to your farms. Sarah's is ready now and just needs the sides added. It sounds like you all enjoyed yourselves today. How is your corking coming along?" There are smiles and eager comments. "Soon you will have a long enough piece to make a pot holder. I will show you how to sew it together. Bye for now. I'll see many of you on Tuesday morning. Have a great week."

Tim and James talk with them as the remainder of the cleanup is being carried out. "Do you want me to go ahead and put the butter moulds together?" Tim asks. "Or should we make it a project for next week to have the girls hammer in the nails?"

"I think we should let the girls do as much as they can," Brenda suggests. "Look at how eager they were to do their own carving. Even ones we thought might be too young were eager to do it and were very careful with the sharp tool. James, thanks for all your help today. How did you feel when you were working with the children? Is this something you would like to do on a regular basis?"

"I enjoyed very much working with the children. How about I come out every other Thursday afternoon and work with the girls for an hour. When would be the best time?" James Ellis asks.

"How about we plan the art lesson right at the beginning of the session? That way the children will be the freshest. I am really glad you will be able to join us. Thanks James. We will see you around town," Brenda says as she closes the door on his waving figure.

"We will have to come up with something for the younger girls to do next week while the older ones are finishing their carving," Brenda notes.

"Perhaps we can have them start the sanding for the sides of their moulds," Tim suggests.

"Maybe they like to colour and can do that," Beth adds.

Tim says goodbye and heads back to the furniture shop to put in another hour of work before the end of the day. Jack has encouraged Tim to take a couple of hours to work with the children, realizing what a great opportunity it is for both him and the children. Jack hopes that one day something can be organized for the young boys as well.

The women are ready to relax for the next hour before it is time to help Mary with supper. It has been a busy afternoon and Brenda, Tim and James were glad that Beth and Katie were there to help. Patricia was working on the loom at Lydia's and Barbara was experimenting with sewing quilt blocks on the sewing machine. Patricia and Barbara arrive shortly and tell of their experiences during the afternoon.

"Tomorrow afternoon let's go for a walk along the bluff out the back gate of the fort. We must stay within sight of the fort. It will be lovely to see the fall colours of the trees along the river."

The view across the river is always a pretty sight, but with the leaves changing colours, there is extra beauty to behold. Katie has her sketching pad with her and sets up her easel to capture some of the scene. An hour quickly passes as she shuts out the world and concentrates completely on adding colour to her picture. The others have strolled a little further down the bluff and are happy to be out in the crisp air. When they return to Katie, they admire the picture she has made.

Katie positions the girls for a group picture. She quickly sketches Brenda, Patricia, Barbara, Beth and Ruth and then spends a few minutes filling in a little of the background. She has learned a lot from James and is soon ready to add some colour to the drawing. Another hour has flown by and it is time to pack up and head to the fort.

During his evening walk with Beth, Tim suggests that they go canoeing upriver tomorrow. It will be one of the last opportunities to be out on the water before it gets too cold for the girls to be out. Beth agrees that it is a good idea and assures Tim that they had nothing specific planned.

"I'll see who I can round up to come with us. We could put two girls in a canoe, but we will need at least one other man. Brenda still doesn't have the knack of canoeing," Tim chuckles as Beth smiles in agreement. They have been out on the water several times but Brenda always lags behind the others.

"Perhaps Mike would like to join us for something different. We can offer to watch the children later so that Mike and Mary can have the evening to themselves," Beth suggests.

"That will be good for Mike. He doesn't often get included in outings as he has so much responsibility with his blacksmithing. He has become an excellent wheelwright and that keeps him even busier than shoeing horses."

"We are back at the cabin now. Let's check with Mike and Mary." Mike gladly accepts the opportunity to get out on the water, a pastime he enjoyed years ago but hasn't taken any time to do since being in Boonesborough. Mary looks forward to spending the evening with Mike.

With baking, weaving, sewing, rug hooking, quilting, painting and helping the children with their projects, the week quickly speeds along and before they know it, Saturday has arrived and they are off to the river for their canoe trip. Tim and Brenda share one canoe so that Tim can be the power to keep the movement going; Mike and Patricia are in another canoe, while Beth and Ruth paddle in the third. That leaves Katie and Barbara to work together in their canoe. Tim gives a few instructions on how to steer the canoe, the job of the person in the rear.

The forests on either side of the river are ablaze with colour. Tim notices that there is a little thin ice forming at the edges of the water. The air is nippy but soon the group has warmed up and they are happily enjoying their time together. It is hard work paddling against the current, but once they turn around it will be easier for the return trip. Tim reminds the girls from time to time to look at the beauty of the scenery around them. The pairs of canoeists are evenly matched for strength and all are moving along at a similar pace. After an hour and a half, Tim calls for a short break then it is time to turn the canoes around and head back.

"Thanks, Tim and Mike, for a good time this morning," the girls chorus as they return to Boonesborough.

"That will be the last time for canoeing this fall. Soon there will be winter activities to take part in," Tim informs the group. "Enjoy the rest of the day."

Sure enough, just as Tim predicted, a few days later the world is white when the girls wake up. They quickly dress up warmly and head out to enjoy the snow. The snow packs nicely and just for fun Katie tosses a snowball at Brenda who returns the fun. Before long Barbara and Patricia have joined in. The next thing they know the young boys are starting to come out and there is a real free for all. What a great way to start the morning! Time now to head for Mary and Mike's for breakfast; the girls are even a little late having enjoyed the early morning in the snow.

After breakfast the girls offer to take Isaac, Sarah and Ellie outside. Beth is working today and Mary has some shopping to do at the General Store. The sisters head out together.

This is the first time Ellie is able to crawl around in the snow and before long she has tried eating some. When the children's clothes are quite wet and they are starting to get cold, Katie herds them inside and Brenda, Patricia and Barbara help to get them into dry clothes and hang up the wet ones near the fireplace to dry. Then there are indoor toys to play with until lunch time. By that time Mary has returned and Barbara jumps up to help her with lunch.

After lunch, Barbara and Patricia head to Lydia's so that Barbara can sew quilt pieces together and Patricia wants to do some work on a loom. Patricia is thinking of asking Tim if he is able to make her own loom, perhaps one that will fold up in between work sessions.

Then she will be able to do some designing. At the moment, when she goes to work on the loom, she continues with whatever project is in progress. She has learned a lot from Linda and Lucy over the past couple of months.

Katie is spending her afternoon drawing. She sketches from memory a scene from the morning in the snow. She still gets together with James Ellis twice a week, but it is more for companionship than actual lessons. Only occasionally does Katie require a tip as she has progressed so well. She has been sketching Mike and Mary and the four children separately over the last couple of weeks. She now wants to take those sketches and put them together in a picture of the family to give to them for Christmas. She may do a second picture with Beth included as a gift for her. She has been thinking about what she will give the other girls but is still allowing her mind to work on that. Maybe she can follow the girls around and draw them at work learning their new skill. Wouldn't Patricia be pleased to have a picture working at the loom, and Barbara bent over the sewing machine? Brenda has really blossomed working with the children but just for fun, Katie is thinking about a funny picture of Brenda soaking wet trying to get the hang of canoeing.

Patricia decides to take a walk to the Wallace Furniture Shop to talk to Tim about making a loom for her. She walks in and is welcomed by Jack and encouraged to check out what the men are working on and to admire some of the finished pieces. The cabinet that Tim has been making for the Hancocks is nearly finished; he has added some lovely carving and soon will be ready to varnish it.

"Tim, I have a new project for you." Tim looks at her as she continues talking. "I enjoy working on the loom at the Pattersons, but I never get to finish a project or design my own items. I work on whatever project is in progress on the loom. I would like to have my own loom so that I can experiment and grow in the skill."

Tim responds, "I will look at the looms at Lydia's, see how they are made, and decide if I can design one."

"There is one problem though, Tim. I don't have the room in our cabin to leave the loom out all the time. I wondered if it would be possible to make it in such a way that it could be folded up in between my work sessions."

"I'll think on it, do some research and perhaps talk to Richard Patterson, and see what I can come up with. I'll get back to you within the week with plans. How does that sound?"

"That would be great Tim. I'm heading over to Lydia's now to do some weaving."

"I'll come over with you and see what I can learn." They head out together where Tim takes measurements and is soon in deep discussion with Richard. He leaves with the good beginnings of plans for making a loom for Patricia.

Tim has been thinking ahead to Christmas and wants to make something special for Beth. He has been working on the butter mould from the design she drew, but he wants to make something more. Beth gets a letter a couple of times a month from her parents, and the Brownleys write regularly as well, with Charles usually adding a few comments but up until now he has not made any plans with Beth. Tim wants to move on with his life, hopefully with Beth, but Charles always remains in the background. Tim plans to continue enjoying the time he has to spend with Beth. They are getting to know each other very well. Even after all these months it is still amazing to him to learn something new about Beth. From time to time Beth also comments that Tim has just shared something new about his past.

The next morning as the young women are getting ready for the day, Brenda asks if they have any more ideas of things to do with the girls.

Patricia says, "I heard Mary talking the other day about making candles. I wonder if she would help us work with the girls doing that activity. Let's ask her at breakfast."

When asked, Mary is willing to teach the girls. "What works best for you, Tuesday morning or Thursday afternoon?" Brenda asks.

"How is Tuesday about mid-morning this coming week?"

"We will be happy to work around your schedule, Mary."

Tuesday morning Mary brings supplies with her and begins to teach the girls how to make candles. She has bear and moose fat, bayberries and beeswax. "When we melt the bear and moose fat to make candles, the smell is not very pleasant. With the addition of bayberries or beeswax and even some vanilla, the aroma is more pleasing. Let's put some fat and bayberries in one pot over the fire. In the second pot we will put beeswax and bayberries. While it is melting, I will explain about making candles. There are two methods to use. Hand-dipping takes a long time. We will try some this morning. A much faster way is to use candle molds and I have some with me today.

"We will start with the wicks. Thomas Hart, Eliza's father, makes rope and has provided us with some that we can use for wicks. We will take several strands and twist them together. We will tie three on each stick so that you can each work on making three candles. It takes a long time to dip them to make a candle big enough. Let's get the wicks ready on our sticks now." Brenda and Mary help the girls tie the wicks on their sticks.

"The tallow is now ready for the first dipping," Mary says as she brings the pot over to the table. We will put the pot on this sturdy stool to make it easier to work with. Hold your stick on both ends and dip the wicks into the pot being careful not to touch the hot pan. Lift the stick back up and let it drip for a moment. Then hang your stick between two chairs. We can hang several sticks on each set of chairs. You may want to mark your stick so that you will know which one is yours. By the time each of you has dipped your stick, the first person can dip theirs the second time."

After half an hour, Mary is ready to show them how to use the molds. "These are plain tin molds that will make a dozen candles at a time. We make the wicks the same way by twisting the rope and threading it through the holes for each candle. We tie it at the top to hold it in place. What I like to do is to make the wick long enough that I can tie both ends together around the mold so that I don't have to worry about losing the wick when I pour in the wax.

"I have six molds, and I see several of you brought molds with you. Everyone will have a chance to use a mold. Let's work on the wicks and get them all ready. You can mark your mold with a coloured thread so that you will know which is yours.

"Thanks for your help Brenda. It looks like everyone has their wicks ready. We will use a metal ladle to dip the wax into the molds. Remember, the wax is very hot. Don't touch the wax or the pot. Six of you can work at a time pouring wax into your molds. Let's start with the youngest ones first. In the meantime, the rest of you can continue dipping your candles in the other pot.

"Paula, Kizia, China, Esther can start ladling the wax into your molds. Linda and Jemima can help with this group. Very carefully pour the wax into the molds. The mold will heat up as you pour in the hot wax so make sure you hold on with the cloth to protect your hands."

Once all the molds are filled, the groups switch. The filled molds are carefully placed on a shelf that Tim built just yesterday. The wax will harden during the week.

"Jemima, Fanny, Linda and Lucy can you stay behind for a few minutes after the others leave today? The rest of you it is time to head home for lunch." The girls put on their coats and thank Mary for helping them today. Mary turns to the older girls. "I would like to teach the four of you how to make soap. Jemima you may have helped your mom make it." Jemima nods. "Have the rest of you done this?" They all shake their heads. "We make lye from the ashes that we collect from the fireplace with all the wood we burn. The lye is very strong and will burn your hands. We will put wet cloths around our mouths and noses so that we do not breathe in the fumes. Laundry soap is made a little differently than hand soap. I have some unique ways of making the hand soap. Would you like to learn how to do it?" There are choruses of agreement. "What day works for you? We will need a sunny day, or at least one that isn't raining or snowing as we will be working outside." The girls are flexible so Mary decides that the next morning will be a good time. "I will arrange with Katie, Barbara or Patricia to watch the children as I don't want them around while we are working. Brenda, you will be able to join us I hope."

"I was hoping to be included. I am very interested to learn with you, Mary."

"We will start right after breakfast as it will take us awhile. Let's go to the cabin for lunch now."

The next morning Katie and Barbara are watching the children. Patricia has asked to join the group learning how to make soap. "We will remove the temporary fence that I had Mike make around the ash hopper. I added water to the barrel yesterday so that the lye would already have leached out for us to use today. Patricia and Brenda have been dumping ashes in this barrel for weeks. Did you ever wonder why we put the ashes in the barrel?"

"I know we always had to be sure that the ashes were completely cool before putting them in the barrel," Patricia says. "Otherwise we could start a fire in the barrel."

"Linda and Lucy what do you do with the ashes from your fireplaces?"

"I never asked and haven't had to do that job. Johnny and David always look after them. I wonder if Johnny puts some in his garden around the flowers, or mixes it with the dirt," Linda comments.

"We will have to ask to find out," Lucy says.

"Let's get a fire going and put the soap pot on to heat the water and animal fat. We will make laundry soap first. After the fat is melted, we will add some lye and a little borax. When we are ready to add the lye, everyone make sure they have their wet mask around their mouth and nose so that you don't breathe the fumes. This is the most dangerous part of the process. Lye is strong enough to burn your hands and the fumes can burn your throat."

"What is borax?" Fanny asks.

"Borax is a whitish crystal made from a natural mineral boric acid. It helps to soften the water, whiten the clothes, and remove stains and odours. Borax is always stored on a high shelf because it is poisonous. We never want the children to find it."

"The fat is melted now," Patricia notes.

"We call the melted fat tallow and it helps to weaken the lye so that it won't burn the skin. I'll get the lye bucket and add some of it to the boiling mixture."

"I see what you mean about the fumes," Lucy and Linda say and the other girls nod their heads in agreement. They each take a turn stirring the mixture for a few minutes and are then glad to move away from the pot. When the ingredients are well mixed, it is time to take the pot off the fire.

"The soap is now poured into metal trays and left to harden. It can then be broken off to use for the laundry or cut up into bars," Mary explains. The trays are placed out of the way on a bench and covered with a clean cloth.

"To make soap for washing, we start the same way with animal fat and water and then add lye. We will get that ready now." Brenda and Jemima help to put the fat and water in the pan over the fire, making a large pot of the mixture.

"For washing up and for baths, it is nice to have a fragrance in the soap, at least for the women. I have been working with your brother Johnny over the past few months," Mary says to Linda and Lucy. "He is very knowledgeable about perfume fragrances. The most common additions to soap are bayberry and wild ginger leaves. The fragrant flowers that Johnny has been growing can also be used in soap making."

"Wouldn't you have leaves and flowers in your soap?" Lucy asks.

"What I like to do is to wrap the leaves or flowers in a piece of plain cloth, tie it with a string and hang it into the soap mixture. Some flowers and leaves can be mixed together for a very pleasing scent. In order to experiment, I like to make the pot of plain soap and then dip some into smaller pans to scent each one a little differently. Cedar makes a lovely soap, perhaps a little more manly."

"What about pine needles? I always like the smell of them when we walk in the woods," Brenda asks.

"I haven't tried pine needles. That is a good suggestion. Does anyone else have any suggestions?"

"What about lilacs? In the spring they are a welcome smell," Fanny suggests.

"Strawberries have a lovely smell. Perhaps they could be added to soap," Jemima suggests.

"As long as you have lots of strawberries to eat and have a few extra, you could certainly try them. You can try anything and if you are not pleased with the result you can make a note of it and not use it again. There will be some things that just won't transfer a fragrance to the soap. It is a matter of trial and error.

"I asked each of you to bring a pot today. I have several items to use for perfuming the soap. You can choose what you would like to try and wrap it in a piece of cloth. I will add the lye to the boiling tallow. Does everyone have their wet mask over their mouth and nose?" The girls indicate they are ready.

"Do the berries, leaves or flowers have to be crushed before putting them into the soap mixture?" Lucy asks a few minutes later.

"That is a good suggestion. The flowers and leaves break down very quickly in the boiling mixture but the berries take longer. One of you could experiment with crushing the berries before adding them."

Mary has been stirring the mixture while the girls get their cloth packages together. "The mixture is ready to add the fragrances now. Each of you can bring your pot over and we will ladle some of the soap mixture into each. Then you can add your bag of leaves or berries. Once everyone has their pot ready, we will remove the large pot and hang the smaller pots over the fire."

"How long does the soap have to be over the fire? How do you know when the fragrance is strong enough for the soap?" Patricia asks. Others nod that they have also been wondering about that.

"I go by smell. It will be a little more difficult having six pans around the fire, but you will be able to lift your pot off and sniff it carefully to see if you think it is ready. It is all about experimenting. A half hour is sufficient for many of the fragrances, others will take longer."

"Juniper berries might make a nice fragrance too," adds Fanny.

"Once we start thinking about it, there are many possibilities," Mary agrees. "Next time you are out for a walk, take time to smell different flowers and trees. You may have to wait until the spring though."

"Let's make a note on each pan of soap of what fragrance we used. We could split each pan into at least seven bars of soap and have a sample of each one," Patricia suggests.

"You will have twelve bars from each pan so that will work out well," Mary informs the group. "Does anyone think their soap is about ready? Carefully pour it into a pan. If there is too much for one pan, I may have to hunt up some additional pans."

"I'll run over to Mom's and get a few extra pans. She has a stack of them for when she makes soap," Jemima offers. "Will someone watch my soap? It has bayberries in it which I didn't crush so it will take a little longer."

Fanny and Lucy pour their soap mixtures into pans and carefully mark what ingredients they used. Soon Linda and Patricia's are ready, followed by Brenda and Jemima returns in time to pour hers into a pan.

"I have a suggestion for some of the leftover mixture. What about if we mix several of the soaps together and see what we come up with?" Brenda is always eager to experiment. Everyone agrees to put two scoops of their mixture into a pan which will make a full pan of the conglomerate mixture.

"Mike put some temporary shelves up on the side of the cabin so that we can store the pans of liquid soap for the mixtures to harden. By morning they should all be hard and we can cut them into bars. Anytime tomorrow you can come by to cut your bars and take your soap home with you. You may want to wrap each bar in a different colour of material. Or you may want to wrap them all the same and be surprised when you open a new bar."

"Thanks Mary for working with us today. It has been fun working together and learning about making soap and adding a special touch to it," Brenda says and the others chime in.

Chapter 22 – Adoption

Each hunting trip for meat takes the men farther from the fort as the game is scarcer. In the winter there is no problem keeping the meat, but in the summer salt is a precious commodity. In January 1778, when salt is running low a party of thirty men which includes Daniel Boone and Tim Eadon, go to the Blue Licks on the Licking River, about one hundred miles north of Boonesborough to make salt from the water. The large salt-kettles are loaded onto pack-horses, the only way to traverse the narrow, rough wilderness trails. It is a time-consuming process to boil the water down to make salt. It takes eight hundred and forty gallons of water to make a bushel of salt. The first group of men is to camp at the Licks for a month and will then be relieved by a new party. These reliefs are to continue until they have a year's supply of salt. Three men take pack horses loaded with salt back to the fort and arrive safely.

Salt-making is dangerous as the Indians also know about the licks. Salt-making parties have to go out in force and be prepared to defend themselves at all times. It is almost time for the relief party to arrive and the men are thinking about seeing their families in Boonesborough. The Indians usually keep close to their villages in Ohio during the bitter weather, the reason why winter is the best time for this activity, and with the fires going the men keep warm. Three scouts are in the woods at all times to provide advance warning of any Indian trouble, and to hunt for meat to feed the men.

In early February, Daniel Boone heads in one direction while his son-in-law Flanders Calloway and a companion, John Holder, go the other direction. Daniel shoots a buffalo, cuts up the meat and packs it on his horse and heads back towards camp through a blinding snowstorm. He is leading his horse along the riverbank when he notices his horse is nervous. He looks around and four Shawnees are close behind him. He leaves his horse and takes off on the run giving them a merry chase for half a mile. His tracks are obvious in the snow and he cannot hide and the braves are closing in. Daniel knows Indians and he knows when he has had enough. He halts in his tracks with no way of escape and surrenders to the warriors. They disarm him and march him towards their camp on Hinkston's Creek, not far from the Blue Licks.

As he comes into their camp, Daniel is amazed and horrified by what he sees. In a sheltered part of the valley, around a long fire are more than a hundred Shawnee warriors fully armed and painted for war. The chief, a short, sturdy warrior, is Blackfish whom Daniel has met before. It doesn't take Daniel long to realize this is not an ordinary raiding party. He quickly notes that there are white men with the Indians which makes the situation that much worse. White brains are directing Indian savagery. Charles Beaubien, a French-Canadian hired by the British as an Indian agent is there, along with Louis Lorimier, a French-Canadian with a lot of influence with the Shawnee. Worst of all are George and James Girty, brothers of Simon whose name spreads terror among the pioneers. Boone realizes he is in a dangerous situation. The presence of the white men shows that an attack has been carefully planned and encouraged by the British. The band is strong enough to overwhelm Boonesborough in a few hours.

Three months before while in an American fort on a peace mission "King" Cornstalk, the great chief of the Shawnee was murdered by soldiers. The Shawnees want revenge and are out to bring vengeance on any whites. The British have taken advantage of this situation to spur on the Indians' hatred of the whites, that being the reason they are on the warpath in the winter.

The Indians admire Boone knowing that he is as good a woodsman as any of them, and a far better shot. Daniel hates killing and is never cruel. He is respected by the Indians. Blackfish tells Daniel, "My band is going to attack Boonesborough. Who are the men at the salt springs which my scouts have discovered?"

After being unsuccessful in evading an answer, he says, "They are my own men."

Blackfish blandly says, "I'll go down right away and kill them." Daniel does some quick thinking, knowing that the fortifications at Boonesborough are in bad shape, knowing that thirty men are with him and the relief party is on its way, leaving Boonesborough almost empty. He doesn't want everyone killed, or forced into captivity with a long march for the women and children in the cold weather. He will do whatever he can to prevent any bloodshed or suffering. He knows he has a slim chance. If the Indians have one victory they might be satisfied and go quietly back to Ohio.

Boone tells Blackfish, "I'll go with you and persuade the men at the salt licks to surrender, but you must promise that the men won't be tortured or forced to run the gauntlet." Daniel goes further to say, "It is too cold to move the women and children now; the spring would be a better time to take them to Detroit."

Blackfish agrees but adds, "If you fail to persuade your men to surrender, your own life will be the penalty."

The next morning the war party sets off, reaching the salt licks by noon. They are within two hundred yards of the salt-makers, and have completely surrounded them without being discovered. Boone is sent down a hill toward them, under surveillance of warriors following a little way behind him but near enough to shoot in case of treachery.

The spring has been flooded with fresh water for several days and the salt-makers, unable to work, are resting quietly in camp. They are not worried with Boone's absence as scouts and hunters are often gone for days at a time and the other two scouts are also still out. Seeing men approaching through the woods, the salt-makers look up from their blankets, supposing it is their relief coming from Boonesborough. Then, seeing Indians, they leap for their muskets.

"Don't fire!" yells Boone. "If you do, everyone will be massacred." Hurriedly he explains, "You are surrounded by Indians and I have agreed with them that you are to be treated well and as prisoners of war you will be given up to the British officers at Detroit." What a shock to these men who have been thinking about their soon return to their families in Boonesborough. Timothy Eadon quickly grasps the situation is as Daniel indicates and encourages the men to do as Daniel says; there are too many warriors for them to resist. The salt-makers form a circle and stack their guns. A large circle of warriors emerges from the woods, surrounds them and orders the twenty-seven men to sit down.

The Indians hold a council to determine whether they should kill their prisoners in spite of promises. They propose to spare only Boone as he will be useful at Boonesborough in the spring. The council continues for two hours with warriors rising to speak for mercy or for death. With no knowledge of Shawnee, the men have no idea that their lives depend on the outcome of the ceremonious Indian council. Tim watches what is going on. He too notices the presence of white men amongst the Indians and realizes this is not a good sign. The white agents whom the British have sent along sit silent while Daniel Boone is permitted to make the closing speech.

"Brothers!" says Boone as his words are translated sentence by sentence to the Shawnee. "What I have promised you, I can much better fulfill in the spring than now; then the weather will be warm and the women and children can travel from Boonesborough to the Indian towns and all live with you as one people. You have all the young men; to kill them would displease the Great Spirit, and you could not then expect future success in hunting or war." He goes on to explain that the men will make fine warriors and excellent hunters to kill game for their squaws and children. "These men have done you no harm; they were engaged in a peaceful occupation, and surrendered to you without resisting when I told them that it was the only safe thing to do." This is the first speech the startled prisoners have understood and now for the first time realize the peril they are in.

Knowing his friend quite well, Tim analyzes what Daniel is saying and asks himself why Daniel uses the words he does. He wants to grasp the reason behind the words. He knows that Daniel hasn't sold out to either the Indians or the British. His friend has a conscience and has family in Boonesborough. Timothy has spent many hours with Daniel since working with him in 1775 building the Wilderness Road. Although he can't yet understand everything, he knows things are not as straight forward as they sound. He picks up on the blown up story of how strong a fort Boonesborough is and that it will take many more than a hundred warriors to take the fort. Could it be that Daniel is trying to protect the rest of the people in Boonesborough? Tim continues to listen closely as Daniel says it would be too rough on the women and children to travel in the winter and the spring would be a better time for the Shawnee to come back.

It is a tight vote being won by Blackfish and the older chiefs for mercy. The group of reckless, brutal young braves who cry for blood have lost.

All has turned out as Daniel had hoped. The Shawnees are satisfied with a big haul of prisoners and plenty of glory as well as plenty of profit. Prisoners are useful as slaves and can be sold to the British for cash. Why go on to Boonesborough through the snow and risk a hard fight for nothing, when they can now slip safely back to Ohio with prisoners, much glory, and no losses?

Blackfish is greatly impressed. The white comrades of the Indians try in vain to urge the Shawnees on to the attack. Once the retreat with the prisoners has been decided on, it is promptly carried out. Three hundred bushels of salt are thrown away. Then the war party files off to the north through the white and silent winter woods, with their prisoners under close and careful guard.

In the meantime, Flanders and John are successful in finding deer and load the meat onto their pack-horses and head back towards camp. They return to an empty camp and at first think the salt-makers have wearied of waiting for the relief and have gone back to Boonesborough. Kindling a fire, they prepare to camp for the night, but they soon discover an Indian bow, some arrows and moccasin tracks. Then they observe that the precious salt has been thrown into the snow. Leaving the remaining salt-kettles where they lay, they rush off by night to warn the advancing relief whom they find in a camp along the way. After hearing their story, the relief party head for the fort at full speed.

After weeks of hearing nothing from the men who have disappeared from the salt lick, Rebecca Boone thinks that Daniel must be dead and she decides to return with her family to North Carolina to stay with her father; her grandparents Morgan and Martha Bryan live nearby. It is a sad parting for Beth when Rebecca leaves as she has been a big help in teaching Beth during much of the early days of her time in Boonesborough and a real friendship has grown over the past months. Beth stays on with Mary and Mike. It is a tough life as pioneers. For the second time, Tim is likely a prisoner of the Indians.

I wonder if Tim is alive. I have to hope so, as he has come to mean a lot to me, Beth muses.

As part of her hope chest, Beth adds hand-hemmed towels and embroidered pillowcases to the many items already in the chest in Boston. It is an occupation young women are encouraged to start working on from their early teens. Crocheted doilies and dresser scarves, dishes handed down from parents or an aunt, pots and pans and blankets are other items. Beth has often thought of her wedding dress and has a design in mind. She isn't sure yet who she will be marrying but she begins work on her wedding gown. It is a beautiful periwinkle blue material, soft with a little sheen. It will have lace around the neckline and at the bottom of the long sleeves. There will be a pattern of seed pearls and clear beads on the bodice. It is a big job and Mary and Beth work on it together when they have an hour each day. While Tim is gone it gives Beth something pleasant to think about. Mary and Beth have some lively sisterly conversations as they work together.

Winter passes into spring. The water in the Kentucky River is flowing swiftly and has flooded over its banks as the ice melts and begins to break up. The settlers are glad they built the fort on a plateau away from the river and there is no danger to those in the fort. Some of the outlying cabins have problems with flooding because they built too close to the river.

Every morning someone from each cabin makes the trip down to the spring to fill pails with water, often the women have to make an additional trip each day, one of the reasons the women keep encouraging the men to finish digging the well. A few more feet are dug and then the project is abandoned.

Chapter 23 – Escape

In the meantime, Tim is living in an Indian village and thinking about his life, and writing it in a journal. "We are always guarded and tied up at night. Wood chopping is one of our chores, but as the days flow into each other, we go on hunts for meat, being used to carry the kill back to camp, not being trusted with a rifle for the actual kill. The first two weeks are the biggest adjustment settling into life in the village. Gradually we are guarded less when it is seen that we aren't trying to escape. We have to bide our time."

Good thing Beth and I decided to only be friends, Tim thinks. *It would be terrible for me to be gone all this time and have her worrying about me, wondering if I was even alive, if I was coming back. On the other hand, she will probably be wondering about me anyway as we get along so well together, enjoying spending time together, doing many different activities. We can talk about a lot of different subjects too. I'll keep looking for the opportunity to escape and make my way back to Boonesborough.*

"It is on the minds of all of us that we will escape one day and return to our own people. I pick up a pebble each day to keep track of the days. In the evening, I take out my pebbles and count them up, seven, fourteen, twenty-one, twenty-eight, will I ever escape?" he notes in his journal.

Tim's time finally comes to escape and he strikes out for the fort.

He has learned how to cover his trail and uses all the tricks he can to make his escape and not be caught. He walks down streams, walks over rocky areas, always heading in the direction of Boonesborough. He brought a little dried meat with him, all that he was able to save from his meals. That lasts for the first day, supplemented with water from the streams. The second day is tougher with only water to drink, but the burning desire to get home is always present to keep him moving as swiftly as possible. He is able to find plenty of berries to help fill his stomach and knows some plants growing in the wild that are filling. The fifth day he sees the welcome sight of the fort walls and safety. He is exhausted but so thankful to be back.

"Hello, the fort," he yells. "Open the gate for me."

"Who are you?" It is dusk and the individual is not in plain view.

"It's Tim, the blacksmith's helper."

"Tim! It's been a long time! Come on in." The gates are opened and then shut again behind him. All the men quickly gather at the Tavern to hear his story.

"We were surprised by a large party of braves, being completely surrounded with far too many of them to make resistance of any use, other than for us all to get killed. Many of us were adopted into the Indian tribes."

"What about Ronald Calloway? Do you know what happened to Tom and John Luttrell? What about John Floyd and the Pogue brothers?" Tim is peppered with questions.

"I saw Ronald about two weeks ago when we were out hunting. In the last month I saw the Luttrells and Pogues at different times. The four Williams brothers were with me in the same camp, but we were always prisoners and kept apart. We could never plan an escape together. It was always each man for himself."

"What about the Bentons? What about Ballard?" others asked.

"I don't believe I saw Jesse Benton, Bland Ballard or Pemberton Rollins after the first day. They were among the first group to be taken away. It was only as the day progressed that it became apparent what was happening when a small group of men were taken off on a branching trail every few miles. I think some might have been taken on to Detroit.

"It's been a long trek back. I suspect others will escape one day. I suggest we get this fort in tip-top shape, filling in the gaps in the stockade walls, finish digging the well inside the fort and in the meantime get as much water in storage in the fort as we can manage. Let's work together to make our lives here as secure as possible." Tim has a meal at Richard's Café, then sleeps for a few hours before heading to the O'Neills to find Beth.

Beth is so ecstatic to see Tim. She has a big hug for him this time. Those six weeks had seemed long, with the uncertainty hovering of when or if Tim would return. No one had been left dead at the salt licks, so that allowed for hope and most of the time Beth succeeded in being cheerful and hopeful.

"You learned some things from the Indians while you lived with them, Tim."

"Yes, it was a time when I was very observant, taking in everything I could, both for survival at the time and always looking for the chance to escape."

"It certainly is great to have you back," Beth says as she beams at him.

"It is great to be back. Although I was treated okay, I was a prisoner, always longing to be free."

"Freedom is something to treasure," Beth agrees.

After Tim's long capture, his escape after months as a prisoner, and his successful return to Boonesborough, he has another conflict, feeling it is not fair to a woman to cause her such anguish. Tim is sad, remembering his mother's words when he returned from that fatal trip away from home several years ago, convinced again that he and Beth are meant to be good friends only. Now that Tim has returned, there is more hope for others to come back.

Every week another man returns, having escaped from the Indians and made the journey back. It is encouraging to the women to have the men return.

Chapter 24 – Another Surprise

"A group is arriving!" the sentry calls out. Everyone within hearing distance rushes towards the gate. It is a Sunday afternoon at the end of May and many people are outside enjoying the beautiful weather.

Beth has just called on Ruth and they are planning a walk down to the spring. They eagerly rush forward to greet the newcomers. There are about thirty people in the group but all of a sudden Beth lets out a gasp.

"What's the matter Beth?" Ruth asks in concern. "Is there someone you recognize?"

"It's my father! And my mother! It has been two years since I saw them. I never expected to see them in Boonesborough." Beth rushes forward to hug her father as soon as he steps off the horse he is riding. Her father holds her tight and then helps his wife down so that she can also greet her daughter.

"Look who I brought with me," Jacob points behind him.

"Mr. and Mrs. Brownley, how wonderful to see you. Katie will be thrilled. She is watching the children for Mary and Mike this afternoon. I'll take over for her in a few minutes," Beth smiles in welcome. She looks a little further and also sees the Smileys, the Townsends and the Fultons. Won't all of the girls be excited! She hugs each of them in turn.

At that moment, Mary and Mike arrive and Mary is enveloped in a long hug by her father. "It's been too long, Mary. I have missed you so much. What a thrill to see you! You are looking well." Mary just clings to him as the tears run down her face. He lets her go so that she can greet her mother. Mike shakes hands with Mr. Worthington, the Smileys, Townsends and Fultons. He knew them all in Boston but it has been a long time.

"You must be tired after your long trip. Let's get you settled in and you can freshen up before supper which you will all be having with us tonight," Mike says as he leads the way. "We have two cabins with a connecting door for two couples. Then we have three places for the others. Who would like to stay together here? The Pogues have farms and have offered the use of their cabin while you are in Boonesborough." The Smileys and Fultons agree to share the Pogue cabins. Their belongings are unloaded and brought inside and they are left to get themselves organized.

"Mom and Dad, we have a special place for you to stay. It is across the fort and fairly close to our cabin. With all of our children, and the girls sharing meals with us, we don't have room for you to stay and have any space for yourselves. James and Sally Ellis are delighted to have you stay with them." They arrive at the door and James and Sally are there to welcome them in and help get them settled. Mary stays behind to give them a hand.

Mike takes the Brownleys and Townsends to the far end of the fort where they are welcomed by Flanders and Jemima Calloway and John and Fanny Holder. "Take your time getting organized and settled in. Someone will be by in a couple of hours to bring you to our cabin for supper."

"No need to send someone, Mike. I will be happy to bring them up to your place," Flanders offers.

"That would be a big help. Thanks. I will leave you now and see you later." Mike heads back to their cabin. In the meantime, Beth has found the girls and told them there are visitors in town. She sends

Brenda and Patricia over to the Pogue cabin as she has kept an eye on where Mike has taken people. She lets them be surprised when they arrive. She sends Katie and Barbara to Jemima's as it looked like that was where Mike was heading. When Mike gets back to the cabin, she is free to leave and go to see her parents at the Ellis'. Beth and Mary spend another half hour with their parents and then leave them to get settled in while they work on supper preparations.

Beth and Mary are talking non-stop. "Mary, you knew they were all coming. You have kept another surprise for me. What a wonderful surprise for myself and my friends! Who would have thought two years ago that Dad and Mom and their friends would be in Boonesborough?"

"It has been two years since you saw Mother and Father. It has been much longer for me. It wasn't until I actually saw them that I realized how much I have missed them," Mary says as the tears of joy run down her cheeks again. Beth gives her a warm hug.

"When I started out on my trip here in the spring of 1776, you know that Father travelled with me for the first three days. He said at the time that he wished he could make the whole trip with me. I had forgotten about that until now," Beth continues.

"It is great that Robert is able to look after the family business for six weeks so that Father could make this trip. I am amazed that Mother has come too. She was never as adventuresome as Father."

"Mother was always rather timid. When I read your letter to her asking me to come here, her first reaction was negative. She did come around and assist with preparations, add items for me to bring along, and offer words of encouragement," Beth adds.

"Father has a way with words. His excitement for this trip was enough to have the Smileys, Fultons, Townsends and Brownleys come along. It is great that they each have an older son or two to help in their businesses for the time they are away," Mary shares.

"Have you and Mike made any plans for when the parents are here?" Beth asks.

"Everything is tentative, not knowing the exact day they would arrive. An overnight trip is planned to the Pogues and Stagners, possibly a canoe trip to the Calloways, a hunting trip for the men, and walks in the area. We can probably pick wild strawberries and raspberries and maybe plums will be ripe."

"All of us will want to share what we have been doing in Boonesborough, at least with our Mothers," Beth continues. Maybe they would like to try some of the things we have been learning. For sure our mothers have never done any rug hooking, working on a loom, nor have they ever used a sewing machine."

"We will be a little crowded in here tonight. There will be twenty-one of us, but I wanted to have everyone here for their first night. Jemima and Fanny will have meals for the couples staying with them. James and Sally will have some meals with Father and Mother but we will often have them here. I am not sure about those staying at the Pogue cabin. They may join us for meals as well, or they may cook some of their own meals."

"There is always the Holt Campbell Tavern and Richard's Café. We have lots of options," Beth adds.

"The food is almost ready. Mike can you go and round up the girls and their parents? Here are the Brownleys and Townsends now. And look, here comes Brenda and Patricia with their parents. They know what time supper is! Looks like you will just need to collect our parents, Mike."

"I'll be back in a few minutes," Mike calls as he heads to the Ellis cabin.

"Is it supper time already?" Jacob asks. "We have been having a great visit with James and Sally. Are you ready Sally?" She smiles and nods her agreement as she stands up, takes her husband's hand and they follow Mike to his home.

Everyone finds a chair around the table and Mike and Mary stand together with their arms around each other. They bow their heads and offer thanks for the safe arrival of their families and for the meal they are about to eat. The platters and bowls are passed around for everyone to help themselves, with the children being assisted whenever needed. It's a merry group around the table with many conversations going on. After all appetites have been satisfied, the men help Mike to dismantle the extra table arrangements so there is room for them to sit around the fireplace. The young girls help clean up, insisting that their mothers go and sit. In short order everything is done and all are enjoying time together.

Soon it will be bedtime for the children and Mary notices that the mothers are looking tired. Mary nudges Mike and asks him to send everyone to their lodgings. Brenda and Patricia are happy to take their parents to the cabin, and Barbara and Katie look forward to the trip to the end of the fort to get the Brownleys and Townsends settled for the night. Beth offers to put the children to bed so that Mike and Mary can spend some time with their parents and the Ellis'. It will be a good break for Mary after all the hard work she has put in on the preparations.

After an hour, Mike and Mary say their goodnights to Mary's parents and the Ellis'. Mike suggests, "How about a coffee and treat at Dan's?"

"That would be a lovely way to finish off the day! I don't feel quite ready to head home yet," Mary agrees. In a little while they walk to the cabin hand-in-hand with Mike stopping part way to draw Mary into a warm hug and a deep kiss.

The next morning Brenda and Patricia call on their parents to bring them to Mike and Mary's for breakfast. The other three couples are being looked after by their hosts and hostesses. Today has been planned as a low key one with a chance to get to know the fort and some of the people. The first stop will be at the Ellis' to pick up Jacob and Sally Worthington. Then Beth introduces everyone to Lydia and Richard Patterson and she stays to put in a morning's work at the seamstress shop. The rest meet up with the Brownleys and Townsends and the girls give them a tour of Boonesborough. The last stop before lunch is the General Store. The women talk among themselves and decide that they will be back on their own to spend more time here. Soon the men are calling them to go and they head to the Holt Campbell Tavern for lunch.

A social evening is planned for the Saturday evening for everyone in Boonesborough and the surrounding area. Everyone will have a chance to meet the visitors and have some fun around a bonfire. Charlie has his fiddle, Mabel is at the harpsichord, Mike O'Neill plays his harmonica, and Ben his accordion. Barbara and Beth are encouraged to sing a few duets and let their voices harmonize for the enjoyment of the listeners. Mabel draws Patricia to the harpsichord for her to play a few classical solos.

Just before it is time to eat, the visitors all gather together and Jack Worthington raises his arms and calls for quiet. "We have all looked forward to this trip to Kentucky. Our daughters Beth and Mary, as well Katie, Brenda, Patricia and Barbara, have written to us and whetted our appetite for seeing it for ourselves. We have heard about many people who have touched the lives of our daughters and it has been wonderful to meet some of you already and now be able to put a face to a name."

Mike O'Neill takes over from his father-in-law, "We have enjoyed having our sister, Beth, with us for the past two years and we are happy to hear that she has agreed to stay with us longer." There is much clapping and cheering at this announcement as Beth has been a positive influence in the lives of many. "We wanted to do something really special for her." Mike and Mary draw Beth between them for a warm squeeze.

"Tomorrow is Beth's birthday and Ruth has prepared a lovely cake to celebrate the occasion." Mabel picks out the cords for "Happy Birthday" and everyone breaks into song. "We'll have some of that delicious dessert in a few minutes," Jack continues. "First we want to unveil a special gift that we brought along from Boston with us. Richard Patterson has been helpful in assembling it for us.

"We have tried to keep it a secret and have told only a few people about it. I don't think our friends have even shared it with their daughters. Am I right?" There are nods of agreement from the parents and shaking of heads from the girls.

"I think Richard was even able to keep it a surprise from Lydia, although that was more difficult as he had these mysterious times away from home that he didn't share with her." Richard smiles and gives Lydia a squeeze.

"Okay, Beth, you can pull off the cover." Beth eagerly moves forward, having no idea what might be underneath. Beth cannot believe her eyes! It is a sewing machine! Her very own! She touches it lovingly and her face just glows. Her parents, Mike and Mary, the Smileys, Brownleys, Townsends and Fultons have been watching Beth and are thrilled that the surprise means even more to Beth than they had hoped. It was well worth the effort of packing it here.

"Speech! Speech!" calls someone in the crowd.

Beth blushes as she turns to her family. "This is the most wonderful surprise I have ever had. And I have had some very special ones in the past year with my friends' arrival," she says as she turns to smile at them, "and then the arrival last week of my parents and family friends," she acknowledges them. "I will cherish this gift and produce many lovely outfits on it. A big thank you to all of you." She moves forward to hug each of them as the crowd cheers.

"Food is ready. Line up and enjoy."

A little later Lydia comes up to Beth and says, "I hope this doesn't mean I am going to lose my excellent assistant."

"I don't have any plans in that direction at this time, Lydia," Beth assures her. "But who knows what may occur in the future. Are either of your daughters interested in learning more about the seamstress trade? They are both very proficient on the loom. Are either of them drawn to the sewing machine?"

"To tell you the truth, I haven't encouraged either of them in any of my activities. I'm not sure why. I'll approach them on Monday morning and see what they have to say. They are old enough to help me out. I guess I never wanted them forced to do what I like to do, and now that we are talking about it, I believe I may have discouraged them from even showing an interest. Thanks for your help, Beth, in getting me to think about it."

"That's what friends are for," Beth smiles as she gives her a warm hug.

Many people come up to Beth to personally wish her a happy birthday and to offer some personal words of what she has meant to them in the time she has been in Boonesborough. Beth never realized how much she has come to mean to the people. Beth treasures each comment and each individual who shares with her. What a wonderful evening is spent together with the people of Boonesborough.

It is almost the middle of June, a perfect time for a weekend trip to the Pogue and Stagner farms. Abraham and Sarah Smiley and James and Joan Fulton are especially looking forward to meeting them and to thank them personally for the use of their cabin. Sarah and Joan have been experimenting with cooking some of their own meals, usually breakfast and lunch. It is handy having the connecting door between the cabins.

They will travel with horses and wagons and stay overnight for an early return the next day. Mike and Mary are coming along with their four children. Ruth Hancock and Paul Holt are part of the group, as well as Tim. Eight soldiers can be spared from the fort and will accompany them on horseback. Mary and the girls have prepared food to take with them and Ruth has been busy making cookies and loaf cakes and has along six loaves of bread. There is one big wagon with bales of straw around the outer edges with blankets covering the straw. The children sit in the middle of the wagon. There is a buggy to hold six adults and that's where Tim, Beth, Ruth, Paul, Katie and Brenda ride.

It's a merry group heading out with everyone talking excitedly.

The two hour trip passes quickly and soon they see the Pogue farm a short distance ahead. The noise the group is making gives an early announcement of visitors arriving. Brothers John and William Pogue hurry in from the fields to see who is coming. Laura and Jane gather their children and head outside to welcome everyone. Barney Stagner is helping the Pogues in the fields today.

The wagons pull up the laneway and all are happy to climb down and stretch their legs. Everyone is introduced and invited to sit under the shade trees beside Laura and Bill's cabin. Cool water from the nearby spring is provided for everyone to quench their thirst. Barney hops on a horse and hurries home to bring Helen and their four children to join in the festivities. All work stops to enjoy the break from routine. The children are playing nearby and the men have gone off together to check out the farm. The soldiers are keeping an alert eye out for any sign of Indians.

"We are so thrilled to meet the parents of five lovely women," Jane says. "We have shared many hours together with them."

"Patricia has made some lovely rugs during her time out here," Joan Fulton says. "You have been wonderful teachers for her, Jane, Laura and Helen."

"We have enjoyed spending our time with Patricia. She has been so eager to learn what we can show her. She has taught us a few things along the way. When you teach another person how to do something that you have been doing for years, you learn important things when the other person asks questions," Laura adds.

"Things we never thought of had to be examined, explained and ideas only half formed and done automatically needed revision," Helen interjects. "We have a few more designs for you Patricia. Are you able to transfer them to the burlap easily?"

"Katie has been helping me as she is better at drawing than I am. I have the knack to make the picture come alive in the rugs."

"It is great to be able to keep learning throughout our lives," Sarah

Smiley joins in the conversation. "Patricia started me working on a rug on my second day."

"That's a new skill for you to take back with you when you return to Boston. Good for you."

"What about the rest of you? Have you started on any projects?" Helen asks.

"I always enjoyed drawing," Mary O'Neill says, "But with the young children I never pursued it. Katie has really learned a lot from James Ellis and I am going to start lessons once a week with him."

"That's great to hear Mary," Beth encourages. "While we are around, we can watch the children for you for a morning or an afternoon, although my time is limited working with Lydia."

"We are always happy to mind the children," Brenda pipes up and the other girls nod in agreement. "Just let us know when you need us and we are glad to help."

"You have been so warm and friendly and helpful to us while we have been in Boonesborough, Mary," Barbara says. "We want to contribute wherever we can."

"Speaking of Lydia, she has been a welcome addition to the town. We have used her services a few times. The girls were all at the shop one day when Laura and I stopped in to be measured for a gown," Jane adds. "Lydia taught them how to take the measurements."

"I have been doing some work on Patricia's loom," Joan Fulton adds. "That's a relaxing occupation."

"Although it is not a new skill for me," Dorothy Townsend adds, "I have been working with Barbara on some quilting. She has shown me how she uses the sewing machine to do part of the work. That is certainly a new idea. She is planning to take me to Lydia's this coming week for us to work on it together."

"Actually Mom, we will be able to use Beth's new machine while she is at work. That way we won't be slowing Lydia down. Beth and

I talked about it yesterday," Barbara informs.

"I have seen a few sewing machines in Boston, but I have never used one," Dorothy adds. "Helen, Jane and Laura, we brought a sewing machine from Boston for Beth for her birthday."

"That was a wonderful surprise for me!" Beth exclaims. "I have had only a few minutes so far to use it." The women express their happiness for her.

"There is so much to see and do around here," Catherine Brownley adds. "We always thought of Boonesborough being in the wilderness, which it is, but never would have imagined that there were so many opportunities available. The girls peaked our interest over the past few months."

"Now you have an idea of why we wanted to stay out here longer," Katie adds. "We have each developed a skill to take back home with us."

"Our girls have enjoyed the few times working with Brenda. They talk about it for days afterwards," Helen Stagner comments. "Margaret made her first batch of butter the other day and used her own butter mould. Mary helped to fill her new mould. The rest of the butter went into my plain moulds."

"We never knew there would be quite as much excitement as there was in making those moulds. The girls were eager to do as much as they possibly could. Margaret actually carved out the design in her mould," Brenda added to the conversation. "Even the seven year olds wanted to use the sharp tool and carefully make their designs."

"With a little encouragement, it is amazing what children will try," said Sally Worthington.

"Let's go inside and see what we can put together for lunch. I imagine you are all hungry and the men will be back soon. They always know when it is time to eat! Girls will you stay outside and keep an eye on the children?" Laura asks. The girls agree and the mothers head inside.

"It looks like you brought a lot of food with you. Let's organize it and see what we should add. Jane, do you have enough fresh milk?"

"Yes, Laura, I'll take one of the women with me and we'll bring it from my house." Jane and Joan Fulton head out.

"Sally and Catherine will you pump some water from the well? Here are two buckets." Off they go to fulfill the request.

Sarah, Dorothy, Mary and Helen work with Laura in organizing the food. The desserts are put aside on the counter. Plates and cutlery are put out. It will be buffet style as there are too many people to sit at the table. The weather is conducive to sitting outside. Soon everything is ready, the children are called to wash up and sure enough the men are in sight of the cabin. William asks the blessing on the food and then the plates are filled and everyone finds a place to sit and eat.

Katie, Brenda, Barbara, Patricia and Beth eagerly set about cleaning up after the meal. Barbara enjoys washing the dishes while Katie and Brenda dry them. Patricia and Beth help Laura put the leftover food in the cool cellar. They talk with Jane about what they will prepare for the supper meal which will be at her cabin.

The women and girls want to see the vegetable garden and the barn and the animals to get a deeper appreciation for the life lived out here so far from town.

Laura and Jane each have two extra rooms in their large two storey cabins for four couples to sleep. Helen and Barney have one extra room. There are plenty of blankets to make pallets in the large living rooms at Laura and Jane's. The young women can stay at Laura's, and the young men at Jane's. Twelve year old John Stagner is happy to have ten year old James O'Neill bunk with him. The O'Neill's will use the spare room at the Stagners where everyone will meet for an eleven o'clock feast the next day before it is time to head back to Boonesborough.

The Stagners and Pogues are so thrilled to have visitors and show it with their fine hospitality. In the evening after supper there is some impromptu entertainment. Patricia plays the harpsichord while Barbara and Beth sing some duets. Mike O'Neill brings out his harmonica and accompanies them. They get a sing-along going and the children eagerly join in the familiar songs.

There is a ten minute ride to the Stagners and the soldiers agree to accompany the Stagners and the O'Neills. The soldiers make the trip without incident and return to Jane and John's for the night. Half of them will be on sentry duty first, and then will switch in the middle of the night. All have been trained to be alert the hour before dawn. There is no point taking any chances.

Ruth is up early to make fresh biscuits to supplement the oatmeal, eggs and bacon that Laura is preparing with the help of the other girls. The coffee brewing is enough to bring the Worthingtons and Fullers down. With the table extension Will quickly puts up, there is enough room for the fourteen of them to sit down together for breakfast.

Soon it is time to head for the Stagners for lunch. Their house is situated on high ground and there is a lovely view of the countryside. The grain is ripening in the fields. Many fresh vegetables are ready in the garden and are a tasty supplement to the staples of deer, moose or bear meat. Chickens are kept penned up at night and they provide eggs and meat for the family.

Chapter 25 – Return

"Hello, Fort," calls a long-unheard voice. "Open the gate. It's Daniel."

The gate is quickly opened to admit him. Daniel wants to see Rebecca first and then calls a meeting of all the adults. But before he goes to his cabin, he is informed that his family left two months before for North Carolina having given him up for dead. This greatly saddens him.

"Tim, good to see you are back. It's been a long time," Daniel says as he shakes his hand.

The men head to the Holt Campbell Inn and Tavern to celebrate with a drink and to hear all about Daniel's time away.

"We were first taken to Old Chillicothe, on the Miami, where the Shawnee chief Blackfish had me run the gauntlet, and then adopted me into his family under an imposing but painful ceremonial." The Chief liked Daniel's courage and determination. Daniel pointed to his head to show that all his hair, except a tuft four inches across on the crown of the head, was plucked out; the remaining hair grew to a length where feathers and ribbons could be added. "I had to wash in the river to cleanse me from the taint of white blood. My face was painted, and Blackfish made a speech to complete the ceremony.

"I was kindly treated by the Indians, but I sure missed my family and friends in Boonesborough. When I discovered that the Indians were planning to attack Boonesborough with a large group, I decided to attempt to escape to do what I could to save my family and friends."

"How long has it taken you to get here?"

"I have been travelling for five days. I started out with a horse and then carried on by foot, always being conscious of hiding my trail to elude any pursuers."

Some of the men express doubts about Boone's loyalty. They accuse him of surrendering the salt making party and then living quite happily among the Shawnees for several months. This idea is especially strengthened by the men who escaped and made it back to Boonesborough telling about how Daniel told the men not to resist the Indians, and even told the Indians that Boonesborough would surrender.

"What happened to John Calloway? He's my nephew and I haven't seen or heard from him," questions Colonel Richard Calloway.

"What about my nephew Ben Logan? Do you know where he is? You surrendered them at the salt licks. Where is he now?" Captain Benjamin Logan sneers.

Tim always stands by Daniel, having gone through similar rites of initiation, knowing it hadn't been a picnic living with the Indians. Mike remains a true friend as well.

Tim has to fight his attitude towards the men knowing that he has to put those negative thoughts behind him. Beth is a real help encouraging him to let them go, encouraging cooperation and teamwork, even as she encourages Dorothy to see the good in the men who have survived their time among the Indians.

Daniel, Tim and Mike have a private meeting while Daniel has a meal with Mary and Beth. He asks Tim to go with him to get his family; Tim immediately agrees.

"We must prepare for an attack. The Shawnees will be coming soon. Mike, you are in charge of the preparations. Make sure all the walls of the fort are secure with all the gaps in the stockade filled in.

Have all the animals brought inside after they have eaten their fill of grass each day with lookouts watching for the first sign of trouble. Harvest whatever food you can from outside the walls. Bring as much water into the fort as possible. Can you think of anything else?"

"We'll have to make more bullets and gunpowder."

"Great. I'll bring some back with me if I can. Can you think of anything else? I want to travel light and return as quickly as possible with my family."

"Go with God's protection, Daniel. May you return swiftly."

That evening Tim says to Beth, "It was great to have Daniel come back today."

"We never knew if he would come back. Even Rebecca had given up about his return."

"He has suffered a lot since February. I know what it was like running the gauntlet. It was not pleasant. How long it must have taken to pull out all the hairs on his head."

"That must have been painful for quite some time."

"We were always watched although our captors were lulled into less watchfulness as the weeks wore on. They expected us to stay with them for the rest of our lives. They didn't understand that the white man would never be an Indian. We always wanted to return to our own people."

"Look at Hannah Wilkes. She was captured and lived with the Chickasaw Indians for fifteen years. She thought her husband was dead. Jonas thought she was dead."

"It wasn't easy for them to take up their former lives where they left off. There was a lot of healing, forgiving and accepting that had to go on," Tim responds. "Look at the suspicion there was on Daniel when he returned today. They thought he was living the life of a king. Sure, he is an outdoorsman. He loves to hunt and trap and fish. But he had a whole family of his own back in Boonesborough."

"He must have thought about Rebecca, Lavina, Becky, Israel, Danny and Jesse every day wondering how they were managing with him gone so long. And even though Jemima and Susanna are married, he would be thinking of them as well."

"He was often gone for weeks at a time. Rebecca was often alone. But this time was different. He wasn't just out hunting but had been captured and his fate was unknown. I'm leaving with him in the morning to bring his family back. You look after yourself while I'm gone. Stay close to the fort."

"I'll miss you Tim. No evening walks and talks at the end of each day. But you will be a good companion for Daniel on the trip."

"We'll take two horses and make the trip as fast as possible."

"I'll ask Mike to take the news to Will and Steve and the Bryans of Daniel's return. With Daniel making the trip to get his family, I believe Will and Sue, Steve and Anne will get married after you get back. There will be more than one thing to celebrate," Beth says.

Tim pulls Beth into his arms and holds her tightly for a long time before walking her back to the cabin. He almost says he loves her but doesn't want to go against the arrangements they have made with each other.

Tim and Daniel set off the next morning on horseback, making good time on the now much travelled roads. Daniel is eager to find Rebecca. What a welcome he receives, the hug warm and tight, unbelief quickly changing to joy, a beaming smile on Rebecca's face. They gather a wagonload of food and ammunition and leave the next day for Boonesborough, realizing the urgency of the need for their return. With the wagon, it takes twice as long to return as it had for Daniel and Tim to make the trip, but within two weeks, they are welcomed back to the fort.

Beth has thoroughly cleaned the Boone cabin and has everything ready for them to take up their daily life. Tim and Beth have their own reunion that evening with a walk around Boonesborough, holding hands, gazing at the stars, finding a private nook for a long, warm hug. Sometimes Tim feels like he wants to do more than hug Beth, but those are the boundaries they agreed on several months ago and he wants to continue to honour them.

Will and Steve stand with their brides for the wedding ceremony the day after the return of the Boone family. Beth and Tim are standing side-by-side and Tim reaches for Beth's hand. They still stubbornly insist they are only friends, but both of them feel the beginnings of longing as they listen to Squire Boone's words. Beth has made herself a cheery yellow summer dress with a flowery bonnet. They have a fantastic time at the dance after the meal, thoroughly enjoying the different rhythms and speeds of the music. They dance well together. Will and Steve each have a dance with Beth, while Tim takes Sue and then Anne for a spin around the dance area.

The jokes are made to Tim, "You better ask Beth or someone else is going to make a move on her. She's a lovely girl." Tim smiles but makes no comment. Beth never sits out a dance as there are many eager bachelors ready to be her partner. Tim tries not to let it bother him when other men are dancing with her, but he has his jealous moments. He keeps his eyes on her all the time. Other than the brides and the bridesmaids Tim reserves dances only with Beth and her four friends. Whenever it is Tim's turn to dance with her, Beth feels lighter, happier and more relaxed. Some of the men are somewhat clumsy, some only shuffle along. With Tim, Beth floats and twirls and her heart sings. Ruth Hancock and Paul Holt are constant companions and Ruth is nearly always dancing with Paul. It looks like another wedding soon.

"Don't Naomi and Ruth look lovely in their pink gowns? They are a nice contrast to the brides. What a thrill for them all to be together for this double wedding," Beth comments to Tim.

"It was a great reunion for all of them last May. Now their family is extending with the addition of two more sisters," Tim responds.

Beth is happy that her friends and their parents are here to join in this celebration. It is a special thrill for her to be able to introduce

Daniel and Rebecca Boone to her parents and their friends.

"Your name has become well-known in Boston circles, Daniel. I am pleased to meet you," Jacob Worthington says.

"You have two lovely daughters. Mary has been living near us for years and we have shared many hours together with her and Mike," Daniel says.

"It has been good these last few weeks to be close to her. She has been gone from home a long time," Sally and Jacob agree.

"Beth has fit right in and been a real help to her sister and she has reached out to many of us and has a warm place in our hearts," Rebecca adds. "Let's get together tomorrow evening so that we can talk more. Come over to our cabin after supper," Daniel and Rebecca invite the Worthingtons. During the course of the evening, the Brownleys, Smileys, Fultons, Townsends and O'Neill adults are also invited to the Boones' the following evening. They are able to spend time in interesting conversations about Daniel's adventures in North Carolina and Kentucky. Daniel has many stories to tell.

Tim wants more than his "friendship only" agreement with Beth. He will have to start working on her. Flanders and John made the move last year to get married and now Will and Steve. Each of them is beaming from ear to ear every time Tim sees them. There must be something to getting married. He decides he will try to kiss Beth again on their next evening out. If only her situation back east could be straightened out. He has spoken to Mr. Worthington about his feelings for Beth and been assured that everything will work out, probably by the fall.

All too soon the six weeks are up and her parents and friends are planning their trip back to Boston. Tim and Ruth are very aware of the turmoil this will cause for Beth and plan to be an extra support to her at this trying time. Mary suspects that she is pregnant again and Beth feels it would be wise to stay and help out. It was a tough decision to make as she is really torn between staying in Boonesborough and returning with her parents, friends and their parents to Boston. After having her parents here for a visit, and after having her four friends with her for the past six months, it will be very quiet for her.

Chapter 26 – Siege

Preparations continue over the next two months, never knowing what reserves of strength will be required of them in the coming days. Blackfish knew that if Daniel came with settlers, more and more would come and the land would no longer belong to the Shawnees.

The British want control of the colonies after ousting the French, but the settlers want to become their own independent country and have a say in their own government. The colonists are made of sturdy stuff and don't just cave in when trials come. Being a pioneer means sacrifice and trials are part of life.

The rains begin during the last week of August. The ground is soggy and everything is damp. Apples, peaches and plums are picked in the woods during short breaks in the rain, often the pickers end up soaked to the skin before getting back to the cabins. Some of the fruit is dried or preserved for later use; some is made into apple butter and fruit pies. Other fruit is mixed in cakes. Ruth and the older children try to get out every afternoon so they will have fruit for special items for the bakeshop. Beth often goes along with the group, having arranged her time working with Lydia in the mornings during this time. Now that the wedding dresses have been made, Lydia is not quite as busy and Beth has more free time. Often she has her nieces and nephews to care for as Mary is even sicker than with Ellie. Sometimes she brings five year old Isaac, three year old Sarah, and one and a half year old Ellie with her and they are content to play while Beth works with Lydia.

Tim values Beth's opinion and they continue to enjoy walks and talks together daily, fitting time in whenever they have a few minutes to spare in the day. The well is finally finished and that is a big help to the women who can draw some of their water inside the fort rather than having to make the trek down to the spring several times a day lugging the heavy pails up the slope to the fort. Most of the women still enjoy the walk to the spring once during the day for a change of pace.

Tim and Beth often hold hands, sometimes walk and talk, sometimes find a quiet spot to sit, other times just stand and gaze at the sunset or sunrise, or the beauty of nature around the fort.

At the beginning of September, the letter from Boston arrives telling of Charles's engagement to the girl of his choice, Diana Campbell. They are to be married the following spring. Although Beth is happy to have closure to the situation in Boston, there is a little twinge of hurt that a plan by her parents, that she has been well aware of for several years, has not happened and she has an adjustment to make in her mind. There is a little sadness connected to it, even though Beth has been having doubts about the parental arrangement for several months. She decides to go for a walk to the spring to think things through. Just as she is heading out the gate, Ruth calls to her and asks if she can join her. Maybe Ruth's company will be a good thing she thinks as she smiles and waits for Ruth to catch up. Ruth is her usual bubbly self as they start out, telling about their latest happenings in the bakeshop. Paul Holt's name comes up often in Ruth's conversation.

All of a sudden Ruth stops talking mid-sentence sensing that something is bothering her friend. "Okay, Beth. I have had my say, now tell me what's bothering you. I have been chattering away since we left the fort and you have been lost in your own world."

Beth smiles briefly before she begins to share with Ruth about her upbringing and her parents' plans for her and Charles. "I decided to walk to think it through. It's one thing to have a decision made and another to accept it. I'm not saying it's a bad thing. It's just that now there is an end to the dream and there is a letdown. Funny how the mind works isn't it? I have wanted this very thing for months and now that it has happened there is some sadness too."

Ruth listens intently while Beth talks on for a few minutes, and then she responds, "That's only natural with a situation you have grown up with. Give yourself another half hour of sadness and then put a smile on your face and look ahead to the future."

"Ruth you have really helped," Beth laughs. "I was feeling silly for being sad but you have reassured me and helped me through this."

"That's what friends are for. Let's fill these buckets and head back to the fort. It looks like it is going to rain again soon. We have had a lot of rain in the last couple of weeks." The girls hurry back to the fort arriving as the first few drops begin to fall. They each rush off to their homes.

"Mary, it's starting to rain. Ruth and I had to hurry back. We had a good chat. You know I got a letter today Mary. Mother sent me a separate one from the family one because she wanted to tell me that Charles is engaged to a girl from Boston. I was sad to hear it at first but Ruth helped me through it."

"Now you have closure and can move on with your life," Mary states.

"You never know how you will respond to situations until you are presented with them. I never thought this would make me sad."

"It's been on your mind for years. Now it has ended. It's okay for you to experience a little sadness. Do you feel like you have been jilted?" Mary asks.

"In a way, yes, I guess I do feel that I wasn't good enough for Charles. In spite of our parents' wishes, which were commonly known, he didn't choose me."

That night while Tim and Beth are walking around Boonesborough, Tim notices that Beth is very quiet. They find their favourite bench and Tim asks her what is wrong. Beth tells him about the letter and says how it has upset her. She is still trying to come to grips with it.

"It's like I have been rejected, as though I'm not wanted." In response to that comment, Tim draws Beth into his arms and this time he does more than hug her. He kisses her long and deep and she melts in his arms. The stars shine brighter, the air crackles, her blood courses through her veins, her heart soars.

"Wow! You are one special young woman."

"Oh, Tim! That was amazing."

"You have lots to offer to the right man. Now it's time to get you home." Each evening they now end their walks with a deep kiss.

A week after the letter arrived, the Indian alert bell rings out, and with stomachs clenching everyone gathers quickly at their battle stations. Before any shots are fired, negotiations are called for. Daniel, Tim and a few others leave the fort to meet with the native representatives. The Indians want Boonesborough to surrender, but the settlers are determined to fight. This is their home and they love Kentucky, knowing there is room for them and the Indians in this land.

Four hundred Indians and twelve French-Canadian companions hired by the British surround the fort for the attack. The British didn't want the settlers to go into Kentucky. They didn't agree with the Cherokee selling their land to the white settlers. There are many different tribes of Indians. There is a treaty for the Shawnee to stay north of the Kentucky River and it is the land south of the Kentucky River that was sold to the Transylvania Company. But the Shawnee are the worst attackers of the white settlers.

Chief Blackfish figures that Daniel Boone won't fight him but will surrender and return to his tribe since he adopted him as a son. Just goes to show how wrong he was. Daniel was his own man, had his own family and his own way of life, only enduring life with the Shawnee until he could escape, having no desire to return to a life living with the Shawnees.

The negotiation team has to appear to consider a surrender to give those inside as long as possible for their preparations, and to hope for the arrival of an army regiment expected soon. All during the negotiations, the women in the fort have performed a ruse to make it look like there are more men in the fort than there actually are. Beth leads the women in dressing in men's clothes, hair pulled up under hats, poking their heads up all around the fort, with faces lowered of course. They fool the Indians. While negotiations are going on the Indians permit the settlers to go back and forth for water at the spring. They bring as much extra water back with them as they can, making as many extra trips as possible without the Indians becoming suspicious.

When the negotiating comes to an end, Daniel tells Blackfish that the people of Boonesborough will not surrender. The battle begins in earnest. Tim has coached the men that they should only shoot at an Indian and shoot to kill, for they will be fighting for their lives. In the past three months all of the women have been drilled on how to load the muskets. They have become quite proficient at it and the fastest woman can load a musket in twenty seconds, being only slightly slower than the fastest man who can do it in fifteen seconds.

It is tricky business but Daniel has been making gunpowder over the past couple of months and they now have a good supply. The women and older children put out fires started when the Indians shoot flaming arrows into the fort. Dorothy is quite feisty leading the group under her charge to put out every fire as quickly as possible.

Beth takes her position by Tim`s side, loading the extra muskets in between his shots. Many Indians fall that day. Tim takes careful aim hitting his target each time in an effort to protect the people in the fort. The battle rages on, with the Indians being very serious about this battle, aided by the British, the added drive for the Indians.

By the evening of the first day, everyone is exhausted but they cannot let down their guard or all will be lost. Half the group sleeps while the others stand guard, changing halfway through the night. Long before first light all of the men are alert and at their stations and the battle resumes.

Tim keeps encouraging and coaching the men, successfully attempting to keep their spirits up. Some of the women are on cooking detail to provide nourishment for the men involved in shooting. Beth leaves Tim's side every couple of hours to check on the women, encourages them with a patriotic song, or an amusing quip, or provides them with an update on what is happening outside the fort.

The settlers first notice what appears to be muddy water in the river. They wonder what is happening. They build a watchtower above Judge Henderson's two-storey blockhouse and are able to see that the Indians and British are digging a tunnel, appearing as though they plan to get into the fort by going underground, or that they are planning to dig close to the wall of the fort and then cause an explosion. Mike O'Neill and Richard Calloway begin to dig a counter-tunnel to intercept them which they can easily defend with few men.

All of a sudden, at least that's how it seems to the people of Boonesborough, the Indians clear out. The Indians have tried flaming arrows and flaming torches but both sputtered and went out due to all the rain there has been – a blessing for the people. Whenever it rains, they are able to collect rainwater from the roofs of the cabins. After being sure that the Indians have really gone, it is discovered that the rains on the already water-logged ground have caused the tunnel to partially collapse and so the Indians abandoned it as well as the siege on the fort, believing that there are a lot more people inside than there actually are. When the Indians leave, the animals are let out to graze, being very hungry after the seven day siege. It is still a few days before a regiment of eighty men comes to help them and brings supplies.

After the siege of Boonesborough, the Indian situation settles down and many more settlers come to the area wanting to farm, living in cabins outside the fort. Neighbours are a long distance away from each other. A shindig at Boonesborough draws everyone in from the outlying areas to enjoy a good visit, especially important for the women who need to talk to other women, to share problems and triumphs, that all important female contact. However, the men thoroughly enjoy these times as well, sharing farming stories, and embellished stories about hunting expeditions, sharing challenges they have met, asking for guidance for other issues. The children enjoy games with others their own ages, being a time for them to share with someone other than a sibling. The next spring many more settlers come and build cabins and start farming. They grow mostly corn and that year a bumper crop is harvested.

Chapter 27 – Barriers Gone

After the long siege in September when Beth and Tim worked side by side each day, life settles down and they have time to spend together on a regular basis again. On a crisp morning in late September, Tim takes Beth for a walk down to the river.

"We have been through many things over the past two and a half years, Beth. We met when you nursed me after I got an arrow in my shoulder. We enjoy walks and talks. You are so easy to talk to. Then you were kidnapped by Indians and I was part of the group who rescued you."

"What a welcome sight you were to our eyes!"

"Then I was captured by the Indians and Daniel and David rescued me. When they brought me back to the fort, you nursed me for the second time."

"We have had our high moments and our rough times."

"It was hard for me to share my past with you. You listened to me and encouraged me to talk about it. We have often talked about my sister Kathy since that day."

"I'm sure I would have liked her." Tim smiles and nods his head in agreement.

"We have fished together, gone for horseback rides, canoed on the Kentucky River, and picked berries together. Do you remember the bear we had to quickly get away from, but you were determined to hold onto your full pail of berries!"

"I didn't want to give them up to the bear after all the time we spent filling the pail. And do you remember the pies and other desserts we enjoyed afterwards?"

"Yes, it was worth the extra few minutes it took us to get away, and we did outwit the bear. We had some good times around the fireplace at Mike and Mary's during the blizzards, sometimes just the two of us enjoying the warmth of the bright blaze, sometimes playing checkers or chess with your sister and brother-in-law."

"Lots of good memories shared. Chess requires too much thinking for me. You taught me a lot about the stars, something I had often wondered about."

"Remember the first time you tried snowshoes? It was quite a funny experience. I had to be careful not to laugh at you. You looked so funny trying to walk daintily on those two big, wide shoes."

"I'm sure it must have looked funny. I might not have taken too kindly to you laughing at the time as I was concentrating so hard in order to be able to walk in them," she chuckles in remembrance.

"You are a real trooper. What else have you learned since you came here?"

"Patience is the big one for me. I wanted to know how to do everything right away, but many times I have had to slow right down and take challenges in small steps."

"I didn't know that about you, or didn't give it any thought. I have always seen you as eager to try new things and you catch on quickly. You jump right in, sometimes without knowing the dangers but ready to give it your all," Tim says, smiling with a twinkle in his eyes.

"What incident gives you that smile on your face, Tim?"

"I can still picture you almost falling head first into the water out of the canoe," he laughs. "You just stood up tall and jumped right in and almost kept right on going."

"I watched others afterwards to see how it should be done," Beth blushes.

"We can learn a lot from others. I value my time around Daniel, always trying to learn from him. He was perceived wrongly at the salt licks when we were captured. We were surrounded by a large party of braves, we were far outnumbered. Most of us were adopted into Shawnee village tribes, although some were taken to Detroit where the British paid the Indians for them."

"There were a few we never heard from again. But most of them escaped and made it back to Boonesborough; all those with families returned."

"I remember being questioned about some of the other men when I returned. I was the first one to make it back."

"Your return gave everyone hope especially when you could tell them about their men."

"I learned a lot from the Indians in that time. It was nothing like the first time. I still shudder to think of that time," Tim continues.

"When you were recuperating from that episode, I did a lot of talking about Boston. You wanted me to describe my home and learn about my parents. This past summer you got to meet them. How wonderful it was to have them here. What about your parents, Tim? Are you planning to go and see them?"

"Yes, it is time. I'm ready to face them and stand up for myself."

"Maybe in the meantime your mother has mellowed and is waiting to ask for your forgiveness for what she said."

"Maybe, but likely she won't back down from what she said. I've never known her to apologize."

"How about your father?"

"I'll be able to talk man-to-man with him away from Mother."

"It's sad how some people go through life with a big chip on their shoulders. You could have become a very bitter person, but instead you have dealt with your inner anguish and decided to move forward with your life. I'm glad to see that."

"It took a long time with you actually being the catalyst to get me started really thinking about what had happened. Up to that point, I still fully blamed myself without having thought it through. I mostly pushed thoughts of it out of my mind. Now I'm able to talk about Kathy and remember her as a wonderful sister." He pauses as he thinks for a moment and pictures her in his mind. "Thanksgiving and Christmas were great celebrations for us and all the people of Boonesborough. I treasure the belt buckle you gave me the first Christmas, and you look attractive in the dress and bonnet you made from the material I gave you."

"Shortly after the New Year you went to make salt with a group of thirty men from the fort and surrounding farms. It was great to have three men return with pack horses loaded with salt. But then we heard nothing more. When the two scouts returned to camp, they found lots of moccasin tracks but no dead men around the salt licks. That was a promising sign."

"That was a difficult time for us, still prisoners even though we were adopted into various Indian villages. We didn't have contact with others, although occasionally we would see some of the other men. We were never allowed to visit with other white men, always being kept separate."

"It was a long six weeks. We didn't know whether you were still alive, whether you would ever escape. What a thrill it was to have you return!"

"It was great to be back. We had a busy summer preparing for the siege and then we were surrounded by a large number of Indians who expected Boonesborough to surrender. Daniel Boone negotiated as long as he could to give us valuable time to continue our preparations. He finally told the Shawnees that we would not surrender. They were surprised that we would fight them, but our freedom meant more to us than living with the Indians as part of their tribes."

"What a thrill it was when we discovered that the siege was over, the Indians had packed up and left. We had all survived."

"We have shared so many things together Beth."

"Yes we have. I spoke with Mother and Father when they were here and told them about you and my feelings for Kentucky. They released me from the thoughts and plans they had for me. They spoke with Charles' parents, hesitantly at first not knowing what their response would be. I spoke personally with Mr. and Mrs. Brownley in the summer. They said Charles had met someone special and they were hoping to be able to allow Charles to make his own choice of a wife."

"Amazing how things work out. We have certainly seen that in our own lives here." Tim pauses a moment, then turns to Beth and says, "I would like to spend the rest of my life with you Beth. Will you be my wife?"

When she nods and smiles broadly, Tim draws Beth into his arms and holds her tight. After a few minutes, the yearning grows and Tim reaches for her mouth and kisses her long and deep, having finally exorcized his demons, having finally found healing, having finally found his soul mate in Beth.

"Let's get married tomorrow. You can wear any of your dresses. It doesn't matter to me. I don't want to wait any longer."

"Oh, Tim, I'm so happy! But about a dress, I have a story to tell. When you were gone all those weeks in the early spring, Mary and I made a wedding dress. I wasn't sure who I was going to marry at that time but it kept us busy."

"You have waited a long time for me."

"The wait has been well worth it."

"Let's make the announcement to the folks around town and get the plans in motion! In the spring how about we travel back east to Boston for our honeymoon? I can see your home and we can spend time with your parents."

"Maybe we can fit in a trip to your family as well, Tim."

"That's a great idea."

THE END

Resources for "Arrows, Indians and Love"

http://donchesnut.com/genealogy/pages/fortboon.htm Boonesborough Settlers

http://www.archive.org/stream/boonesboroughits00ran/boonesboroughits00ran_djvu.txt

Boonesborough - ITS FOUNDING, PIONEER STRUGGLES, INDIAN EXPERIENCES, TRANSYLVANIA DAYS, AND REVOLUTIONARY ANNALS

by George W. Ranck

CPSIA information can be obtained at www.ICGtesting.com
261240BV00001B/57/P